Pelican Books

Secrets of Strangers

Alice Thomas Ellis was bor[n] educated at Bangor Gram[mar] Art. She is the author of *The Birds of the Air (*Penguin 1983), *The 27th Kingdom* (Penguin 1982), nominated for the Booker Prize in 1982, *The Others Side of the Fire* (1983, Penguin 1985), *The Sin Eater* (1977, Penguin 1986), *Unexplained Laughter* (1985, Penguin 1986) and *Home Life* (1986, Fontana 1987). *The Birds of the Air* and *The Sin Eater* are winners of a Welsh Arts Council Award. Under her own name (Anna Haycraft) she has written two cookery books, *Natural Baby Food* and, with Caroline Blackwood, *Darling, You Shouldn't Have Gone to So Much Trouble* (1980). She is married to Colin Haycraft, chairman and managing director of Duckworth publishers, of which she is a director and the fiction editor. They have five children.

Dr Tom Pitt-Aikens writes: 'Childhood meant a Scottish manse full of evacuees, Polish officers, Italian POWs, his mother, grandmother, aunts and his minister grandfather, who had been Chaplain and Governor at Duke Street Prison, Glasgow. His apprenticeship was served accompanying his grandfather visiting the Parish aged, needy, "boarded-out" children and TB sanatoria. By the time his father returned from the war a calling had been established. Peace brought moves with his Brewmaster father to homes in England, Ireland and British Guiana and education at the Dollar Academy, Christian Brothers College, Cork, and Taunton School. He qualified in Medicine at Bristol in 1963. Hospital work and a spell as a ship's surgeon were followed by psychiatry and psychoanalysis with posts at the Tavistock Clinic, Home Office and Cassel Hospital. Medical journals, including the *Lancet*, have published his articles on the elderly and adolescence. His chief preoccupations are in the areas of delinquency and cancer and their relation to his "three generational theory of the loss of the good authority".'

SECRETS OF STRANGERS

Alice Thomas Ellis
&
Tom Pitt-Aikens

PENGUIN BOOKS

PENGUIN BOOKS

Published by the Penguin Group
27 Wrights Lane, London w8 5TZ, England
Viking Penguin Inc., 40 West 23rd Street, New York, New York 10010, USA
Penguin Books Australia Ltd, Ringwood, Victoria, Australia
Penguin Books Canada Ltd, 2801 John Street, Markham, Ontario, Canada L3R 1B4
Penguin Books (NZ) Ltd, 182-190 Wairau Road, Auckland 10, New Zealand

Penguin Books Ltd, Registered Offices: Harmondsworth, Middlesex, England

First published by Duckworth 1986
Published in Pelican Books 1988

Reproduced, printed and bound in Great Britain by
Hazell Watson & Viney Limited
Member of BPCC plc
Aylesbury Bucks

Contents

Setting the Scene

It is often said that Freud would have been a magnificent novelist. Certainly he was concerned with the mainsprings of human motivation, which is what most novels aspire to portray, and he was not uninventive. Best and most useful of all, he had access to what few novelists have – the secrets of strangers.

Most writers of fiction need to rely on their knowledge of themselves and their covert observations of others to build up imaginary characters to populate their work. This can be perfectly satisfying until they start worrying about it, when the word 'liar' tends to recur in their thoughts; which is illogical and unfair but needles away at the writer, who then begins to yearn for *real* people to write about. Having written several novels depicting completely imaginary people – although they seemed at the time as real as anyone in the outside world, inducing in me fondness, dislike, interest and boredom – I began to feel like a child who, after playing for years with dolls, begins to hanker after actual babies. I would pass houses in strange streets and wonder what was going on inside, and what the occupants would say if I should bang on the door enquiring if I could look round and see what they were having for supper and how their relationships were progressing. I knew, of course, that in most cases they would instantly send for the police. I could not write freely about my friends, not only from feelings of delicacy, but because the mere fact that I already knew them put them, in a sense, beside me, so that I could not see them clearly or objectively. Knowing them well I yet did not know them well enough, and it is extremely difficult to ask fresh questions within an established relationship; rather as one cannot suddenly ask the name of a person to whom one has been chatting throughout an entire dinner party. Nor could I attain the position of observer without falsifying and distorting the scene by removing myself from it. What I wanted was a family of strangers who would permit me to learn about them. What I wanted were the privileges of the analyst which clearly were not available to me.

The irony is that often when psychoanalysts, who have been made free of the psychological histories of their patients, write down their

1

observations, their work is boring – being done, as it were, from the head of the couch at an odd angle and leaving out the day-to-day details of dress, comportment and domestic surroundings which are so important to the novelist and sweeten the experience for the reader. Too often they seem only to be writing for each other in the curious language which members of a club or a cult will use in order to evade the importunate outsider. 'But what does it mean?' asks the layman impatiently, only to be fended off with a yet further hopelessly opaque exposition, so that the discipline is sometimes seen as existing independently of human kind on a par perhaps with the higher mathematics, holding very little relevance for the bewildered man in the street who may or may not understand the processes by which the patient gets better.

My co-author is an analyst who is happy to use ecclesiastical as well as psychoanalytic terms, and his particular interest is in crime and its genesis. He works with many families who have delinquent members and also, I hasten to add, sees patients with no such problem. I met him first because I had suffered a loss with which I found it impossible to come to terms. My whole family were suffering also – it transpired – not only from their own grief but from my seemingly unprecedented inability to cope with everything. After a time, with no overtly dramatic signs I found that we were all better, that a certain sort of demonic madness had left us, that we were beginning to live in ourselves again. The grief was still there but without the dreadful rage. The sceptical would say that time was responsible, that time heals all, but I think they would be wrong. I do not think that we would have emerged from the nightmare without help. This realisation disposed me in his favour. He was unlike the few other psychiatrists whom I knew and his methods seemed to me original and fresh as well as apparently efficacious. I am as interested as the next man in evil and delinquency and when I ceased to be his patient I suggested that we might write this book together. I had already written about a delinquent boy in a novel and, being surrounded by teenage children, was still fascinated by the problem of the seemingly inherent awfulness of the human race.

All parents have to suffer some degree of disobedience in their children: occasional unruliness, temper tantrums, the unexplained absence, untidiness, cheek, and quite often petty pilfering. Most parents are able to cope with all this by dint of patience, example, reasoning and the odd slap. They may get very tired but on the whole they are not overwhelmed, and with any luck the children develop into the sort of adult that society is content to accept. Some parents, of course, raise delinquent children because they are themselves delinquent, and while society still frowns the family members muddle along together quite happily because they understand each other – 'Gary, love, just nick that packet of fags for Mummy and slip it in the pocket of your little rompers.' They stick together, the Law is regarded as the enemy and the family is outraged when one of its members is apprehended in evil-doing and punished for it. The law-abiding tend to imagine that all criminals spring from this one class: morally and educationally deprived, badly housed and nourished, raised on TV violence and surrounded by drunkenness and disarray. Then there are the children of the upper class, alternately spoiled and neglected by their fun-loving parents who spend their time getting divorced, skiing in Klosters and sunbathing in the Bahamas. These children grow up to drive fast cars, steal the family silver to buy heroin, smuggle cocaine and frequently become involved with the other criminal class. While examples of these stereotypes undoubtedly exist the image of delinquency that they present is at once reassuring to the ordinary citizen and misleading. Bad parents and a poor environment do not necessarily give rise to delinquency, and sometimes seemingly ideal parents of impeccable honesty, hard-working and devoted to their children, will find to their appalled bewilderment that they have a monster in their midst.

Geoffrey Hutton was one such.

At the age of 6, he was referred to a child-guidance clinic, his parents having discovered in him a tendency to pilfer. Three years later he was referred to another clinic for the same reason, and for his frequent bedwetting. He was sent to three separate assessment centres (which I find confusing and imagine the family did too). At 12 he was at a Comprehensive School, where his behaviour was described as 'very disruptive, both in and out of school'. He had no particularly close friends but sought attention and bought friendship with cigarettes. A year later he was caught stealing money from a sports club changing-room and brought before a Juvenile Court. From then on he was constantly stealing from home, still bedwetting, and thieving bicycles in Barking, which again brought him before a Juvenile Court. He was remanded to the care of the Local Authority for twenty-one days and was placed in yet another Observation and Assessment Centre. At the same time he was suspended from the Comprehensive for persistent disruptive behaviour. His behaviour at home had also continued to deteriorate, with more thefts of money and cigarettes, and his parents were beginning to speak in terms of 'having him removed'. In December of that year he stayed out all night for the first time, was picked up by the police and explained that he and his friend had run away from home. After promising that he would stop 'mucking around' he was reinstated at the Comprehensive, but his school reports showed that there had been no improvement in his behaviour. He continued stealing, and his aggression towards his mother and siblings was becoming more physical. That year he was charged with six counts of burglary and the theft of a motor-cycle. He was openly rude and rebellious at home. He was then admitted again to the Observation and Assessment Centre and started regularly playing truant with some of the other boys. He was sent 'home under supervision' since the younger members of the staff had been unable to restrain him from doing virtually what he liked, and he attended the Centre daily in the 'unschoolable' group. After a violent struggle with his brothers, parents and a social worker, he was returned to the Centre and then transferred for a brief time to what is somewhat ungrammatically described as a 'Maladjusted Boarding School'. A month later, aged 14, he was admitted to Orwell House, described as a Community Home with Education on the Premises, where Tom Pitt-Aikens (henceforth TPA) was Consultant Psychiatrist.

He began his career here by 'going missing quite a lot'. On his week-end visits home he continued to steal from his mother's purse and smash things, especially things belonging to his brothers and sisters. Back at Orwell House he got into serious fights with other boys, and after a while he exposed himself to two young girls. For this he was cautioned by the police but, nothing daunted, carried on doing it several more times. He was then discovered peeing from the roof in front of the other boys but claimed, on a note of injured innocence, that he was merely exposing himself. In August he stole a great deal of female clothing, and a month or so later broke into a house and exposed himself to two further girls. He denied exposing himself and also denied that he was carrying a flick knife. One of the girls had been cut, though it was unclear how this had happened. In December he stole some female clothing from a number of shops, and early in the New Year appeared in court on this charge and was found guilty. In the same month he had a nasty fight with another boy at Orwell House, and the next month he stole some more girls' clothes plus a bicycle, which he did in fact return, though minus its pump.

At 16 he left Orwell House. Some time passed without apparent incident until he was hauled up before the court again on yet another charge of indecent exposure, and later the same year he was back in court on three counts of theft. The following spring he was again charged with indecent exposure and the theft of a blouse from a washing line, and in June of that year he was charged with arson. He had attempted to blow up an immersion heater in the loft of a church and had caused £42,000 worth of damage. At this he was sentenced to a term of penal confinement and packed off to Borstal, where as it happened TPA worked. There he spent about a year. On his release he was almost immediately taken again into custody on suspicion of having stolen some scaffolding poles and remanded on bail, only to be found not guilty owing to lack of evidence. At Christmas time he proudly showed his father a CB aerial which he had constructed – out of scaffolding poles.

*

Many people only come to the notice of the public and the authorities when they commit an offence. As far as most of us are concerned they and their families might never have existed until we read of an offence in a newspaper. The Huttons were unknown to TPA and certainly to me until Geoffrey arrived at Orwell House trailing his long list of misdemeanours like bunting. We wondered for some time how to portray the delinquent Geoffrey without defeating our own main purpose of depicting what is not revealed by newspapers.

During an informal and somewhat baffled discussion we put the problem to my 13-year-old daughter. She only confirmed our difficulty, suggesting that we should simply describe him drily and factually until we came to the 'truth' – as though indeed that only began from the moment when Geoffrey met us. This innocent suggestion reinforced for us the point of this book, which is to describe as fully as possible, without fantasy or rhetoric, the workings of a real family.

Nevertheless, here is the delinquent as seen through the Orwell House dossier. The dossier on Geoffrey was almost a book in itself. It occupies fifty-eight pages of typescript and is frequently bewildering, giving an impression of being at once repetitive and incomplete. Its purpose, apart from providing a record of past and present misdemeanours and 'occurrences', is obscure, since despite some sketchy 'pen portraits' of the family the picture which emerges, of both the family and Geoffrey, is unfocused and sometimes self-contradictory. I, for one, would not recognise Geoffrey's mother and father from the brief and shallow descriptions offered. Of course, it would be impossible to write lengthy 'in depth' analyses of all the families who come in contact with an institution, but to describe Mr Hutton as 'withdrawn and quickly depressed by Geoffrey's behaviour' is quite simply misleading, and would not be particularly helpful to, say, a new social worker attempting to familiarise himself with the case. Nor would he gain a very clear picture of Geoffrey's various placements, since at times he seems to have been simultaneously in several Observation and Assessment Centres.

But these are the faults of bureaucracy and no doubt we must learn to live with them. More interesting are the occasional comments which appear to have been made by a human being rather than an automaton. The poignant 'Geoffrey presents as a very unhappy boy' says more than 'Geoffrey's problems are deep-seated', which could mean anything or nothing according to which school of thought you favour. I learned little from the contents of the Assessment Report on Geoffrey, which are listed as follows: Personal Details, including Pen Picture; Home Circumstances; Family Relationships; Personal History (chronologically set out); Personal History (continued); Psychological Report; Psychiatric Report; Medical Report; Educational Report; School Record (school reports if available); Employment Record; Leisure Time Activities; Observed Behaviour; Summary; Recommendations; Case Conference Minutes. Amazingly enough, these details take up only fifteen pages. At one point someone has noted:

> The family has apparently experienced considerable anxiety and tension as a result of Geoffrey's stealing from the home. The parents say they are concerned about the adverse effects on the siblings' behaviour. They maintain that Geoffrey has rejected their efforts to devote more time and attention to him. Have seen Dr Quick but felt they were being offered no realistic help. Both parents appear to distrust psychiatric help – possibly reluctant to examine their own problems in depth.

There may be some truth in the last observation, but only I think because Mrs Hutton especially was desperately seeking help and was constantly disappointed. Mr Hutton, though often severely critical of TPA's approach and interpretation of the problems presented by Geoffrey, contined doggedly to attend the family meetings for eight years, which suggests a certain faith in psychiatry even if it stemmed only from a despairing sense that there was nowhere else to turn.

Meanwhile back at Orwell House they were continuing to wrestle with the problem that was Geoffrey. An assessment put together by a trainee psychologist, using various 'tests', had been sent on to them from one of the Centres, and while it is rather moving (Geoffrey had to look back over two or three years to find a happy memory), it strikes me as unhelpful insofar as by now it was richly apparent to everyone that Geoffrey was a naughty, disobedient, miserable child.

It concludes: 'By implication he sees himself negatively as a bad boy who gets into trouble and then faces punishment.'

The Assessment Centre's psychiatrist's report which came next in the dossier is more illuminating, though not much, and ends with the observation that 'there is a hidden conflict between the parents and it seems that a scapegoating situation is necessary'. I, perhaps naively, do not believe that to be the case at all. One does not need to be a trained psychiatrist to discern conflict between a married couple. One merely has to dine with them a few times or spend a weekend with them, and provided they do not stint on the alcohol the state of their relationship becomes swiftly apparent to anyone sufficiently interested to look closely, or in extreme cases, to *anyone* – interested or not. I know very few happily married couples and those I do know are unmistakable. They stand, as it were, side by side, facing the world and its vicissitudes together; whereas the unhappily married stand face to face, glaring at each other, swapping recriminations, and are so wrapped up in their mutual hostility, each so concerned to lay the blame for the children's faults, and even those they find in themselves, on the other, that they scarcely see the world, which could be going rapidly to hell for all they care. The Huttons certainly do not seem to me to fall into the latter category.

Halfway through the dossier comes a heartfelt account of Geoffrey's demeanour during his time in one of the Observation and Assessment Centres. He had clearly been wreaking havoc, and the staff were at a loss to know how to deal with him. He had been 'a totally disruptive influence on the children presently residing here. His catalystic approach within the group situation is having adverse behavioural effects on what would be a manageable situation'. He had been 'involved in numerous incidents' and had 'found each staff member's limits and pushed beyond'. Neighbours had reported indignantly that he was derisive and rude to them – he would climb trees in the garden and shout abuse at local people. He regularly left the premises without consent and created a public nuisance. He had illicitly entered the nearby Electricity Board's sub-power house, and the staff 'feared for his own safety' – which was magnanimous of them in view of the circumstances. The account ends on a pitiful note: 'Any attempts by staff to counsel this boy as to his anti-social behaviour have been thwarted and have met with a barrage of verbal abuse.' They finally cracked when Geoffrey and another boy attacked a staff member with a piece of wood because he had the temerity to atempt to curb them, and Geoffrey was then despatched to Orwell House.

He had been assigned a Social Worker, Mr Dowe, representing

the Local Authority, who now assumed responsibility for him. Geoffrey was permitted weekends and holidays at home, but three months after the arrangement between Orwell House and the Local Authority had begun, his father telephoned to say that Geoffrey had not had a very good half-term leave. He had been mixing with his old friends and staying out late at night. His parents would now prefer him to come home on leave one in four weekends only. A month later he did not return to Orwell House after his weekend leave and the police and social services were alerted. He had set out but had gone back to the house in the early hours of the morning and then run off again. He returned to Orwell House the following day. Shortly afterwards a staff member, sensing something wrong and hearing a shout, betook himself to Pets' Corner where he found Geoffrey crying loudly, soaking wet, very red in the face and with a swelling under his right eye, while another boy stood over him. There were three more boys present at this scene and the staff member was hard put to it to come at the truth of the matter. When Geoffrey gave his version the other boys became abusive and called him a liar. His ear swelled up and he was taken to hospital, still sobbing and in a state of shock thirty minutes after the incident. The same month there was an outbreak of violence between him and another boy during a lunch-hour, though in this case it seems he was more sinned against than sinning. Fortunately a staff member was present to take prompt action. Otherwise 'the dining-room would have been a shambles'. On the brighter side, he went to Yorkshire with a group, joined in all the activities and had a successful trip.

Then there was an incident at the end of a lesson when Geoffrey knocked some wooden blocks to the floor, was told by the teacher to pick them up and 'indicated by his mannerisms that he was not going to do this'. He worked himself into a tantrum of temper and had to be restrained on the floor. Shortly afterwards he got a crack on the head when another boy pushed a swing door, and he had to go to hospital for stitches. Some weeks later he slipped in the changing-room after swimming and bruised his mouth on a bench.

So the saga continues for page after page, lightened by occasional spasms of virtuous behaviour. Geoffrey was as good as gold when helping out at a garden fête, collecting, erecting and dismantling stalls and public address equipment, looking after three side-shows and handling money. His behaviour was described as exemplary and he worked extremely hard over a prolonged period. Sadly, the next day he had to be taken to task for his part in bullying another boy, although the report admits that this was out of character. One day he spent the afternoon helping mentally handicapped young people exercise in the gym and 'performed some very valuable work'. Then a few days later his mother telephoned Orwell House to say that he had been stealing money from her purse while on home-leave. The next day his father telephoned to say that Geoffrey had been picked up by the police and had admitted in the presence of himself and Mr Dowe that he had exposed himself to two girls – and so it went on. After a while the transvestism came to light, and the theft of female clothing. Geoffrey went on fighting other boys, and when he wasn't doing that he was proving himself to be still accident-prone, cutting his hand when trying to open a sticking window in the common room. He continued, says the report, to behave in a bizarre fashion, and because of his 'sexual difficulties' the staff were always suspicious when he was missing for any length of time. One day when he had disappeared for two separate periods of an hour each and was finally tracked down he said he had been on the roof – a most dangerous enterprise, carrying the risk, if caught, of the loss of a weekend's leave as well as the risk of death. Geoffrey was white-faced and agitated. I wonder what he had been up to.

The flashing and transvestism went on; the police were in and out of the place like a fiddler's elbow, the parents were at their wits' end, and the staff were baffled. The Principal of Orwell House even arranged for Geoffrey to see a clinical psychologist, which TPA regarded as something of a waste of time, knowing full well that Geoffrey would inevitably be up on the roof or down at Pets' Corner when required to attend sessions. Geoffrey himself was not keen on the idea and, while shamefacedly admitting that he needed help, asked whether he could at any time opt out of seeing Dr Adams and was assured that he could. Then he had another fight, and then he went missing from the midday assembly. Finally he was found returning from Pets' Corner where he had already been twice fruitlessly sought, and the Principal said that he was never – in no way *ever* – to be allowed alone near Pets' Corner. Next day a staff member encountered him there, holding the keys, and full of assurances that he was in charge of feeding the pets. The staff member writes plaintively: 'Despite my statement on many occasions to him, that he is not to go to Pets' Corner without an escort of another boy or a member of staff, he still continues to do so. The dangers are obvious in his case. He has again been guilty of stealing women's clothes and hiding them to further his transvestite tendencies. We have of course,' the report ends hopefully, 'this meeting arranged with Dr Adams, the clinical psychologist, who has taken an interest in his case.' Unfortunately Dr Adams, owing to a misunderstanding, did not turn up at the appointed hour, and had to make fresh arrangements.

Then Geoffrey went missing again, prowled round somebody's garage, drank some beer, smoked some cigarettes, had another fight, stole some girls' clothing, stole a bicycle, stole twenty-four more bottles of beer and was caught and charged for it. He was 16 by this time and therefore due to leave Orwell House. The report reads:

> His Social Worker was enjoined to find him a job quickly so that (a) he could be tried at home whilst employed and (b) it would minimise to an extent the bad name he was giving this establishment with the locals.

It ends:

> Geoffrey to leave today to go home and hopefully to work.

There must have been similar dossiers in each institution that Geoffrey visited, describing his circumstances and giving a blow-by-blow account of his behaviour. They are certainly not boring, but neither are they particularly revealing, and it is hard to escape the conclusion that all those words were written to give people the sense that they were doing *something* in an impossible situation; as though by writing him down, Geoffrey could somehow be made more containable. Apart from the times when he is noted as 'unhappy' and the observation that he is fond of the pets and loves swimming, he is never seen or represented as a whole person, merely as someone who does very bad things very often and sometimes, in surprising contrast, quite good things. This, I suppose, is fair enough, but it makes it difficult to get a clear look at Geoffrey, who remains nebulous and elusive. Again, to be fair, it must be admitted that dressing up in girls' clothes is a somewhat dramatic aspect of personality; yet the concentration on his bizarreries does have a distorting effect. Between the behavioural extremes of very bad and quite good there seemed to be an empty space.

After I had read the dossier and had come to grips with the 'paper Geoffrey', TPA wanted me to see some more cases before allowing me to meet the Hutton family in the flesh. He got permission for me to visit Orwell House where Geoffrey had been four years before and I humbly had to revise a few of my opinions. I was appalled by some of the children with whom he dealt. They were exactly as he had described, strangely empty; and I felt them to be dangerous. As one of my own sons puts it – the light was on but there was no one at home. They had a lost, feral air of not belonging, of not even seeking for somewhere to belong; content to drift and damage like wrecked hulks; purposeless and randomly inimical.

Once I was no more disposed in favour of social workers than anyone else. If I had been writing a novel about one I would have given him a straggly beard or, if female, baggy dungarees and striped socks. Either way my social worker would have talked about 'meaningful dialogues' and used phrases like 'at this moment in time', and I would have despised him and tossed him about as though I were a cat with a mouse.

It is fashionable to despise social workers. They are regarded widely as wet and incompetent: addle-pated do-gooders, given to feather-bedding people who, some believe, would benefit more from a short sharp shock or a taste of the birch – for which remedy however there is no positive evidence whatsoever. I no longer despise social workers. I have watched them at work and I now think them admirable. I find delinquents frightening and baffling and boring and quite without glamour. The ones I have met have seemed empty and inhuman and humourless. At one instant I suffered a deplorable moral lapse, thinking that the easiest and most economical thing to do would be to take a great big gun and shoot the lot of them. They seemed to me to be beyond communication and therefore beyond help. I met a social worker who had just been thrown to the ground by a large and recalcitrant child and had chipped her knee-cap and I thanked God that I earn my living in the way I do. If I was starving, I thought, I would not throw in my lot with those horrid antinomian young who, empty as they were, seemed possessed by devils. The people charged with their care admittedly did look somewhat worn, but on the whole gave the appearance of being completely committed to their thankless task. TPA spoke to me severely about this very matter, reminding me that I was now writing about real people and was not at liberty to caricature or traduce. Quite apart from the danger of inadvertently libelling someone, I was on my honour to be truthful and straight, and not allowed to gibe for the fun of it. This, he observed repressively, was no time to give rein to my 'sardonic' streak which was appropriate only to fiction. Quite right. It is, in fact, I think, unfair even to invent a character merely to despise him, and real people deserve truly thorough appraisal. I had grown impatient with the dossiers, often muttering 'So what?' as I came across some seemingly flat-footed observation; but, as I have already admitted, my own response to the problem was entirely reprehensible and not helpful in the least. These people were struggling to *do* something. Social workers, staff and psychiatrists, all in their various ways, were attempting to alleviate impossible situations.

Now psychiatry is rather like post-ecumenical religion. The adherents of the varying disciplines and schools of thought have to strive against a tendency to regard each other with pity if not contempt. I myself, even as a layman, get quite steamed up when some Freudian wiseacre remarks that the pen with which I write is a penis. 'A penis is a penis,' I snarl. 'This is a *pen*, you fool, and as a medical man you should be able to tell the difference.' Of course, the Freudian, on the grand old principle of heads-I-win – tails-you-lose, will observe knowingly that I protest too much, and in all probability I then lose my temper. Nor have I cared for Behaviourists since I once walked into a room to discover a naked one, together with his mistress, also naked, waiting, I suspect, for me to join them in a romp. I may be unfair but I have always felt that had he not been a Behaviourist he would not have behaved so. From such small incidents great prejudices arise. I am fortunate in being able to walk away from the source of irritation and dismiss it from my mind, but I feel compassionate towards those who have elected to spend their lives probing, from their various standpoints, the secrets of the human psyche; sitting, as it were, in a circle around truth and viewing it from different angles, yet forced, lest they scandalise the laity, to muddle along together with as good a grace as they can muster. I get rather the same feeling when the Archbishop of Canterbury visits the Pope. Internecine strife is not reassuring to the outsider.

A person finding himself at odds with himself or with society may seek help or have help thrust upon him, and it is a matter of luck whether or not he immediately feels at ease with the therapy offered. I myself once marched straight out of our medical centre when, having gone to consult a physician about my state of extreme weariness, I found I had been shunted off to a man who wanted to talk about vaginal orgasms. Sometimes, no doubt, such chat is appropriate, but not when one knows perfectly well that one's exhaustion is caused by lack of sleep due to a healthy but insomniac baby. What one wants are knock-out drops for the baby. But this, of course, is one of the major problems of psychiatry – it so frequently presents to the layman as a mixture of straightforward commonsense and sheer perverted thinking, and it is often extremely difficult to follow the thought-processes involved. Geoffrey was seen by several practitioners without apparent effect, although this is possibly because after one or two consultations he thereafter failed to turn up for treatment, clearly either having no faith in its efficacy, or perhaps merely denying that he needed it. Mr and Mrs Hutton on the other hand, although sometimes bewildered by his methods, assiduously attended almost every meeting offered by TPA and would, I think, agree that without this support they would have found the situation even more difficult than they did.

*

Several people who have looked at the unfinished MS of this book have remarked upon the seeming absence of Geoffrey, the difficulty of getting a clear look at him: 'We want to know about the *boy*,' they cry. 'What was he *like*?' But this near invisibility is one of the commonest features of delinquency. The delinquent is, in a sense, absent from himself. He has a mercurial elusive quality and he is unexpected. He does unexpected things and is found in unexpected places – up trees hurling insults, or in other people's houses without their knowledge or consent. He is defined only by his surroundings and the effect he has on them. He does not offer himself voluntarily for treatment. When appointments are arranged for him he does not turn up. '*Of course he doesn't*,' says TPA, almost with exasperation. 'That is precisely the nature of the beast; not turning up for therapy is one of his symptoms, and not due to mere lapses of memory or lack of the bus fare.' The delinquent is not autonomous; he is empty of himself and possessed of evil projections. He does not know why he does the things he does and so is amenable neither to reason nor to punishment. 'But what about free will?' asks an intelligent reader, perhaps worrying, as others have done before her, that since Freud the concept of sin has been made meaningless. The answer is that the delinquent does not – perhaps only temporarily – have access to his free will, being possessed. It is these 'evil spirits' which must be recognised and subdued. As in all probability they emanate from a parent and the other children may well be at risk from them, the family are required to be present at therapy sessions quite as much as the bad child himself.

*

Mourning, that is the realisation and eventual acceptance of loss and its implications, is, it seems, entirely necessary for psychic health – not only of the bereaved person but also of his nearest and dearest. A loss – it need not be a death – severely curtails any sense of omnipotence that one may be harbouring and offers a chance of understanding, of coming to grips with reality; but, denied or thwarted, the now unconscious sense of loss can create havoc. There are many factors which can interfere with mourning, of which perhaps the best known, if not the most important, is guilt. An overwhelming sense of loss can seem unbearable and so inadmissible. In some cases a person may never have had certain kinds of reality – parents, home, security – and will never know what he has missed, and therefore be unable to mourn in the usual sense of realising that he has lost something. Sedation, obviously, can interfere with the mourning process, and so can lack of support. It can happen that, without help, someone may simply not have time to mourn. After a while it may appear that all is well with the bereft. But do not be deceived. In the case of a parent of a delinquent child, it will always be found that he has himself been deprived of the authority of his own parent or parents, by death or desertion for instance, and has failed to come to grieving terms with his loss.

Now we are finding trouble with co-authorship. TPA has expressed quite clearly what happens in the case of a child whose unconscious is screaming that something is amiss, who is behaving appallingly in order to draw attention to the state of affairs. I could not, I remark, have put it better myself. But TPA is loth to believe me. Writing, he says, is not his job. I am supposed to put it in my own words because, since he has explained it to me so often, I know the theory as well as he knows it himself. This is all very fine and large but I feel like a person being invited to ride a bicycle which already has someone in position. Two bodies cannot occupy the same space. Besides I have found dealing with the concept of mourning extremely difficult, not for technical but for personal reasons. As I wrote of grieving I felt tears streaming down my face. It is all very well to insist on the importance of mourning, but people are abashed in the presence of sorrow. They want you to stop crying and get on with life and work. Also, crying is exhausting. I have been told that tears are not sufficient, that the bereaved need to sob and sob; but too much sobbing leaves one feeling ill. I have found that screaming very loudly is more useful. You lose your voice and greatly alarm any bystanders, but it is a release. As the years go by, one is told, the sorrow of bereavement lessens. Sometimes this is not the case. Regrets and guilts and terrible inexpressible pity can linger and fester, and often with the best will in the world they prove inaccessible for years both to the bearer, who would gladly relinquish them if he could locate their source, and to the therapist. But then perhaps a simple awareness of one's plight is better than nothing. This book is really an account of professionally supported, uphill mourning which has extended over eight years. This rather gives the lie to that popular and attractive notion that, no matter what the crisis, a good cry, an aspirin and a cup of hot sweet tea will enable the sufferer to pick up the pieces and get on with life.

The unconscious realms are dangerous, however. Here be dragons. I should not like being submerged in the murky depths of the unconscious without the protection of the analyst. It is like Loch

Ness – so dark down there that you cannot tell whether or not you are upside down. Patients must often feel wildly angry at being required to visit depths they would prefer to ignore the existence of. They don't want to think about loss and grief. They want to go out and play. Even now as I write thinking about all this I find myself totally reverting to infancy. At one point there I was lying in my pram watching the statutory sunlight dappling through the statutory leaves. I had better get on with it.

TPA has written, quite unexceptionably in my view:

> It seems that the parents of delinquents have, as a result of their own deficient rearing, certain psychic deficits, some of which take up particularly shaped spaces – or 'psychic holes' – which are then exploded out of the parent's psyche, invasion-like, into the psyche of another individual (in my experience often their own child).

That seems to me perfectly clear, although I have to remind myself that on first acquaintance with this theory I found it almost incomprehensible. (Some remnants of this incomprehension are still discernible as I strive throughout the book to understand the complexities of each meeting.) I was worried at that time about my children, and when told by TPA that once *I* was all right *they* would be too, I thought he was crazy. He continues by explaining that the 'projections' swamp the child's personality, more or less crippling his ordinary mental functioning, and that intermittently or constantly the body of the delinquent is pervaded and run by a different spirit – the origin of this different spirit deriving from the delinquency of the grandparent, who by his dereliction of duty – either by deserting or dying (dying is no excuse, says TPA repressively: the result is the same) – gives rise to 'the non-provision of good-authority models' for identification by his child – the parent of today's overt delinquent.

> The terrible truth about the swamping phenomenon is that the projecting parent has no conscious awareness of his psychic deficit, nor that he has sent salvoes of these deficits devastatingly into his nearest and dearest.

A delinquent grandchild personifies the meaning of the loss of the good authority, providing the opportunity for its reinstatement, or in some cases bringing an awareness for the first time that it has always been lacking. The grandchild, the medium, may cause enormous anxiety; but that is the means by which everyone is made aware that all is not well and one should not be put off – especially, remarks TPA, if one is being paid to help. Failure to understand that the child is a vehicle for evil projections will mean that each child in the family will in turn be unconsciously advanced as the vehicle, offering the opportunity of regaining the lost good authority. Once all the children have fallen victim the loss of good authority will be depicted in some other form, often a 'loss of control' medical condition in a parent. Leukaemia, for example, has shown its ugly face more often than TPA is inclined to regard as coincidence.

*

It took us some time to decide on precisely what form this book should take. We toyed with the idea of writing it as a novel and presenting the Huttons as fictional characters, but this would not have been in accord with our original purpose which was to stick grimly to facts; to tell the truth insofar as it seemed apparent to us; to write, without polish or artifice, about real people. It would have seemed disrespectful to the Huttons to reduce them to story-book figures and the temptation to add to and mould the tale would have been almost irresistible. Dickens pointed out that writers never dream about their characters and we have certainly dreamed about the Huttons. They are not the stuff of fiction, even though of course their names, like all the names in this book, have been changed for the sake of confidentiality.

We also wanted them to speak with their own voices and the children said very little at the Family Meetings. We would have been tempted to put into their mouths the things we thought they would say if they spoke. But the whole point was that they did not speak – although at home they were unusually outgoing and fluent – and it is difficult to sustain interest in a novel if half the cast is mute. If we had followed them round for days recording all that everyone said then we would not have had a true picture, because an alien presence would inevitably have brought about a change in environment and attitude. Besides, the level of perception, in that case, would have been inadequate, since the real interest lay in unconscious realms and had to be uncovered, drawn out and exposed by the therapy. Few people make their problems and complexes, or even the fate of their ancestors, the subject of tea-time conversation. If they do, they are, of course, wildly boring and we avoid their company. It was in the meetings that the real fascination lay: where it was appropriate, where it was expected that the talk should be of old mysteries and sorrows and matters of the psyche.

Perhaps, after all, we wanted to present not a finished tapestry, hanging primly with its back to the wall, but 'work in progress' –

unfinished in all senses, since life itself remains unfinished as long as life is long – with its seams, its loose ends, its completed cameos and its areas of puzzling incompleteness all open to view; to leave it to the observer to colour in the spaces, and to see whether the structure left exposed reminded him of anything, of the underlying warp and weft of human life and trouble.

*

New experiences are frequently bewildering, especially when you find yourself in the hands of practitioners of an unfamiliar discipline. I sympathise with the Huttons as they approached their first family meeting. They had had a rough time with Geoffrey who had proved too much for the staff at the Observation and Assessment Centre, running away and climbing his trees in order to be rude to neighbours from this vantage point, and generally making life difficult for those around him. His parents, now that he was to be ensconced at Orwell House, must have felt half despairing, half hopeful at the fresh development. I imagine they were greatly in need of reassurance that their son would finally be unravelled, understood and persuaded to behave, and I wonder how they felt in the strange atmosphere of a Family Meeting which can have met few of their preconceptions. The clerk of the meeting naturally enough did not record the description of the 'format and philosophy' of the meetings, in full, so we shall do that for the benefit of the bewildered reader. It should be added that the structure of these meetings was slowly evolved by TPA over many years. The rigid format is intended to provide that vital element – a framework, without which all edifices would collapse. But first we shall hear Ian Hutton's own version of his family history.

A Family History

by Ian Hutton, Geoffrey's father

Michel Pierre Huytens, b.1810

My great-great-grandfather. He was born in Bruges but quarrelled with his family and to annoy them turned Protestant and emigrated to England, where he established a successful coach-building company.

Robert Claude Hutton, b.1845

My great-grandfather. Whether he had brothers and sisters is not known; but there seem to have been some, judging by sporadic references to distant relations. He made a fortune by patenting a new hansom-cab wheel and lost it by insisting that motor taxis were a passing craze and keeping his money in hansom-cabs. He was naturalised British at some point, changing his name to Hutton. His wife Freda was a forceful character. When her eldest son was dropped as a baby by his nursemaid and broke his first tooth, she pursued the poor girl up three flights of stairs brandishing a carving knife and screaming: 'An eye for an eye and a tooth for a tooth. I'll kill the bugger.' When the unfortunate girl was finally cornered in the loft, Great-grandmother Freda had seen the funny side and collapsed with laughter. During the First World War she was required by the Defence of the Realm Act to report to the police once a week as married to an alien. The air in Bethnal Green police station was quite blue on Thursday mornings with her opinions of this requirement and they dreaded her visits. At her death, her grandson Charles Robert Hutton, my father, was amused at the inscription chosen by my grandfather for the tombstone: 'She walked in meekness all her days.'

Michael Robert Hutton, b.1868

My grandfather. He had six younger sisters and one younger

brother – Marcel Joseph, a dentist who, with one of his sisters, married to a Roberts, started a firm of instrument makers, Hutton & Roberts. He made a packet but kept it to himself. Serving in the Yeomanry in the Boer War, Michael Robert Hutton later rose to be a colour-sergeant, as an instructor of musketry. He was a crack rifle shot and won medals at Bisley. He worked as a travelling salesman. The family were outraged when his fancy bit from Liverpool, previously unknown, turned up for his funeral. He died of cancer in 1914.

William Horner, b.1876

My maternal grandfather. Born at Kirby Malzeard, Yorkshire, he was a teacher who was ordained in the Church of England. He married Sarah Williams, also a teacher from Chesterfield. He was appointed curate near Cardiff in 1914 and then moved to North Wales, where he was rector until he died of a stroke in 1934. A likeable man, with a great sense of humour, he had a talent for painting, especially in water-colour. The Bishop had a habit of passing unwanted guests on to him. One of these was a condescending English lady who decided to go out and patronise the villagers on Sunday afternoon. Borrowing the pony-trap, she asked him the Welsh for 'Good Afternoon'. He duly provided her with a Welsh phrase and she drove around sweetly telling the villagers to 'Go to Hell'. Fortunately they knew and understood him, and anyway few spoke Welsh. When he died, even Chapel folk went to his funeral and he was still remembered twenty years later on one of our family holidays.

Charles Robert, b.1892

My father. He joined the Territorials as a private and fought throughout the war. He was wounded in the leg and, when recovering, was sent to Dublin after the Easter Rising. Later he was badly gassed on the Western front, and this affected his health. Finishing the war as a Captain, he remained in the Territorials to become a Major. He became a senior civil servant. He was very successful, and met and married Daphne. He died in 1940 of heart-failure while suffering from pneumonia, which he had developed after a family visit to an old flame who by then was married with several children. The family had gone home after tea but he stayed to play bowls with the husband and, after being caught in a thunderstorm, would not change his clothes. He may also be said to have been killed by his own laziness, for the probable cause of his heart-failure was a black-out blind falling with a loud crash. It had been secured by a cord passing from behind it when rolled up and over a hook in front, but the hook had rusted and rotted the cord; instead of replacing the cord he had knotted it and the cord had to be balanced by the knot on the hook. On the fateful night the blinds were up and the top windows open for fresh air. A breeze must have dislodged the cord, and the blind fell, its wooden roller hitting the window-sill with a loud bang. He was found dead in the morning.

Father was a strict but good, if slightly distant, parent. He had a rather regimental sense of humour and scandalised mother by singing mildly bawdy barrack-room songs to his children. He liked bad puns and spoonerisms – it was ten years before I realised why he went so red and shut up quickly after spoonerising 'The Kitchen Front'. He was not very practical but liked making things. He had a tendency to miss the obvious. On one occasion he took us out on a lake in a motor boat. The engine stopped and we had to be rescued. It seemed quite clear to me that all that was wrong was that he had taken his foot off the pedal and had only to replace it for the engine to go again. I did not dare tell him, for he hated to be 'shown up' in any way, even more than he disliked having attention drawn to him in public.

Malcolm, b. 1894

My uncle, second son of Michael Robert. He served in RNAS in the First World War – the only family naval connection. He worked as a technician for *his* uncle Marcel Joseph and married Margaret (Maggie). They had one son, Joseph, who is now married with two sons. He was killed in an air-raid in the Second World War when a bomb took out two outer walls of his bedroom leaving him pinned in bed by the chimney, which had fallen across his legs, with the floor in imminent danger of collapse. He was rescued by a fireman, who was awarded the George Medal, but died of exposure.

Michael Claud, b. 1896

My other uncle, youngest son of Michael Robert, a good example of the Anglicisation of family names. He won the Mons Star in the First World War but was killed in 1915. Severely wounded in a night raid, he managed to crawl several hundred yards in the dark but, with the luck of the Huttons, went parallel to the front line and died through loss of blood.

Daphne Horner, b. 1906

My mother. The only child of William and Sarah Horner, she lived with her parents until her teens and then went to school in Gloucester. Later she stayed with a doctor friend in Torquay and attended secretarial college. She was an accomplished pianist and violinist. She went to London and entered the civil service, where she met Charles Robert Hutton whom she married in 1926. After his death she refused to put the children into an orphanage, as had been suggested she should, but kept the family together. Once her youngest child Freda was old enough to go to nursery school she took a job with an accountant in London. She was later employed as a secretary at an art college, and in 1951 became secretary to a Conservative agent. She retired in 1966. Two years later she moved to Worcester and is now somewhat remote from the family. She would like to move nearer but refuses to make the decision. As she is now 78 and lives alone, she is a worry to all the family.

Kevin, b.1927

My elder brother. When he was about 5 he had an accident as he was riding off on my indoor tricycle to prevent me getting it. He fell onto a needle on the floor, and the tip broke off and lodged behind his knee cap. He was in hospital for over a year, while unsuccessful attempts were made to remove it. He had to wear a calliper for long afterwards and was never able to play games at school.

James, b.1933

My younger brother. The only memorable occasion in childhood was when Kevin had him 'executed' by a firing squad, which consisted of an air rifle. He was chosen solely because he could wear my overcoat on top of his own – Kevin believed in taking some precautions. Always a little distant from me, James resented my attempts to emulate Kevin. He developed the habit of throwing things at me when he was annoyed – usually sister Freda's building bricks, but anything handy, even the cat. He would then try to blame me when windows inevitably got broken, saying that I shouldn't have ducked. He joined the army in 1951. A mathematical genius, he got into computers on the ground floor and is now a senior manager and systems analyst. In 1965 he married Silvia, a nice and infernally capable female. They live in Kent and have two sons.

Freda, b.1940

My younger sister, the daughter Father had always wanted. She was brought up by three brothers in three different ways. Outwardly she had an uneventful childhood. She married David, a friend of James's, who was also in computers, but while James stayed put in one company David changed his job several times, improving it each time. He is now making a go of his own computer firm. They have two sons and one daughter. The latter, born in 1970, was a difficult pregnancy which followed a miscarriage.

Ian Hutton, b.1929

Myself. I was born at Clapham Common (in a nursing-home) when the family lived at Lavender Hill. In 1937 they moved to Kent. I hero-worshipped my elder brother, Kevin, to the extent that, in exchange for a toy bulldozer of Kevin's that I coveted, I agreed to take the blame for Kevin's misdeeds, even though the bulldozer was always taken back again until next time. I was always willing to execute Kevin's bright ideas. Once, supervised by Kevin who was safe from retribution, I went crawling through long grass armed with a pair of pliers purloined from Father to cut a hole in the wire mesh of a large chicken-run so that Kevin could catch the runaway chickens. He would then return them and earn praise and reward. On another occasion Kevin filled the spare room, his chemistry laboratory, with chlorine gas and sent me in wearing his gas mask to test it. Fortunately it worked.

I was always in trouble off my own bat too, and usually caught for it. I was sad at Father's death and missed him very much, though in later life I was taken to task by my younger daughter when she heard that I hadn't cried when told the sad news. I had few friends, but those I had were close. I was rather shy and tended to get picked on at school, but liked attention. I was often in trouble with teachers because of a tendency to the sort of practical joke that flouted authority. I was evacuated during the war to the Lake District with James, and enjoyed it. Far from brilliant at school, my usual report was 'Could do better if he tried', which was quite true. I just scraped through the School Certificate in spite of the headmaster's opinion that it was impossible.

After school, I worked as an errand boy for a chemist for 18 months, during which time I managed a week's cycling holiday in Holland, by myself, at the end of October 1947. In 1948 I joined the navy as a seaman. I soon discovered I was in the wrong branch but managed to find a side route to an office job. In many ways the navy was just like school.

In 1954 I went to a friend's wedding as best man. There I met Anne, who was a bridesmaid, and three months later, to the surprise of both of us, I proposed. Anne never actually said 'yes', but we both accepted it as agreed and married in 1955. In October 1956 I was sent out to Suez, returning in May 1957.

We had a bed-sit at Tooting Bec Common. But when I landed a shore job in Portsmouth we got a flat in Havant and later married quarters in Portsmouth. After a year I joined *HMS Mauritius* for what was to be my last sea-going commission – a good one with plenty of foreign travel. During this time I managed a 18-day holiday in Malta, Tangier and Spain with Anne. On that ship I was Commander's Writer and began at last to take life seriously. For my last year in the navy I was ashore at Devonport and lived with Anne in Plymouth. I used this period to complete the growing-up process and to prepare for civilian life.

In 1960 I left the navy to join Her Majesty's Customs & Excise. I spent the first 18 months in training and as a supernumerary in London. At first we lived with Mother in Kent and then in a flat in Richmond. Late in 1961 I was transferred to Northern Ireland Land Boundary Patrol at Newry and we got a house in Warrenpoint. This was an interesting and enjoyable job, which enabled me to learn to drive. The family could visit Anne's home.

It was during this period that the family was assembled. Anne worked on an inverse ratio: when we had no children she wanted six; when we had two she thought four was plenty; when we had four she felt two would have been ideal; and when we had five she didn't want any. That is of course an exaggeration. Anne has always liked, and still likes, children. The problem was not so much the number as the frequency of the arrivals:

Sean

Born in Plymouth in 1960. There was some difficulty with his birth, which was prolonged: the first indication was at 11 pm and he was not finally born till 5.30 pm the next day. The delivery was difficult and he needed oxygen and an incubator.

Geoffrey

Born in Kent in 1961. At that time I was in digs in Northern Ireland and the family moved to a hotel in Newry less than three weeks later.

Margaret

Born in Northumberland in 1964. She arrived about a fortnight late, but otherwise no problems.

Louis

Born in Kent in 1965. There was some trouble with the birth – he turned blue.

Claire

Born in Plymouth in 1966. There were no problems with her birth, but when she was only a few weeks old she developed gastroenteritis and was in hospital for many weeks. Partly because of this and partly because of Anne's disaffection with the Church, she was not baptized, for which she has never forgiven us.

I was transferred to Dover in 1965. The family stayed with Mother in Kent until November when they moved into a house in Folkestone. This was the family's first venture into home ownership. In 1968 I was promoted and posted to London. I bought a house in Barking, Essex, and was fixed at Gravesend. I became interested in training on a part-time basis and became involved in staff training in that capacity. As the years passed, I was frustrated at not getting promotion. I was active in the Union and began to make myself an essential part of the local staff on both a welfare and social basis. In 1971 I joined the Scouts and, as disaffection with the job developed, I drew fulfilment from that.

By the late 70s increased disaffection with my job plus family troubles led to a move to Portsmouth, effected in 1980. It is interesting to note that this was the tenth move in twenty-five years of marriage, and the eleven years in Barking were the longest period I had lived in one house in my whole life.

The move to Portsmouth signalled the end of my hopes of promotion but failed to give any added job satisfaction. Without Scouts as an outlet I became more interested in freelance philatelic journalism. I began seriously in 1976. During 1983 I found renewed interest in work when I was employed at Southampton, but that too collapsed. I am now again at a loose end in the Department and looking for a suitable peg on which to hang the purpose of my life.

Margaret Anne, b.1933

My wife. The daughter of Robert Goldie, a New Zealand soldier, and Jean McKinnon, an Irish woman of Scottish descent, she was born at Ballymena, Co. Antrim. She lived at Broughshane with grandmother McKinnon, who died when she was 5. She went into a convent. The exact circumstances are somewhat blurred, but she seems to have become a ward of court; the parents were presumably divorced. She remained in the convent until she was 16, giving the poor nuns a load of trouble, it would seem. As many of the girls stayed long after 16, she must have had to leave, possibly because of her legal status. Anyway she was packed off to London to a job. Her mother, living in Manchester and apparently married to another New Zealander, or possibly an Australian, did get in touch, but Anne had been warned by the nuns against possible exploitation and gave her the brush-off. The warning may have been due more to the divorced status of her mother.

Anne had an argument with her employer and walked out. A stranger in a strange city, she was refused at a C of E hostel because she was RC and approached a bus inspector, thinking from his peaked cap that he was a Garda (policeman), and asked if he knew where she could stay the night. Fortunately she picked the right one and he took her to a friend in a hotel and got her a job. The next few years are known only to Anne, but late in 1953 a friend from the convent, Maria Hobbs, who was engaged to be married to a sailor, asked her to be bridesmaid. The fiancé, Jim Hines, told her about me, his best man, who he said was very shy and reserved. Anne decided she would have a date with me. Meanwhile Jim had warned me about Anne, who he said was 'flighty'. At the wedding reception Anne managed to monopolise me, at one point placing a vase of flowers between me and another Irish girl sitting opposite me at the table. At that time she was working as a domestic help, living in, with a family in Golders Green. I lived in Kent. Anyway, Anne got her date. More followed, in spite of the distance, and somehow this match of opposites succeeded.

Once 'safely' married to me, Anne proved to be very capable. She is a person to whom people (and animals) take very easily and she got on very well with my family. It was probably fortunate that, with me in the navy and not there all the time, we were able to ease into the marriage. At the same time the parting was not too severe, and after six months I took a shore job that kept us together for a year. She was keen to have a family and was quite disappointed when no baby came, though I wasn't really worried one way or the other. Perhaps I preferred not to have the responsibility. Anne took medical advice and made me have a check-up too, but there was no medical problem. When I got a shore job on my last year in the navy, Anne more or less gave up trying, on the grounds that it would be better to get settled in civilian life first. Of course she immediately became pregnant, and Sean was born a fortnight before I began my terminal leave.

When the family were living in Ireland we visited Anne's old home, which I had no trouble finding with Anne's directions. It was occupied by a woman who remembered Anne. She told us a curious story, though it is a bit disjointed. A relation of Anne's, a cousin possibly, called Paddy McKinnon, had been convicted of manslaughter. Anne did once recall an uncle in the Irish Army.

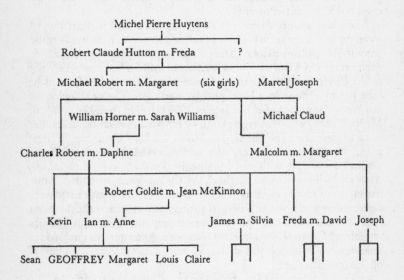

Format and Philosophy of the Meetings

1. The presenting 'delinquent' is, all or some of the time, to a greater or lesser degree, a personification of issues which are unconscious and require to be made conscious in his family. Unless this happens, dangerous situations will ensue in the family: what are known as 'catastrophes on the time horizon'.

2. The presenting delinquent's own personality is more or less, from time to time, or constantly, swamped by alien themes arising from these unconscious, covert familial issues (alien themes, ego alien factors, evil spirits, etc.) He is often too frightened to acknowledge what is happening to his old familiar self. When his 'self' is swamped by these alien themes it tries to rationalise them and their effects. To submit to 'treatment' would be to acknowledge that a terrifying and devastating change is happening to the 'self' which is not explicable in rational terms, i.e. he must be mad. Individual 'therapy' is therefore avoided by the presenting delinquent except as a manipulative manoeuvre, e.g. to placate authority figures. Clearly also, if the delinquent did co-operate, such individual therapy would leave the family unwittingly in a position of jeopardy.

3. The family, at any rate initially, tend to limit the problem to the delinquent rather than to address themselves to issues which are by definition unconscious. They do not see themselves as in need of 'treatment'. But they usually do see the presenting delinquent as needing 'treatment'.

4. A meeting of relevant individuals – professionals and family members – will always be found to contain within it the covert issues which need identification and management.

5. The format of the meeting can:

(a) ensure that the delinquent is not allowed to be the only point of discussion, which would be too threatening for him;
(b) stop the family feeling that they are either on trial or irrelevant;

27

(c) prevent unnecessary anxieties from damaging the ability of relevant people to think.

6. The professionals will be bound to experience first-hand, in themselves, the effects of the alien themes – those covert themes current in the family, which require identification and management. Their overt identification and management of these aliens in themselves at the meeting provides a model for family members, thereby preventing these themes:

(a) from being projected into the 'delinquent';
(b) from being projected into another member of the family, e.g. a younger sibling;
(c) from being enacted in some other 'loss of control' syndrome, e.g. a medical condition in a parent;
(d) from blocking further positive personal and interpersonal development within the family. (That is to say, blocking the family from getting 'better' – necessarily better than it was. 'Better' is commonly thought of as the removal of symptoms; a psychoanalyst may use the term to mean a better-than-before person.)

7. The purpose of the 'meeting', or 'family meeting', is to provide an opportunity for professionals and non-professionals to express, share and discuss feelings about an agreed topic. Attendance can be by invitation, insistence or compulsion.

8. The format of the meetings is as follows. They last exactly one hour and consist of three parts of no fixed proportion: (1) Pre-professionals';
(2) Joint; (3) Post-professionals'.

(1) Preliminary professionals' meeting (i.e. only professionals present):

(a) Election of Chairman and Clerk to the meeting;
(b) Reading, approval and discussion of previous pre-professionals' meeting;
(c) Reading, approval and discussion of previous post-professionals' meeting;
(d) Discussion of anything not felt appropriate for the second, or joint, part of the meeting – called 'taboo topics' – e.g. other relevant cases, preliminary discussion of very sensitive issues, theorising, professional/political issues with indirect relevance to the case. Conversely this part of the meeting does not give a

licence to the professionals to 'gossip', i.e. to discuss matters more appropriate to communal discussion at the joint meeting.

(2) Joint meeting (i.e. professionals joined by non-professionals):

  (a) Introductions of new people and roles, including the meeting's officers – the Chairman and clerk. These new people are given some insight into the philosophy and format of the meetings. There are three methods. The best is for new people to be asked to 'guess' what the procedure is and then to be instructed by the Chairman. (This technique is akin to that used by a doctor when faced with the necessity of telling a patient that he has cancer. The doctor should first ask the patient what he thinks might be wrong. Otherwise the patient will cling to his own fantasies – good or bad – thus blocking off his ability to understand the clearest of explanations.) Alternatively they are simply instructed by the Chairman. Or again they can be requested to 'flounder'. That is, they are asked to tune in as best they can, with the assurance that the Chairman will try to assist them as the meeting progresses. The method used will depend on prevailing factors, such as the number of new people present, the time available for the joint meeting, and whether the new people have had previous briefing by someone already familiar with the procedure.

  (b) Announcements as to who else has been invited, or whose presence has been insisted upon, and why they are not present if known. The decision is made on whether an invitation is to be superseded by an insistence and whether an insistence is to be superseded by a physical compulsion.

  (c) Reading, correcting and final approval of previous joint meeting.

  (d) Decision on the 'agreed topic', which must be understandable, if necessary, to a very young child.

  (e) Individual comments, each person being given one totally uninterrupted opportunity to address the topic. The order of speaking is the same as the order of seating – in a circle, the psychoanalyst usually speaking last.

  (f) Free discussion. The discussion is 'natural', except that the Chairman has ultimate authority. For instance, he may stop two people talking at once if necessary. It is in this part of the meeting that those present decide upon, or decide against, another meeting. If they agree on another meeting they arrange it; it is the only executive event in the entire meeting that is carried into other places or times.

The non-professionals are asked to leave the joint meeting when the Chairman at his discretion decides.

(3) Post-professionals' meeting:

This is the second opportunity for professionals to discuss among themselves, for instance by following up intuitive notions which might be unnecessarily threatening in their undigested form to the non-professionals. The minutes of joint meetings may be given, or sent, to the non-professionals, so the minutes of the pre- and post-professionals' meeting have to be recorded on separate sheets of paper.

1. The first meeting

Venue: Orwell House   20th May 1976
Present: Dr Pitt-Aikens, Chairman
           Mr Dowe, Local Authority Social Worker legally responsible for Geoffrey Hutton
           Mrs Pannell, link Social Worker at Orwell House and clerk to the meeting
           Dr Bolton, trainee psychiatric colleague of TPA
           Mr & Mrs Hutton
           Geoffrey
           Claire
           Margaret
           Louis

At the preliminary professionals' meeting Mr Dowe agreed to remain in ignorance of the format and philosophy of the proceedings till the joint meeting when the family would also be present. There were no 'taboo topics'.

TPA established that Mr Dowe would be leaving the case shortly and that this should be mentioned in the joint meeting. With Mrs Pannell he thought that a suitable focus for discussion would be 'the arrangement between the Local Authority Social Services Department, represented by Mr Dowe, and Orwell House whereby Orwell House looked after and educated Geoffrey'. Mr Dowe agreed.

The family were brought into the joint meeting. Introductions were made. Sean, the eldest son, who had also been invited, was taking exams and so could not be present.

The Chairman asked the newcomers what they imagined these meetings were for.

Mr Dowe guessed that they were to do with Geoffrey's future.

Mr Hutton thought it was to help Geoffrey.

Margaret said they were for Geoffrey.

Geoffrey said he had no idea.

Louis was overcome by laughter.

31

Claire said she didn't know.

Mrs Hutton thought the meeting was 'to try and straighten Geoffrey out and see why he is as bad as he is'.

Louis, on his second attempt, said he didn't know.

The Chairman then defined the purpose of the meeting as a planned opportunity for professional and non-professional people to come together to express, share and discuss how they felt about the arrangement between the Local Authority Social Services Department, represented by Mr Dowe, and Orwell House whereby Orwell House would be looking after and educating Geoffrey. This was followed by a brief outline of the format and philosophy of the meetings.

Mrs Pannell began 'individual comments' by welcoming the family, saying she was glad they were able to come, especially in view of the long journey involved. The staff had seen Mr Hutton and Geoffrey during the previous week at a 'pre-admission visit' and gathered that they felt fairly happy about Orwell House. The staff didn't know what Geoffrey was thinking. He found it hard to express himself, and one of the purposes of these meetings was to discover why he found himself in care and what had led up to it. It was sad for a boy to leave his family and go so far from home, so it was important to understand why such a big step had become necessary.

Dr Bolton said he didn't yet know anything about the family or Geoffrey but, having worked at Orwell House with TPA for some time now, he was wondering whether he could guess anything. Had anything like this happened before in Mr or Mrs Hutton's family? Had an important person left home, as in the present situation?

Louis said, 'I don't know', looking amused and sad all at once. Prompted by the Chairman, he said he didn't think Geoffrey should go so far from home.

Mrs Hutton said she felt that Geoffrey needed to be away from home and from some of the friends he had made. She thought he should have gone to a boarding school when he was younger for his own good, to be given things they couldn't give him at home.

Claire said she didn't know what to think.

Geoffrey said he didn't know either.

Margaret said she wanted him to be here because it was for his own benefit and she knew some of his friends. But he was a load of fun. They had had fun when he came home one evening from Hartland (the Assessment and Observation Centre where Geoffrey stayed before his transfer to Orwell House).

Mr Hutton said he wanted to do the best for Geoffrey. 'We can't do it ourselves – we have had to ask for help from outside. This may be his last chance.' His own father had died when he himself was eleven and he had been evacuated to the country for nine months. Otherwise there had been no upsets in his family.

Here Mrs Hutton interrupted to say that his older brother had died at the age of 17. He added that it had probably been a case of suicide.

Mr Dowe said he agreed with Mrs Pannell's comments on Geoffrey's reticence in expressing himself and hoped that coming to these meetings might help him. He hoped also that Orwell House would meet Geoffrey's needs. He felt that he and the department had let him and the family down. Unfortunately the arrangement by which Geoffrey lived at home and attended day school had collapsed. The situation at home had become very difficult, with Geoffrey going out whenever he pleased. On the whole the children got on pretty well together, but recently there had been confrontations with Geoffrey.

TPA said they should all know precisely why they had made the arrangement. Children were unnecessarily frightened if they didn't understand the reasons for things. Geoffrey might be at Orwell House because Mr Dowe's department had simply said he should be. Perhaps there was no other school for Geoffrey. Perhaps his mother and father needed a rest. He for one wanted a simple, understandable reason. Mr Hutton had mentioned that he had been only 11 when his own father had died. This was common among boys at Orwell House. In every one of fifty-six cases at least one of the boys' parents had lost at least one of their own parents during childhood. This was an important point to remember when thinking about the arrangement.

Mr Cook, one of the Orwell House housemasters, who had joined the meeting late, said that, from what he had seen last week at the pre-admission visit and now, the Huttons seemed different from many of the families they had there. They appeared more stable. He was surprised that Geoffrey was coming here and that he seemed so happy about it. They would just have to wait and see what developed.

In the free discussion Dr Bolton remarked that the children used their hands a good deal, and said it was possible to communicate by actions. Geoffrey might express things to people by actions rather than words.

TPA asked Mr Dowe whether he would be leaving, and he said he would – in September. TPA noted that it frequently happened that they lost the social worker representing the local authority soon after an 'arrangement' started and that this loss of the person in charge was important.

The clerk observed that Margaret was crossing her eyes.

Dr Bolton asked how Mr and Mrs Hutton felt.

Mrs Hutton said she wanted Geoffrey to be straightened out. He needed help. They had tried everything possible and she felt bad because she thought they had failed.

Mr Hutton said he hadn't agreed with his wife in the past, and although they could see there was something wrong he had thought it could be dealt with within the family. Now he agreed that they had to do something else.

TPA said he found this all very interesting. He observed that he certainly tended to connect present situations with what had happened in the past.

Mr Hutton said he thought him a little late. Perhaps it would have been better if something had been tried earlier. Geoffrey was associated with, but had never been completely part of, the family, though he had been his favourite when he was younger.

TPA asked about Sean.

Mrs Hutton replied that he was 16 and was doing exams. He had a rare eye complaint. He was quiet but a bit bossy and liked his own way. He lost himself in books.

Mr Hutton said Geoffrey tended to resent Sean, especially now that he had his own close friends.

There followed a discussion, which was difficult to clerk, about oxygen being given at birth. TPA remarked that oxygen was good, but too much of it could be bad, and occasionally it was known to damage the eyes of some new-born babies.

The discussion turned to the subject of luck: whether people tended to trust it too much. The number 13 was remarked upon – emblazoned on Geoffrey's shirt.

Mr Hutton then said in response to a question from TPA that he was nearly 48, the age his father had been when he died. His eldest son was nearly 17. Kevin, his brother, had been 13 when his father had died and 17 when he killed himself.

Mrs Hutton said that since going to live in that house in Barking they had been very unlucky.

Mr Hutton said it wasn't *very* bad luck and they had lived there twice as long as in any other house.

At the post-professionals' meeting a discussion followed on how things at home and at the Assessment Centre had deteriorated over the months.

Mr Dowe thought his department had let the family down badly.

TPA had a feeling that 'this luck business' was extremely important.

Mrs Hutton, according to Mr Dowe, believed 'in the moon'.

*

What, I asked, as I read through these minutes, did TPA make of that? It appeared to me less than enlightening. He said, first, that they tried to avoid high-falutin' terms but even the word 'arrangement' could seem bewildering. He said they wanted to arrive at a reason for Geoffrey's admission to Orwell House that even a child could understand; that phrases such as 'for his own good', 'for his own benefit', 'the best for him', 'he needs help' were subjective and meaningless. What was needed – since there was a lot of evidence that places such as Orwell House could actually be bad for children – was a clear reason which would make sense to everybody. Next, he said that it was significant that Mr Dowe was shortly leaving the case, involving Geoffrey in yet another loss of authority. TPA had then felt the hint of a fear that Sean might commit suicide at the same age as his Uncle Kevin. Geoffrey had worn a sweater with the number 13 written on it – the age Kevin had been when his father died. Mrs Pannell had said they didn't know what Geoffrey was thinking, and TPA said of course they didn't. The whole point was that it was impossible to know what these children were thinking. Mr Cook had remarked that the Hutton family was a 'cut above' the rest of the families who found themselves with a child at Orwell House and TPA said that social class made no odds to delinquency – those further up the social scale simply took longer to get into the hands of the authorities. He then said that Sean's eye trouble could be retrolentalfibroplasia – damage to the retina caused by oxygen therapy in cases of premature birth. The retina can become detached. He thought that when later the family spoke of corneal grafts they meant the even more delicate business of retinal repair.

2. The wrong speed

Venue: Orwell House   15th July 1976
Present: Dr Pitt-Aikens, Chairman
              Mr Dowe, Local Authority Social Worker legally
                responsible for Geoffrey
              Mrs Pannell, link Social Worker at Orwell House
              Mrs Evans, Houseparent at Orwell House and clerk to the
                meeting
              Mr & Mrs Hutton
              Geoffrey
              Sean
              Margaret
              Louis
              Claire

The previous pre- and post-professional minutes were read. Discussion was resumed on the family's belief in luck and the moon.

Mrs Pannell said she thought Mrs Evans ought to be told what had happened during the four days' holiday Geoffrey had spent at home.

The Chairman in irritation asked Mrs Pannell why she was bringing that up in this part of the meeting – why not in front of the family, in the joint meeting?

Mrs Evans said that anyway Geoffrey himself had already told her.

The family were late arriving for the joint meeting – except for Geoffrey, who had turned up on time and now went off to collect the others.

They all sat down, and introductions were made. The focus of discussion was decided as the same as the last meeting: the 'arrangement'.

Dr Bolton sent his apologies – he had been promoted to a new post. The minutes of the previous joint meeting were read.

Louis and Margaret wanted to change places, but their mother prevented them because it would have caused giggling.

Sean, who wasn't present at the previous meeting, was asked what he thought they were for and said, 'To enquire about the family and see what we are like.'

The Chairman then gave Sean a brief account of the purpose, format and philosophy of the meeting.

Mrs Pannell began 'individual comments' by saying that since they last met Geoffrey had been admitted to Orwell House, everything seemed to be going well and he was fitting in with no problems. He was harum-scarum but cheerful and agreeable. One weekend at home had seemed to be quite successful, but unfortunately on the second weekend he had caused his parents worry and the people at Orwell House were anxious.

Mr Dowe was interested in what had happened at the weekend and would like to hear Geoffrey's answer to his parents.

Louis had nothing to say.

Mrs Hutton said that the first weekend that Geoffrey was home went smoothly. Geoffrey fitted into the family well, neither going out nor seeing his old friends. The second weekend, however, was very different. The family went fruit-picking to make some pocket money for the holidays and Geoffrey (with some help) picked three boxfuls, but his mother overheard things which alarmed her. Also, he had a lighter which he couldn't account for satisfactorily. She concluded that he was back to his old ways and she was deeply upset.

Claire and Margaret both giggled and said nothing.

Sean said that the first weekend was fine, the second not. Geoffrey had insisted on playing a record at the wrong speed. There had been angry scenes and the record had been broken.

Mr Hutton said that during the first weekend Geoffrey had been as he was three or four years before, chatting happily with the family; but the last weekend had been too long. Geoffrey was back with his old friends. Nothing changed overnight and he had revealed that he was still much the same.

Mrs Evans said that Geoffrey would never do as he was told – unless he felt like it or was faced with absolute insistence – but it was never easy to settle in to a new place and he had done as well as anyone. He had told her his parents weren't happy with his behaviour at the previous weekend and that he must only come home every four weeks. It was early days, however, for a change for the better and she hoped he would soon be more acceptable to the family.

Mrs Evans was interrupted by the Chairman at one point who told her that she was referring to Geoffrey as 'Sean'.

TPA said that he felt Sean's ideas about the purpose of the meeting were correct. Louis, Margaret and Claire, he observed, hadn't contributed but had sat throughout as good as gold. No one had mentioned the important fact that Mr Dowe was leaving, that Mrs Evans had mistakenly referred to Geoffrey as Sean, making him older, and yet Mr Hutton had somewhere previously described Geoffrey as being like him some years before. Did something magic happen at this age, which was the age Mr Hutton had been when his own father had died? Sean had just completed his exams – always a depressing time. TPA remembered it as such when he had taken them himself. Hadn't Mr Hutton's brother committed suicide when he was Sean's present age? He felt the family was neither good nor bad but tended to believe in luck, thinking that things would 'turn out all right'. He wondered whether they yet knew enough. Perhaps Mr Hutton had to change suddenly from being 11 to being a man when his father died – ageing at the wrong speed.

Geoffrey had nothing to say.

Mr Hutton opened the free discussion. He thought Mrs Evans had implied that the family didn't wish to have Geoffrey at home, or to allow him to associate with his friends, but this wasn't true. Nor did he agree with TPA, who implied that he was given to looking into the future. The family were going on holiday the following week but as yet had made no plans. He assured everyone that when his father had died no extra responsibility had come his way and his mother had taken the brunt. When his brother had died it had made no difference at all to him.

Sean said that Geoffrey now tried to stop young Louis from smoking, whereas before he had encouraged him.

Mr Dowe said that certain rules must be observed and remarked on how well the family had behaved although they were frustrated by the rigid format of the meeting.

At the post-professionals' meeting they spoke of Mrs Hutton.

Mrs Pannell commented that she had smiled continuously throughout, seemingly worried by nothing.

Someone observed that she was very like Geoffrey, striding along as if nothing was happening, smiling throughout the turmoil, giving nothing away, keeping herself to herself.

TPA said he felt intuitively that it might have something to do with the fact that she had been orphaned and brought up in an institution herself – a convent.

*

These early meetings, compared with the events which had rendered them necessary, seem bland and unextraordinary. The professionals were still feeling their way, the family perhaps unsure of what was expected of them, Mr and Mrs Hutton very worried, Geoffrey still – as he mostly continued to be – silent, and TPA as yet determined to stick to the format. A further graphic account of Geoffrey's transgressions would make more interesting reading but would contribute nothing useful. One of TPA's pet maxims is that in fraught situations where all those involved are at their wits' end with bewilderment and anxiety, while others are lost in prurient fascination, it is essential that someone should be present who is still able to see the wood for the trees: someone who will indeed press on through the wood until light becomes discernible on the other side. This is impossible if everyone is jumping up and down on the spot twittering 'Goodness how awful'. Progress through the wood may appear, at first, uneventful, but it is progress.

In spite of his silence Geoffrey seemed more human in this meeting. He was on time, went to find his family and behaved like the Geoffrey who was kind to pets. Mr Dowe rather oddly said he would like to hear Geoffrey answer his parents, who as far as I could discern hadn't asked him anything. TPA says this is an example of how even the professionals can be thrown by the meetings. Presumably this question had been asked on some other occasion, and Mr Dowe had forgotten that most of the people in the room would have no idea what he was talking about. This fuzziness is not an indictment, but an illustration of the value, of the meetings. Too often people forget that they have said something which is in effect meaningless and might result in their being at cross-purposes with everyone else. The recording of the meetings serves as a useful reminder of what is in, and what is out of, context.

It was perhaps, muses TPA, significant that Mrs Hutton had been brought up in an institution where all was worked out, planned, timed and predictable, where no one was required to think for herself but all were carried along by the rules.

3. Just a temporary phase

Venue: Orwell House   30th September 1976
Present: Dr Pitt-Aikens, Chairman
            Mr King, Local Authority Social Worker legally
                responsible for Geoffrey Hutton
            Mrs Pannell, link Social Worker at Orwell House and
                clerk to the meeting
            Mr Johnson, Assistant Principal in charge of houseparents
                at Orwell House
            Mr Innes, student at Orwell House
            Mr & Mrs Hutton
            Geoffrey
            Louis
            Margaret

Mrs Pannell recorded this meeting in a style quite different from that adopted by the last clerk – the format is not so clear.

A new social worker, the Assistant Principal and a student were present, as well as the family, Mrs Pannell and TPA. At the pre-professionals' meeting they talked about the recording of the last meeting, which was felt to be 'skeletal', non-detailed. Mr King, a new arrival, felt there was a lot for him to absorb and kindly agreed to 'flounder'.

Mrs Pannell said that it didn't seem long since the last meeting and patterns seemed to have changed. Geoffrey had good spells at Orwell House and bad reports from home. He had been allowed fewer weekends but accepted this equably, being a happy-go-lucky character like this mother, who always seemed to come up smiling in the midst of her large family, all of whom appeared to be bubbling with enthusiasm.

Mr Innes thought Geoffrey's presence at Orwell House a peculiar arrangement and rather puzzling, though he supposed there must be genuine reasons why he was there. He seemed, of all the boys, one of the most normal – enthusiastic about pets, 'soft' and kind. Geoffrey appeared to have been going through a temporary 'phase' and would rejoin his family sooner rather than later.

Mr King felt awkward at having seen Mr and Mrs Hutton several times and Geoffrey only once, which seemed unsatisfactory. He hoped to get more involved soon.

At the joint meeting Mrs Hutton said that when Geoffrey telephoned on their return from holiday he had done all the talking, which was unusual. Previously he had hardly said anything – which she had found difficult to cope with. Perhaps he was coming out of himself. She added that her constant smiling, which someone had mentioned, could be the result of the 'nervousness', which often had this effect on her.

Mr Johnson said he would like to pick up something unminuted that TPA had said last time about Geoffrey's being allowed to be a young boy, to play with the pets etc. On the face of it the Huttons seemed a nice family with a normal home, though they had had their difficulties which might have led to delinquency. The older brother was academically brighter, which might have led to extra pressure on Geoffrey – but then there were always pressures. The social worker lived a long way from Geoffrey and from the family, which could be a reason for his not visiting. Was he guilty or merely remiss? Obviously Geoffrey had good family experiences, which showed in the way he behaved and related to people. He was lively and cheerful and able to put a brave face on things, but serious at times, as for instance at this meeting.

Claire and Margaret had nothing to say.

Mr Hutton said he agreed with the two things that Brenda his wife, had said. (Where on earth did Brenda come from? His wife is called Anne.) He continued: A lot of people had noticed that Geoffrey behaved differently when he was alone from the way he behaved when he was with others, including his family, with whom he could be difficult. He denied that Sean was brighter than Geoffrey and referred to the death of his own brother: although he had felt the effect, he said, he had had no extra responsibility. Last meeting's minutes sounded wrong.

Geoffrey had nothing to say.

It is difficult to make sense of the next part of the meeting. TPA gave his view that it could be extremely important to understand something, because the case might be quite different from what had previously been supposed. For instance: Mr Johnson didn't know Geoffrey as well as his father did, and TPA's inclination therefore was to believe the father. There was a connection between the length of time Geoffrey spent at home and the revelation of a different side to him; two days weren't enough to see the true Geoffrey. Again, looking behind mother's smile you saw something different, and Mr Hutton had thought the minutes of the last meeting at odds with the facts. TPA had spoken of Mr Hutton's father's death when he meant his brother's. If such mistakes were allowed to stand, things could be puzzling. In different situations Geoffrey was different. Was that connected in any way with the pasts of both parents? Had they been seen less as individuals and more as part of a group? Mrs Hutton had lived in a residential school and she may have hated being part of a group, without letting herself admit it. For some reason they had got the wrong end of the stick about Mrs Hutton. He suspected that Geoffrey was trying to show everyone that things weren't necessarily what they seemed to be. It would be dangerous if the family persuaded themselves that facts weren't facts; foolish, if when times were difficult they smiled instead of worrying.

During the free discussion, Mrs Pannell wondered how Geoffrey reacted in larger groups at Orwell House, and there was some discussion about children at nursery school. (Mrs Pannell who was clerking couldn't remember in what connection.) Mrs Hutton said that her grandmother was abroad when she had gone into the convent. She was less than 5 and was happy. She made some comments about holidays with Geoffrey being a strain. There were groups of boys around whom she didn't want Geoffrey to be with.

Some questions and answers followed about Sean who was slower than Geoffrey but worked hard. Mrs Hutton said Geoffrey picked things up quickly but then lost interest. She could herself have done better but lost opportunities, wasted them. She saw Geoffrey in herself.

At the end of the meeting Geoffrey breathed a sigh of relief.

In the post-professionals' meeting TPA referred again to 'mistakes', mentioning Mrs Hutton's talking about her grandmother being abroad – didn't she really mean her *mother*?

*

On this occasion there were several new faces. One of the reasons no one ever quite understands what is going on in these families may be that the professionals seldom if ever stay long enough. The way of working keeps changing and therefore the continuity and understanding are lost. Also the flavour of the recording changes with each clerk, who has licence to do it as he sees fit. Any combination of precis and verbatim report is permitted, provided the content can be adjudged a 'useful record'.

I was interested to learn that Geoffrey was good with the pets, having been struck by the thought that I should very much hate to be the pet of delinquent children, and I was relieved that at least the poor creatures had him to look after them. He was described by Mr Johnson as lively and cheerful with 'good family experiences'. TPA sighs at this and says that half the families in the world are asking in anguish 'Where did we go wrong?'

Mr Innes predicted, incorrectly, that Geoffrey would rejoin his family sooner rather than later, and had been going through a 'phase'. People who optimistically use this term have no comprehension of the enormity of what has happened to the delinquent's personality and are lost in wishful thinking.

Mr Hutton, when it came to his turn, remarked that the last meeting's minutes 'sounded wrong' and TPA pounces on this as a first indication that Mr Hutton had a vested interest in 'tense disparity'. 'In what?' I ask.

Mr Hutton is a 'tense tamperer', continues TPA: a 'specialised kind of liar'. This sounds rude, and I still don't know what he's talking about. I don't think he means that Mr Hutton lies like a carpet – just that his Unconscious fools about a bit.

To be fair, the jargon is kept to a minimum in these meetings: to innocent-sounding little terms like 'taboo topic', 'format', 'arrange-ment', 'flounder' etc., which are within the grasp of the meanest intelligence. I think I understand (but in fact I don't) what is meant by schizophrenia, neurosis, hysteria, manic depressive psychosis etc., but I know beyond any doubt that when the psychoanalytical establishment refers to 'archaic super-ego elements', or 'physicalistic pseudo-spatial reification of the mental apparatus', it has lost me. TPA says the stunned layman faced with such impossible terms is allowed to give up – it's easy – whereas more accessible jargon which he could be expected to understand with a little effort is seen as difficult; so that people will unwittingly prefer the impossible while decrying the difficult. (He talks like that, and after a moment's thought it will become clear.)

At the end of the meeting, as Mrs Hutton was speaking, there came a juxtaposition of two ideas about the roots of delinquency. She said that Geoffrey kept bad company – a popular reason for errant behaviour – and also revealed that she had gone into the convent school when she was less than 5. It is the latter piece of information that is deemed significant.

4. Home and away

Venue: Clinic consulting-room   13th December 1976
Present: Dr Pitt-Aikens, Chairman
           Mr King, Local Authority Social Worker legally
              responsible for Geoffrey Hutton
           Mrs Pannell, link Social Worker
           Mr Quatermain, on the residential staff at Orwell House,
              clerk to the meeting
           Mr & Mrs Hutton
           Geoffrey
           Claire
           Margaret
           Louis

It seems to have become a tradition for TPA to chair the meetings, though the clerk keeps changing. The meeting started late. In the pre-professionals' meeting the professionals agreed that it was 'not taboo', when it came to the joint meeting, to discuss the current dispute between the parents and the local authority concerning their financial contributions in respect of Geoffrey's placement at Orwell House.

Mrs Pannell and Mr Hutton were delayed by traffic. Mrs Pannell, on arrival, referred to Mr Hutton's saying that the last minutes were very sketchy and that since she had been clerk on that occasion that was her fault.

At the joint meeting there were yet more new faces and not enough chairs, so TPA (as chairman after all) went off to get some.

Mrs Pannell said that she hadn't actually got much to say and nothing that was very different from what she said last time. She thought the 'arrangement', whereby Orwell House were looking after and educating Geoffrey for the local authority, was working out quite well for Geoffrey but she found it a bit surprising that he should be as happy as he was at Orwell House. She couldn't tell whether this was because he was putting a brave face on it, or whether underneath he really did enjoy it, since there had been times when he had the choice and had chosen to stay at Orwell House rather than go home for the weekend. She wondered whether he stayed because he really preferred to or whether he was avoiding some situation at home.

Mr Quatermain said he thought the arrangement was going fairly well. It had had its ups and downs but now Geoffrey was settling down, especially with regard to his place in the pecking order, although his relationship with the other boys varied. He thought that Geoffrey's approach, which at present was childish, would change and that he·would see things more clearly. He was glad to see that all the family were present and were happy and smiling.

Mr Hutton wanted to query one thing in the minutes. He couldn't agree with TPA that in a couple of days one didn't see the true Geoffrey. He thought that was putting things totally the wrong way round. If he was home for longer periods they might possibly see the other Geoffrey, but the Geoffrey they generally saw was the true one, the one they wanted. During the last few weekends there had been an extremely nice atmosphere. After the weekends Geoffrey would ring up to keep in touch. In the past the other Geoffrey had emerged after a few days.

Mr King said tentatively that Geoffrey's wanting to be home for weekends was an encouraging sign, and it was good that Mr and Mrs Hutton were happy with the weekends too. He was still puzzled by Geoffrey's attitude towards home – his desire to be there and his misbehaviour which prevented it. Also, when discussing the subject of home he would clam up and become awkward. Still, true, he did seem to be fitting in well.

Geoffrey had nothing to say.

TPA was surprised by the clear appearance of happiness in the family. He had been surprised to learn that there had been a long dispute about finances between the family and the social services. It had apparently been resolved now, but he wanted to stress that the family had experienced unhappiness and unease which he, at least, had not known about until the last post-professionals' meeting when he had only learnt of it by the skin of his teeth – it hadn't even been recorded in the minutes. He felt there was a theme of 'clammed-up unhappiness', to use Mr King's words, which was worrying because such unhappiness could sometimes well up or suddenly show itself devastatingly. He would much prefer to hear about unhappinesses when they were small than allow them to go on grumbling silently and invisibly until they spurted up and knocked everybody sideways. He couldn't help feeling that something like that had been showing itself in Geoffrey long before the 'arrangement' had even started. Would he seem all right and then suddenly badly startle everybody?

Perhaps that was another way for him to portray a tendency within the family which may have had some connection with his mother's and father's own families from long ago.

Louis had nothing to say.

Claire had nothing to say.

Margaret didn't know what to say.

Mrs Hutton agreed that the last few weekends with Geoffrey at home had been marvellous, but Geoffrey didn't want to go home with them today as on Wednesday there was a show at Orwell House which he wanted to see.

In the free discussion Mrs Pannell observed that not many boys would deprive themselves of a weekend at home just to see a show. She wondered if Geoffrey liked it *equally* at home and at Orwell House.

Geoffrey said that he would rather be at home all the time but agreed that it was 'all right' at Orwell House – there was plenty to do, which was why he liked being there.

Mrs Pannell asked where Sean was, and was told he was at school doing his exams. She asked Geoffrey what he wanted to do now that he was in his last year of school, and he said he wanted to join the navy.

Mrs Hutton said her husband had applied for a job in South Africa, and there was a discussion about the other children's education.

Mr Hutton said they might go to a boarding school in this country, but he would quite like to take them as well for the experience.

The children said they would prefer to go to South Africa.

TPA thought that today most people would regard South Africa as the last place on earth they would wish to go to, yet 'the Hutton family see it differently from the rest of us' and Geoffrey sees 'something' in a show, which means he will miss five days at home.

There followed a discussion about the financial dispute between Mr Hutton and the social services and how this might influence feelings about the 'arrangement' between the social services and Orwell House.

Mr King said Mr Hutton carried on running battles with other agencies where he had to pay or receive money.

TPA commented that this was very time-consuming and asked how much time was put into admittedly legitimate grievances because of Mr Hutton's inability to give up.

Mrs Pannell said Geoffrey seemed not to show grievance and

apparently accepted things – for instance he would forego five days at home for the sake of the show.

TPA said he thought that this family had, at all costs, to be in control of luck – whether good or bad. If there was an issue with the council which you could battle with then you had life under control.

Mr Hutton said that if Geoffrey felt any pressure he bottled it up, so that it came out in peculiar ways. Things tended to happen at home when Geoffrey wasn't at his best. There were breakages. Before the arrangement came about he had felt that Geoffrey would be better off at a boarding school – mainly to give him some experience of living with people other than his own family. It would broaden his experience. He supposed that that was why they wanted to go to South Africa.

The next meeting was arranged. Geoffrey objected to the date, to be told by TPA that he would have to lump it.

At the post-professionals' meeting TPA asked whether anyone else had felt an undercurrent of 'not niceness' during this meeting which hadn't been there before.

Mrs Pannell felt that Mr Hutton had been very antagonistic.

Mr Quatermain thought he felt the need to have a grudge in life.

Mr King saw Mr Hutton as 'the last of a dying race' – the typical British man who would fight to the death for himself and his family.

Mrs Pannell thought that was nice.

TPA remarked that if it was true it was not so nice. Perhaps it was Mr Hutton's wish not to resurrect, but actually to be part of, a dying race.

*

Mrs Pannell had expressed surprise that Geoffrey seemed so happy at Orwell House. There was no reason why he should not be, but she wondered about it. There was something about Geoffrey that made people think. Of another child she might have remarked 'He looks happy' and left it at that, but Geoffrey was another matter.

TPA noted that throughout the meetings Mr Hutton talked about different Geoffreys – the one you saw and the one you didn't – according to how long you were with him. Perhaps this was related to the fact that Mr Hutton had been evacuated to the country during the war as a child, and presumably at that time had visited or been visited by his mother. Perhaps there is something unnatural about visits. The Spanish proverb says fish and visitors stink after three days. TPA says that now that hospitals have more or less open visiting hours people find it awkward; they have to make decisions about how long to stay, working their way through the patient's grapes and making conversation. Geoffrey's personality is frequently perceived by his father as a function of the time spent with him. Geoffrey caricatures that 'visiting' aspect of life. There is a relation between the time people are together and the way they behave and perceive each other. In order to get a crashing bore off the telephone you will agree to dine with him next week. As soon as you hang up he is no longer there – relief. But the dreadful dinner begins to loom closer and you hate him more. Time does funny things to people – to all people, not just the Geoffreys.

TPA remarks smugly that there is a tendency to think of psychiatrists as rather soft. (This is true. There is a widely held view that they are not only nuts but hopelessly gullible. How very odd. The ones I know aren't a bit. They are rather disenchanted on the whole.) But look at Geoffrey objecting to the date of the next meeting and being told by TPA that he can jolly well lump it.

5. Bang, bang, you're dead

Venue: Clinic consulting-room   18th March 1977
Present: Dr Pitt-Aikens, Chairman
           Mr King, Local Authority Social Worker legally
               responsible for Geoffrey Hutton
           Mrs Pannell, link Social Worker, Orwell House
           Mr Johnson, Assistant Principal in charge of houseparents
               at Orwell House and clerk to the meeting
           Mrs Dovey, sociology graduate and participant observer
           Sister Bessant, participant observer
           Mr & Mrs Hutton
           Geoffrey
           Claire
           Margaret
           Louis

In the preliminary professionals' meeting it was agreed that two students might attend as participant observers: Sr. Bessant, a nurse, and Mrs Dovey, a sociology graduate. Sean had been invited but did not turn up as he had a heavy day at school.

Geoffrey was asked what he felt about the 'arrangement' and responded, 'Don't know.'

Mr Johnson said he felt angry at Geoffrey's reply and wondered whether his parents also felt angry. Geoffrey was a delightful boy at times but he seemed to have two sides, both of which had now become apparent – the very bad boy who had had to leave home to be looked after somewhere else and the boy who was part of what struck everyone as a nice family unit. It was exasperating that they didn't seem much nearer to knowing how the events that had led to the present 'plight' had come about. Every time he met the family he was surprised by the behaviour of the other children, who were quite relaxed in a situation which many would find difficult to cope with. They seemed to cope very well and he was impressed, but he wondered how Geoffrey felt about it.

Margaret had nothing to say.

Claire had nothing to say.

Louis had nothing to say.

Mrs Pannell said she felt very much the same as Mr Johnson – puzzled about why Geoffrey behaved in such a way that he had had to be taken into care and ended up at Orwell House. She was always saying this, because they saw a family who seemed to be united and yet one of its members had had to be separated and still no one had a clue as to what it was all about. Geoffrey would be 16 at the end of the year, so time in which to investigate the problem was running out. She wondered what he really thought about things at present and what he would be doing when he was 16. He still seemed so young to her that it didn't seem possible that in eight or nine months he would be entitled to go to work – which was what was planned for him. She would be interested to hear from Mr and Mrs Hutton whether anything had come of the South African scheme. Although they hadn't had a meeting for quite a long time, strangely enough it didn't seem very long ago that they were all sitting in the same room. It was very much alive in her mind.

Sr. Bessant said she had read the minutes of the previous meetings but felt she didn't know how Geoffrey had come to be at Orwell House or what had brought it about. She was in the dark.

Mrs Dovey just wished that Geoffrey would say what he thought – tell them why he believed things had gone wrong and whether he felt they had changed at all.

Mrs Hutton said she was extremely pleased with Geoffrey, thought that Orwell House had done wonders for him and was very happy to have him at home, where they now had no trouble with him whatsoever. She was worried about his leaving school in December since he would have had so little education, but feared that no school, let alone his old one, would take him. Nevertheless she was pleased with him.

Mr Hutton agreed. He said Geoffrey was 'back with them', part of the family; it was just Geoffrey now. He also was concerned about what Geoffrey was going to do and Geoffrey didn't discuss it much. The South Africa plan had fallen through since he had heard nothing more, and he was now looking round for something else.

TPA said that, rightly or wrongly, he felt that the 'arrangement' had something to do with the past repeating itself, or with the fear of that happening, particularly of bad things repeating themselves. He was thinking of Mr Hutton's father dying at 48 when Mr Hutton was 11 and of his brother having committed suicide at 17. He wasn't sure how old Sean was now, or Louis, but he guessed Louis was 10 and Sean 16. He was interested to see that Louis had brought a gun with him to today's meeting and wondered about the significance of that. He didn't know how Mr Hutton's brother had died and it might be important to find out. He wondered what the names of Mr Hutton's father and brother had been. He was interested again, on hearing the minutes, by that reference to 'bottling up'. It had been mentioned how things were bottled up in the family, by Mr Hutton especially – his fights with the council, his reasons for wanting to get to South Africa. His contribution to that discussion, however, was 'If Geoffrey's got any pressures he bottles them up', which seemed a bit of a non-sequitur. It was well known . that people who bottle everything up are in some sort of danger from illnesses such as heart disease, ulcers, etc. He worried about Mr Hutton's health. Was he afraid he might die before 50 like his father? On the other hand perhaps there was also a fear that if Mr Hutton didn't bottle things up *he* might be the one to show another side of himself. They had heard enough about the two sides of Geoffrey, who had indeed shown two sides, but lo and behold Orwell House had got to know them both without evaporating into space, so it might be good if Mr Hutton could reveal his suspected other side, because it might prove to be life-saving.

TPA was also worried about Sean and his exam results, suspecting that Sean mightn't have approached his exams in the right spirit. Sean might be in some difficulties, and TPA pointed out that if it weren't for the 'arrangement' with its incorporated family meetings, they wouldn't have the chance of wondering what was happening to Sean. It might be helpful if Mr Hutton (and Mrs Hutton, for that matter) were to change their attitude somewhat – from the liberal 'Come to the meeting if you wish' to 'Now look, Sean, you're coming, and that's that'. This would give him the chance to feel a little less responsible for himself and to depend more on his parents' authority. Often, if children were worried about exams, there was nothing better than for the parents to take some responsibility for the guilt the children would feel about abandoning their books and say, 'Come on, we're going to the pictures.' But, as he had tried to point out, doing that might have made Mr Hutton feel like Hitler. That was a misconception.

Mr King said he had little to add. Part of his problem was not knowing what had gone before, but on the whole everything seemed quite encouraging.

During the free discussion Mr Hutton said that Sean didn't do a lot of swotting. He didn't do anything. The other children would back him up on that. He spent time scribbling on magazines. Mr Hutton felt it was important that Sean should work at school because he made no effort at home at all. He did badly in his exams and it would be wrong to make him miss school at the moment.

Mr Johnson wondered how Geoffrey felt hearing about his brother doing badly.

Geoffrey said he didn't know how he felt.

Mrs Hutton said she thought Geoffrey did know things, being clever, but didn't like to utter them.

Geoffrey said he didn't know what to say.

Mrs Pannell then asked him what he thought about his brother taking exams, and Geoffrey didn't reply. She felt that this was an example of his not wanting to face anything serious.

Mr Johnson referred to Mrs Hutton's remarks about schooling. He thought that Geoffrey was in a better situation at Orwell House than, given his difficulties, he would be in an ordinary school. Geoffrey might have different hopes and ideas about his future.

Mr Hutton said there was a great difference between Sean and Geoffrey. Geoffrey was good at mechanical things – very good at taking his bicycle to pieces. Mr Hutton was concerned about what he would do when he left school in December.

Mr Johnson said all the job possibilities would be looked at.

TPA asked Mr Hutton again what his brother's and father's names were and how his brother had died.

Mr Hutton said his father's name was Charles, his brother's Kevin. His brother had blown himself up with a fulminate detonator. He had attempted suicide three times before – each time that his girl friend had 'chucked him up'. His brother had been taking exams at the time and was thinking about going to university.

TPA asked what the family atmosphere had been like concerning exams.

Mr Hutton said his brother had taken them in his stride. He himself liked taking exams.

Mrs Dovey then asked what had caused Geoffrey's cough.

Mrs Hutton said she thought it was due to smoking, mentioning that Geoffrey spent a fortune on cigarettes.

TPA asked if she gave him money to buy them.

She said she did, since otherwise she feared he would take them from someone else.

Mr Johnson said the school also provided Geoffrey with tobacco money.

Geoffrey was asked how many he smoked a day.

He replied 15 to 20.

At the post-professionals' meeting Mrs Pannell said she didn't feel they were getting anywhere on this case; they were on a treadmill.

TPA said he thought Sean was in trouble – he had had the idea that Sean was a brainy person yet he had got no exam passes. It must be maddening to be at the mercy of someone who wants or needs two sides of everything – certainly Sean needed education, by all accounts, but he also needed these meetings.

*

Mr Johnson after only four meetings was exasperated that they had learned so little about Geoffrey and what had brought him to Orwell House. TPA says that some people might find it appropriate to look right back to the Fall for the reasons for delinquency and that there are no swift answers. Mrs Pannell was also frustrated that they were not making faster progress and seemed to think that when Geoffrey left Orwell House all would be lost. She could see only from her own point of view and failed to realise that there was no reason why the investigation should not continue. So there were two professionals fussing about time as though there was nothing beyond 16. The exasperation, the impatience, TPA informs me, is a function of the way professionals think. Mrs Pannell for a moment thought there was no life after Orwell House. It could be considered that there was an uncanny connection between Geoffrey's nearly bleeding to death as a baby, his uncle's blood and his great uncle bleeding to death in the Great War – a time span of seventy odd years.

Mrs Pannell went on alluding to time, saying that the last meeting seemed recent but it had in fact taken place three months before. 'She's half way there,' says TPA. If she had realised what had happened to her sense of time she might have understood how perhaps the delinquency and the therapy condense relationships, personalities and situations into a short space of time. Sr. Bessant said she felt 'in the dark', but many people knowing less than she are prepared to try and tackle delinquency head on.

TPA was interested in Mr Hutton's non-sequitur and says it often happens that when you are talking to a delinquent's parents about their own problems you think you're going mad because they will be blithely talking about the child as though answering about themselves. The same sort of thing happened later in the meeting. One might have expected those present to have followed TPA's implied connections between Louis's gun, Sean's obvious difficulties and the tragedy of the explosion which had killed Kevin at the age of 17, but no – the meeting got skewed back again on to Geoffrey's behaviour; even Mrs Hutton, who had said earlier that she was pleased with him at present and found him no trouble at all, seemed to recant and said she was afraid he might hijack cigarettes from someone else.

6. The hedge

Venue: Clinic consulting-room   6th June 1977
Present: Dr Pitt-Aikens, Chairman
           Mr King, Local Authority Social Worker legally
               responsible for Geoffrey Hutton
           Mrs Evans, Houseparent at Orwell House and clerk to
               the meeting
           Mr & Mrs Hutton
           Geoffrey
           Claire
           Margaret
           Louis

The preliminary professionals' meeting began on time although only TPA and Mr King had arrived.

Mr King mentioned that there was an issue which Mr and Mrs Hutton didn't want discussed in front of the children. There was talk about what TPA refers to as the 'confidentiality trap'.

TPA thought that the avoidance of issues might be an important theme in this case. He didn't want to know the 'secret' yet but warned Mr King that if he saw fit he would refer to it later.

Mr King said the parents would be anxious about the children's hearing it.

At this point Mrs Evans and Geoffrey arrived, soon followed by the rest of the family who were shown into the waiting room.

Mr King asked about the 'latest development' and was told by the Chairman that Mr and Mrs Hutton didn't wish to discuss it in front of the children, though if Mr King wished to do so there was nothing to stop him. Alternatively, Mr King could suggest that the children leave the room.

When everyone was gathered for the joint meeting Mrs Hutton apologised for being late. They heard that Mrs Pannell was on leave. Sean was busy at school.

The Chairman procured an agreement that they discuss the 'arrangement' whereby Mr King's department of social services was asking Orwell House to look after and educate Geoffrey.

Margaret said she didn't know what TPA meant.

Claire said she didn't know either.

Geoffrey said he didn't know.

Louis had nothing to say.

Mr Hutton said that after the reading of the last minutes he felt there was a conspiracy to get rid of him. He was very happy with Geoffrey's progress and his behaviour at home. It was still nice to see him. He wanted to know how much his and his wife's attendance at meetings was required. Was it voluntary or not?

Mrs Evans said she was happy to see all the family once again but she wasn't happy about Geoffrey. His behaviour was the same as usual but she wasn't happy. He would be leaving school in six months and she didn't know what would happen. He still seemed a nice boy, but she wished a bit more seriousness would come into things. He always said he didn't know what would happen when he left school, and she wished he would find out and think about his future with more seriousness. He was good with the Orwell House pet animals but she was anxious about him and about the future.

Mrs Hutton said that Geoffrey had spoken of going to a polytechnic but she didn't know whether that was going to work out. His behaviour had improved and she thought Orwell House was doing a lot for him. The children had said in the car that they wished to say something but didn't know how to put it. Geoffrey had said the same.

Mr King was pleased to hear that the children would like to participate and said they weren't the only ones who found difficulty in putting thoughts into words. He was also glad that the home weekends were still going well but wasn't as satisfied as he had been at the last meeting that things looked encouraging: he was a little more pessimistic after various recent happenings. He was also concerned about this particular meeting *and* the meetings in general, which could turn into a sort of ritual, a facade that they put up without actually discussing matters of real importance: 'skating away, perhaps, through a veil of secrecy'. He thought the value of the meetings and their future success was, in a sense, at stake.

TPA said these meetings were certainly part of the 'arrangement' and he was interested that Mr Hutton wondered whether they were voluntary or not. He didn't say whether he liked – or more probably didn't like – them, but by his question he had implied that something was on his mind. If a rabbit ran into a hedge and there was only one hedge, even if you couldn't see the rabbit you would know that it must be in the hedge. Likewise, when the family was kept waiting for fifteen minutes before the joint meeting started – much longer than usual – they must have known that something was being said that went on rather a long time. In other words, they must have seen there was a 'kind of cover-up job' going on. It was interesting that he happened to know that Mr and Mrs Hutton had asked the social worker not to talk about a certain matter in front of the children and Mr King had half agreed. This put him in rather an awkward spot, a 'confidentiality trap'. As it happened, Mr King hadn't asked him not to say anything in the joint meeting, and although he hadn't been told what 'it' was he had a shrewd idea. The point was that if things are covered up as badly as that they are bound to explode into the open. He could do that now. Not even knowing except by hunch what it was that Mr King had been asked to conceal, he could pull the plug out without ever even considering that he was offending people. Covering things up was dangerous because they always came out in the end; often, as in this meeting with the family kept waiting, it was obvious from the cover-up itself that something was being hidden. He knew very well that Mr Hutton must have had a reason for asking his question; otherwise he wouldn't have asked it. It was difficult for the children who had said 'I don't know what you mean'. This expression was often used by people who knew precisely what was meant, so there was some sort of hedging going on. Last time he had thought that people were bored by the proceedings, and they had reached a stage in the game where they had to make a choice – either to go on and on, never finding out why the 'arrangement' started in the first place, or taking the bull by the horns and, as it were, changing their 'way of living' in the meetings and maybe beyond. It was something to do with exposing truth by covering up. The evidence of the cover-up gave the game away. If there was a big cover-up going on it made a whole nonsense out of a lot of things and forced a lot of people to pretend that they didn't know. Sean, for instance, might be a clever boy who was having to pretend to himself that he wasn't – pretending even not to know his schoolwork – and consequently doing badly. Lastly, as mentioned, the meeting was part of the 'arrangement', and he was curious to know why Louis who was with them at the meeting today was looking so miserable. Claire's explanation of 'tiredness' seemed insufficient.

During the free discussion Mrs Hutton suggested that the younger children should wait downstairs so that the 'other problem' could be raised.

TPA asked Mr King whether he would like Geoffrey to leave the room.

Mr King thought it would be an ordeal for Geoffrey but he would rather he stayed.

The other younger children left the room.

Mrs Hutton mentioned the incidents of Geoffrey exposing himself and the shock this had given her and her husband. She felt that though Louis was too young to understand he might copy Geoffrey for a joke. The other children probably knew about it, but she and her husband and the Principal of Orwell House, Mr Butler, had agreed before the meeting that it probably shouldn't be spoken of in front of them.

TPA pointed out how much energy was being expended in covering things up. He felt that indecent exposure was very often confused in people's minds with indecent assault and made people feel extremely anxious, leading to the tendency to 'cover up'. Before these incidents he had felt that the family had been involved in a sort of cover-up procedure. For instance, he would still like to know what lay behind Mr Hutton's wish to work in South Africa, and also the motive behind his query about attendance at these meetings.

Mr Hutton said he felt bored with his work, which had changed so much that he was no longer doing the job he was supposed to do. South Africa had appealed to him, and he had always liked travelling. The reason for his query about meetings was financial – the price of petrol, etc.

TPA said that, as far as he knew, the cost of journeys could be reimbursed. It was agreed that this would be looked into.

Mr Hutton said he was finding the cost of Geoffrey more than he expected but felt it was money well spent. He had seen a big change in him during the past six months.

At the post-professionals' meeting TPA said he thought a breakthrough had been made. If they had colluded with Mr and Mrs Hutton nothing would have come out into the open. He hoped the family would continue to experience the exposure these meetings entailed as decent and even helpful, not as persecuting – indecent.

*

TPA says that in this meeting he was trying to persuade everyone that they must either look at things properly or bury them for *ever*. Geoffrey had provided the family with a mourning focus and the meetings were a mourning device. Since everyone agreed that they were fairly onerous it was only sensible to make the most of them. Geoffrey provided the licence for the meetings which should enable the family to mourn, to learn from the past and not make the same mistakes in the future.

Speaking of cover-ups, we agree that the dirty overcoat is synonymous with what is indecently exposed and I learn in passing that foot fetishists got that way because their mummy came into their bedroom with no clothes on when they were a baby and knowing it was naughty to look at her they had stared at her feet. (It is at moments like this that I wonder about analysts. Do many mummies make a habit of strolling around in the altogether? Wouldn't any normal person, even a baby, glance not at her feet but up at the ceiling or out of the window? Why don't they turn into curtain fetishists?)

Mr Hutton made a rueful semi-joke to the effect that he had felt there was a conspiracy to get rid of him. A week before, TPA had been asked to write an in-house report on Geoffrey – a common device in institutions. Frequently the psychiatrist will be asked to collude with a sort of bureaucratic conspiracy to transfer a child. Not caring to confess that they are fed-up to the back teeth with the little beast, the staff hope that the psychiatrist will come up with some incomprehensible diagnosis which will let them all off the hook. TPA didn't fall for that one, concluding his report with the implication that the onus of rejection should lie with those who felt unable to tolerate Geoffrey's anxiety-making capacity and not in any 'psychiatric syndrome'. Here is the report:

Psychiatric report – Geoffrey Hutton (born 1.12.1961)

Confidential – 1st June 1977

At the moment Geoffrey has been producing some anxiety-making self-exposure episodes.

He actually is dramatising the self-exposure that is not happening in this family, i.e. the covered-up aggression particularly in relation to his father and the other brother.

In the professional discussions which have taken place in relation to the family review meetings which have been proceeding, theoretical fears have been expressed relating to the likelihood of Geoffrey's brother committing suicide and his father dying of some inwardly turned aggression, e.g. coronary thrombosis.

I am relieved that the next therapeutic/family review meeting is to take place shortly, viz. on 6th June 1977.

I feel that if Geoffrey's overt delinquencies are tolerable we should continue on our present course.

Dr Tom Pitt-Aikens
Consultant Psychiatrist

At the end of the meeting TPA kept asking Mr Hutton what South
Africa meant to him. He was wondering whether he was covering up
depression about the job he had delighted in, with its quotient of
intuition, and whether he was preparing to lose his job as a kind of
punishment on earth for not having used his intuition to notice the
clues which might have been around at the time of Kevin's suicide.

TPA thinks he should have picked up earlier the signs of Mr
Hutton's denied guilt.

7. One of our blouses is missing

Venue: Orwell House   22nd September 1977
Present: Dr Pitt-Aikens, Chairman
           Mr King, Local Authority Social Worker legally
              responsible for Geoffrey Hutton
           Mrs Evans, Houseparent at Orwell House and clerk to the
              meeting
           Mr & Mrs Hutton

As soon as the preliminary professionals' meeting began Mrs Evans, the clerk, was already finding things confused and confusing and stated that she was sure it was going to stay that way.

Mrs Evans said that before the meeting she had overheard some senior staff, including the Orwell House Principal, Mr Butler, discussing a muddle to do with Mr and Mrs Hutton's wishing it to be a 'small group' today.

Mr King arrived late, apologising to TPA and Mrs Evans. Mr Butler had just seen the family and it had been decided that the children shouldn't attend.

TPA wondered about the wisdom of making this a special case in that way.

Mr King said he understood that another situation had arisen.

TPA mentioned 'a dramatic form of transvestism' and something else which Mrs Evans, who clerked the meeting, also found confusing.

In a kind of introduction to the joint meeting the clerk – beside herself with confusion – wrote: 'The family were quoted almost verbatim, and some of it does not seem to make sense, but I must leave it as it is.' She added: 'What I have written next I cannot understand, i.e. Mr Hutton "impossible if true", TPA "not bad", Mr Hutton "agreed".' The meeting continued with an agreement to 'express, share and discuss any feelings important and relevant to the case'.

Mrs Evans, not having seen Geoffrey for six weeks, said she was out of touch with what had been happening, but according to Orwell

House's 'occurrence sheets' there had been no incidents since the holiday time.

Mrs Hutton wondered why on earth she couldn't get help. The family would go through a period of calm before the storm, sitting back and relaxing, and then before long everything would be ten times worse. She would be feeling pleased with Orwell House, and then the police would be at the door: lots of girls' clothes were missing. She wondered why the court had to be involved before help could be found for these children.

Mr Hutton said he had nothing to add to what his wife had already said. She and Mr King had talked a lot about Geoffrey's problems.

Mr King said that, following the previous meeting, Mr Hutton had been given financial help. He thought it interesting that Mrs Hutton's cry for help had to go unanswered, that her anger and hopelessness were unheard. Maybe it was too late and Geoffrey had gone beyond the point of being brought back.

TPA said something which the clerk couldn't follow about its being a pity that only newsworthy sensationalism or dramatic interest got things going. Stealing girls' clothes didn't fall into that bracket.

TPA went on about police time and money. The clerk became even more confused when TPA referred to the Union Jack, and described Geoffrey as being 'like a flag'. Mr Hutton was said to be aggressive under attack. The heart was mentioned, for some reason, and Mrs Evans, the clerk, thought that maybe TPA had meant that Mr Hutton would contract heart disease from worry.

TPA said there had been much anxiety about this meeting, which was why the children weren't present. Mr King who, as social worker, was responsible for arranging meetings with the parents had exercised his authority over Geoffrey by not inviting him. He spoke of Mr Hutton's 'sad history' and said he was worried about Sean.

Mrs Hutton interrupted TPA in full flow, assuring him that Sean was absolutely no worry whatever. All the family's worry lay with Geoffrey and she thought that TPA, being a psychiatrist, was the expert who should tell people what to do.

Mr Hutton said he was past worrying.

TPA said that Geoffrey's self-exposure might be a form of showing off – either masculinity or femininity, potency or impotence. Other people might laugh at and ridicule him. He then referred to the meetings and Mr Hutton's attitude to the financial aspect of attending them. They had sent forms to Mr Hutton to enable him to receive help, but he hadn't qualified, not being on social supplementary benefits. Help had come via Mr King, but Mr Hutton agreed with TPA that he would have attended anyway.

Someone said that Mr Hutton spent his life throwing bricks; perhaps sometimes it was a waste of time, but it was masculine to show aggression. It would appear more passive and feminine to admit that they couldn't afford to attend meetings. It seemed that Mrs Hutton would hate to think of the head of the family in jeopardy.

Mrs Hutton said she dragged problems out of her husband and made him talk about them.

Mr Hutton said he fought issues of injustice with councils and the like, but only small ones and only when he knew he could win.

TPA remarked 'like showing off masculinity'.

Mrs Evans said that Geoffrey had shown off his masculinity in the swimming pool, etc., throughout his stay at Orwell House.

TPA added 'or femininity'.

Mrs Hutton mentioned that her daughter's blouse had been missing for a short while, and a carrier bag full of girls' clothes had been missing for months until it was found behind a shed by a neighbour.

Mr Hutton said that perhaps Geoffrey had intended it to be discovered, but this had taken eight months.

TPA observed that the carrier bag had been kept secret; that if Mr Hutton hadn't come today it would have been because of lack of money, but he had come. Not having money would have allowed Geoffrey to shelve today.

Mr Hutton said that in two years any debts incurred would be paid off. Whatever money had to be paid to help Geoffrey would be paid, and Geoffrey would never know of any money worries that the family might suffer. It would all be money well spent.

TPA wondered whether that made Geoffrey appear unwittingly callous.

Mrs Hutton then said that the children were told nothing 'gullible', whatever that meant.

TPA asked whether or not the family worried when the bills turned red.

Mr Hutton answered that the cheques were written and the family unconcerned.

TPA pointed out that it was hardly possible that children couldn't smell parental worry.

Mrs Hutton decried this, saying that all the children realised they must wait for items of clothing which would be bought when the money became available.

All areas of saving were discussed, including Sean's saving schemes.

The Chairman told the meeting that they had gone over time.

At the post-professionals' meeting TPA remarked that Geoffrey seemed to be pushing issues forward – if he didn't, would important themes in the family remain hidden? There was discussion of the family's current attitude, which was considered remarkable; and again TPA said that Mr Hutton was 'not very nice'.

The clerk ended by repeating that she found this meeting a difficult, and at times a confusing, one. Even when she quoted the family verbatim some of it just didn't make sense. Sometimes she had thought it wise to record the meeting 'as it was', but the next moment she found herself 'cheating', trying to make the record coherent and sensible when in truth what was being said seemed neither.

*

The family appear determined to confine the problem to Geoffrey. It is comforting to feel that it is possible to limit a problem, and they clearly find TPA's attempts to extend it highly tiresome. Mrs Hutton in particular wanted to keep concentrated on Geoffrey in a pseudo-simple fashion, going so far as to interrupt someone in full flow, which is quite against the rules, rebuking TPA for mentioning Sean and implicitly criticising his views and his whole approach. Often, says TPA, patients will address him as follows: 'You are the expert and *this* is what you should be doing.' In a much later meeting she attempted the same limitation of the problem – this time in relation to Sean and almost advising everyone not to bother about Geoffrey.

This was a strangely secretive meeting in its very obscurity. I was very tempted to scrub whole bits of it, as it was so muddled and confusing, but then kept discovering that we would have lost something salient. I was myself being drawn into making secrets.

Years later TPA, talking to José, the cook at Orwell House, learned that Geoffrey had often dressed up as a girl in the presence of José's cousin Candida, the seamstress. She had cheerfully continued sewing her seams and hadn't thought to mention it to anyone. There was no particular mechanism whereby below-stairs staff could communicate such information to the professionals above stairs. It remained a jolly joke and a secret from those who needed to know.

Secrecy, as TPA insists, can be self-defeating. Life would be less uneasy without the ill-fitting and precarious lid of concealment beneath which rumour festers and steams. But the passion for secrecy currently so prevalent in society is not our concern here. We are attempting to deal with its more subtle, insidious forms – the secrets that families keep not only from outsiders but from themselves; the secrets unwittingly imposed by the vicissitudes of history, and the difficulties of discerning truth through the mists of time. When writing his family history Mr Hutton had some trouble placing Michel Pierre Huytens firmly on the correct branch of his family tree, thus making him hard to see. The dossiers kept on Geoffrey, though the intention was to clarify matters, were frequently confusing and therefore obscurantist. Secrecy is not necessarily imposed by mischief-makers but can arise of itself, and is almost invariably malevolent, breeding not only prurient curiosity (I except myself from this charge, as I except the therapist) but misunderstanding, with its consequent chaos. 'Tell the truth and shame the devil' is a maxim which should be applied not only to liars but to those given to inordinate concealment.

8. I've got a secret

Venue: Orwell House   22nd November 1977
Present: Dr Pitt-Aikens, Chairman
           Mr King, Local Authority Social Worker legally
               responsible for Geoffrey Hutton
           Mrs Pannell, link Social Worker at Orwell House
           Mrs Ferris, Houseparent at Orwell House and clerk to the
               meeting
           Mr & Mrs Hutton
           Geoffrey

At the preliminary professionals' meeting it was decided that no subjects would be regarded as 'taboo' in the joint meeting.

Some reference was made to a previous meeting when Geoffrey had been invited to attend and then been asked to leave. The reasoning behind this was discussed. TPA felt that authorities must do this when necessary but he preferred to keep it to a minimum. He also felt there was some connexion between the ambivalence this represented and the current main concern of the case, viz. sexuality and the powerful yet pathetic situation epitomised by indecent exposure.

At the jovial start of the joint meeting it was established that Geoffrey had been invited but had said he didn't want to attend. Everyone was asked whether they felt he should be made to, and all thought he should.

Geoffrey joined the meeting, making it clear to Mrs Ferris who collected him that he did so under protest.

The topic for the meeting was agreed to be 'anything relevant'.

Mrs Ferris said that this was the first meeting of Geoffrey's that she had attended. She confessed to some confusion about the case, which hadn't been helped by the confused recording of the last meeting. She felt she didn't know Geoffrey at all yet, but not from lack of interest on her own part. Geoffrey was a boy who tended to make himself scarce round Orwell House, frequently going missing. The picture she had of him was of a rather carefree lad, and this didn't add up in any way to what she had read about him. This concerned her a great deal, particularly since they would soon be making plans for his departure from Orwell House. His attitude towards attending the meeting also concerned her, since he was aware that there were considerable problems but was, in effect, saying: 'I find it all rather boring and I would rather not be there. They can get on with it without me.' She had told him frankly that she thought he was opting out of problems of which he was quite aware and that it wouldn't be permitted. Her main concern was that he should acknowledge what was happening at the moment and face his part in seeking some sort of solution.

Geoffrey said he didn't want to say anything.

Mr Hutton was concerned about Geoffrey's recent problems and said it was interesting that, when he was home last term and they had had a little trouble, Louis had come to the same conclusion as himself – that each time Geoffrey came home on an extended visit they had trouble. Later, discussing the matter with Mr King, they discovered that they had more trouble on short weekend visits. The problem seemed to be increasing on this side, and he had been in favour of Geoffrey's being present today because he thought they were all turning a blind eye, pretending that what was going on was not. It was time for things to come out more into the light. Their problem was that Geoffrey preferred that not to happen and seemed to be taking no active steps to exercise any form of control.

Mrs Hutton said she agreed entirely with her husband.

Mrs Pannell said that one of the things she had noticed about today's meeting was that at the beginning they were all quite jovial. Even when the minutes of the last meeting were being read there seemed plenty of cause for mirth as some things sounded very strange. She kept wondering whether they were just putting on the air of joviality because they felt that everything was really very serious. Geoffrey's problems were serious for everyone concerned – particularly the recent problem, knowledge of which had gone beyond the people who knew him well to people who mightn't make the effort to understand him as they did at Orwell House: people who would take things at face value. She wondered why they tended to adopt this light-hearted attitude, which perhaps was covering up something else. It rather reminded her of Geoffrey himself, who was ignoring the whole thing, not wanting to be bothered. Mrs Hutton had said that Geoffrey had said that the meetings were boring. She could think of many words to describe the meetings but 'boring' wasn't one of them. She was interested to see that Geoffrey had insisted on being at the Statutory Review [all children in the care of local authorities are reviewed six monthly at so-called Statutory Reviews] a few weeks before, where many painful things were said to and about him, and yet he didn't want to be involved in today's family meeting. She wondered whether it was significant, or merely coincidental, that in the evening of the very day of that last Statutory Review he had exposed himself to two girls. She found it quite puzzling and thought she'd leave it at that.

Mr King said that Mrs Pannell had raised many of the points that were in his own mind. He too had been struck by the levity which prevailed through the early stages of this meeting. Now, however, he was struck by the air of solemnity. He referred back to the Statutory Review which Geoffrey had attended and said he felt it must have been an ordeal for him. Geoffrey had been told that the future was in his hands, that soon he would have to get a job and be responsible for his own behaviour – no one else could control him. That very evening he had gone out and committed an act of indecent exposure. This seemed to suggest that he was reluctant to accept the responsibility, or was kicking at what went on at that meeting. It seemed significant, for it happened on a weekend, whereas usually those incidents occurred only on the longer holidays. He was sure this particular incident bore some relationship to the Statutory Review.

TPA said he was keen to understand the meaning of the wearing of girls' clothes and the indecent exposure. He guessed that it could be found if they looked hard enough at the 'mirror of these meetings'. He pointed out that they had learned that boys at Orwell House were like symbols of unrealised difficulties within families, infecting the professionals dealing with the case. He wondered about this expression 'indecent exposure'. Last time, apparently, someone had said something about Mr Hutton throwing bricks, but there wasn't much detail in the minutes to explain what the expression meant or who had said it. The statement was very stark, and 'stark' meant 'naked'. It was just there – almost indecently exposed. What it meant, heaven only knew. He himself had also been quoted as saying in the last post-professionals' meeting that he didn't think Mr Hutton was 'very nice'. He couldn't remember making that unkind remark or, if he had made it, why; but he knew he must have made it, since it was minuted, and now he had, as it were, indecently exposed yet again what he had apparently said last time. It again looked pretty stark, but his guess was that he had said it within a context of other things.

TPA went on to re-introduce a further example from last time. He was almost sure that the clerk hadn't written it down but that Mr

Hutton had been talking about heart trouble. He wasn't going to say any more now but would leave it as stark and indecent as that. That said, he supposed one could now imagine either that there had been a deadly serious conversation or that it was one of Mr Hutton's jokes. If in the future a new social worker were to come in on the case and see this reference to heart trouble he wouldn't know how to regard this small, insufficiently clothed piece of information. [Penis?] That situation could be very dangerous. This sort of thing happened quite often, and the trouble was that you could never know without a context whether something was important, or relevant, or nonsense. It was essential to know, when one talked loosely about hearts, either that it was rubbish – just Mr Hutton joking – or that someone was being serious. That, perhaps, was what Mrs Pannell and Mr King had been talking about – the different feelings of solemnity and joviality. When was it a joke and when not? Some people regarded indecent exposure as a daft joke, whereas others took it very, even too, seriously. He had known cases where the over-seriousness had resulted in the term 'indecent assault' being used though the record actually stated the much less serious crime of 'indecent exposure'. There might be something in the backgrounds of Mr or Mrs Hutton whereby they didn't understand sufficiently what was, and what was not, a joke. A common response among prison officers to an inmate claiming that he was going to kill himself was 'I'll give you the rope', but when suicide actually happens the joke turns sour and there is consternation. Serious things could be turned into jokes, and that was dangerous. Jokes could also turn into serious things. When the joke turned sour it was called 'laughing on the other side of your face'. He thought they were gradually moving towards understanding the symptoms – the wearing of girls' clothes, exposure and so on. He wished they were going a bit faster but felt that at least they were moving forward.

During the free discussion Mr Hutton stated that he felt Geoffrey was similar to himself in that they both treated serious things lightly as a defence mechanism. Geoffrey's shyness was another example of the similarity. Mr Hutton was still shy with people until he got to know them. Geoffrey, however, seemed able to adapt to changed circumstances, as in his placement at Orwell House. Mr Hutton felt that he himself didn't so much bottle things up as sweep them under the carpet. It was far better for things to be brought out into the open.

TPA thought that matters grew serious when problems were under the carpet, because if people didn't know about them they couldn't help.

Mrs Pannell was concerned that Geoffrey's problem, 'contained' in a meeting like this, became far more serious when outside authorities such as the police became involved. Then it was 'out from under the carpet'. Could it be said that in some way, by planning for Geoffrey's future, they were putting the responsibility for him elsewhere?

The clerk thought this question made a particularly abortive end to the joint meeting.

Those present at the very brief post-professionals" meeting felt that there might be a significant lack of continuity in the staff working with Geoffrey.

*

It became clear here that Geoffrey proclaimed that he wanted to be secret. Everyone was talking about it – making him, therefore, by definition, not secret. He 'made himself scarce', 'frequently went missing', like a child carolling 'I've got a secret, I've got a secret'. With the family as a whole TPA always needed to ask direct questions if he was to get answers. It was only by dint of enquiry as to the significance of Louis's gun that he had learned how Kevin had died. Presumably if he hadn't asked he wouldn't have been told.

Mrs Pannell was worried lest the police became involved. Geoffrey and the police, while not precisely strangers to each other, yet saw each other as strangers. Geoffrey in this context would be taken at face value and become only a misunderstood stranger to an important and significant group of other strangers, bringing upon himself all the antipathy that is felt towards strangers. I have already admitted that, when first faced with delinquents, I was worse than any policeman is supposed to be – I formed the impression that it would be a good idea to shoot them. Now I find them more thought-provoking.

At the Statutory Review Geoffrey had been told that his future was in his own hands, but of course that was simply not true. The social services would be in charge of him for a couple of years yet. It had been implied that bad Geoffrey was not prepared to accept a responsibility that, strictly speaking, was not yet actually his.

9. Don't panic

Venue: Clinic consulting-room   30th January 1978
Present: Dr Pitt-Aikens, Chairman
           Mr King, Local Authority Social Worker legally
               responsible for Geoffrey Hutton and clerk to the
               meeting
           Mrs Pannell, link Social Worker at Orwell House
           Mr & Mrs Hutton
           Geoffrey

At the preliminary professionals' meeting they discussed the dilemma of whether or not to raise matters of concern about other members of the family, and Mrs Pannell reported that Geoffrey was still causing a great deal of anxiety at Orwell House.

Mr and Mrs Hutton and Geoffrey arrived for the joint meeting. No Orwell House staff besides Mrs Pannell were free to attend. The focus of the meeting was to be 'anything that was or might be felt to be relevant', whereupon Mrs Hutton attempted to introduce a subject of dubious relevancy.

Mrs Pannell said she had expressed most of her present feelings at the last meeting. There didn't seem to be much change in the situation since November, although it was perhaps a little less serious and the police were no longer involved. She felt they were going very slowly.

Mrs Hutton wondered how much it was tied up with Geoffrey that since November Louis had been giving them problems with stealing, etc. He missed having Geoffrey at home. As far as they knew, Geoffrey had been well-behaved over the Christmas holiday and at the weekend. Sean had had an operation.

Mr King said he shared Mrs Pannell's feelings of doubt about where they were going and how quickly they were getting there. What did the future hold? Mr and Mrs Hutton had been under a lot of stress. They had put up with Geoffrey for several years and now were having difficulty with Louis, worrying that he might repeat the pattern. They were anxious about Sean's eyes and were having a stressful time.

Mr Hutton said what struck him most, looking freshly at the matter, was that when Geoffrey started at Orwell House there were certain problems which had been solved only to be replaced by larger ones. He could see elements of Geoffrey's behaviour in Louis, but it wasn't a carbon copy. He wasn't concerned about minor pilfering – it was worse than that – and Louis had been encouraged by Geoffrey's friends and accomplices. He didn't know what to do. He didn't want a repetition of the trouble with Geoffrey, and he didn't want to make the same mistakes.

There was a pause before TPA spoke. He remarked that both Mum and Dad had got as near as they ever had to wondering what was going on in the family, which might have given rise to stealing and cross-dressing, etc. Previously, when he had put forward various suggestions, the family, particularly Mrs Hutton, had reacted laughingly. Now however they were 'wondering'. It wasn't just Geoffrey any longer. It was more than that. Mrs Hutton had nearly got in a panic twice over the subject matter and something else he wasn't sure about. He felt she would rather ask questions and get the wrong answers than put up with the slowness of this process. That could relate to Geoffrey's cross-dressing, since some people found adolescence a difficult and confusing time to live through. They had unusual feelings pulling them in different directions and had to be able to tolerate that sense of messiness. He guessed that Mr Hutton's brother, who had studied hard, couldn't stand it and had needed someone to support him. He had found it all too much. Mrs Hutton was perhaps rather as he had been and found being in a muddle intolerable. So did Geoffrey. If he felt muddled about sexuality he had to quell the feeling. You couldn't miss a boy in girls' clothing, but Mrs Hutton was far less obvious. She would, so to speak, run to a drawer for an answer, instead of putting up with not knowing how she felt, or what she should do, like the rest of us. If you were like that, the chances were that you would do something wrong. He wouldn't want Mr Hutton to make his wife happy in that way, to give in to her impatient wish to keep things straight. It would be a shame if he became part of doing things wrong. Somebody had said that older boys were influencing Louis to do wrong, proving that we know that people can be influenced to do wrong. Mrs Hutton was very powerful in that way. She knew that it was a 'sin' to speak out of turn in these meetings and yet could make TPA as Chairman feel a swine for rightly attempting to stop her frequent interruptions. He often felt he would rather do wrong and let her interrupt the meeting.

No clerk had so far had the temerity even to record her many interruptions. That was powerful in the meetings and he wondered whether Mr Hutton found it so at home: it was dangerous. They had to discover what went on in the family as a whole. If Mr Hutton was influenced to do wrong by his wife, it could be disastrous. The best thing was to sit tight and not to panic.

Before he turned to Geoffrey TPA gave an example of what he meant by Mrs Hutton's influence. She had indicated to Geoffrey at one point that he should speak – out of turn – and if he had responded it would have made the running of the meeting difficult. It would have created a precedent. Everybody would have felt entitled to speak whenever they chose; panic and chaos would have resulted.

Geoffrey said he had never been round with 'those boys' – they were Louis's friends. He only knew their faces, or the faces of one or two of them.

During the free discussion TPA asked Geoffrey at what point he had decided he was going to say something, and Geoffrey said it was when his father spoke. TPA wondered whether his mother's signalling had influenced him.

Mrs Pannell mentioned the matter of the family 'sitting tight'. Of all the families they dealt with at Orwell House the Huttons were the only ones who hadn't panicked about a subject which could be quite panic-provoking. She saw them as being sensible, trying to come to an understanding.

TPA replied that he hadn't been referring to Geoffrey's misdeeds. The panic about that had been put into the professionals.

Mrs Pannell then suggested that they might have panicked about Louis, or Sean's operation and the strain it put on Mr and Mrs Hutton. There was a lot to panic about, but they hadn't done so.

TPA again said that he hadn't been referring to these matters. He had been talking about the possibility of being influenced or panicked by Mrs Hutton into doing wrong. He wondered whether his comments had rung any bells with Mr Hutton. If they had been true Mr Hutton would know.

Mr Hutton said he could see the point TPA was making but didn't know whether he agreed.

Mrs Hutton also felt she could see the point he was making but didn't know whether it was absolutely right. She wouldn't spend a lot of money without consulting her husband, and sometimes when she wanted him to do something her way he would refuse; but there were occasions when her way would be right.

TPA said Mrs Hutton's demands might be very appealing, but

eventually one could perhaps find them tedious and become bloody-minded. As a result, one could do wrong by *not* pleasing her. The demand might be wrong, or one could be wrong in denying her.

Mr Hutton said that if he thought she was doing something wrong he often let her, and when he did step in to help he often did it clumsily.

TPA wondered whether Mr Hutton let his wife get on with things simply for peace and quiet or to teach her a lesson and let her learn from her mistakes.

Mr Hutton felt it was 'due to resignation'.

TPA wondered if that was the same. He asked whether Mrs Hutton could give an example of these sorts of situation.

She replied: 'I know I am doing things my way but I can't help it.'

TPA picked up this point as very useful, saying it was the first time he had heard Mrs Hutton say she couldn't help something. In that respect she was like Geoffrey who, it seemed, couldn't help what he did.

Mrs Hutton quoted the example of washing-up. She couldn't stand it hanging around. She always wanted to get on with it and get it over with.

Mrs Pannell asked her if she sometimes did things she knew weren't right because she felt she had to.

Mrs Hutton said that more often she did things without thinking and then realised about them afterwards.

TPA asked her about medical investigations, since they were something that could take time. He wondered whether if, say, a medical examination were set for some time in the future Mrs Hutton might forget the appointment because she was impatient.

She replied that she only acted impatiently and impulsively on little things, never on important ones. She did get impatient – but that was all – with Sean.

TPA asked whether Sean had been told to 'wait patiently'.

Mrs Hutton said he had had the operation on his eye.

Mrs Pannell asked whether he had had a further accident, since he had needed more than one operation.

Mr Hutton replied that he had. The stitches had come loose and needed re-doing. In future he would have to have them removed under local anaesthetic, which was something he really hated.

TPA asked why he hadn't stayed in hospital while the stitches were in.

Mrs Hutton said that allowing him out early was normal practice.

Mr Hutton said he did take care, but not enough.

TPA said that perhaps their 17-year-old boy couldn't be careful enough and took after his mother.

Mrs Hutton said she tried to make him wait and relax while his eye was recovering but he wouldn't.

TPA thought that Mrs Hutton had previously implied that Sean was a sensible boy.

Mr Hutton said he wasn't always and could be silly.

TPA said that if Sean should lose an eye because of this it would be an absolute disaster, due to his inability to wait, in a sense, in the dark; not knowing what was happening. He asked whether Sean wore a pad over the eye and was told he did, especially in crowds.

Mr Hutton said that in another two years or so Sean would have to have the other eye done. Sean still wanted to go to discos now.

TPA pointed out that there had already been one tragedy in the Hutton family, involving a person of exactly Sean's age – Mr Hutton's brother. Sean appeared to take after Mrs Hutton, and for him that could be disastrous. He needed to be the exact opposite and take his time, so that his eye would recover. If he lost his eye he might become very depressed and it would be a dangerous situation for him.

Mrs Hutton felt that Sean took after her husband more than herself.

TPA said Sean seemed unable to stand being in the dark and it was no surprise that the subject had erupted so graphically. He wondered whether Geoffrey's cross-dressing was a form of lampooning his mother. There was a brother of 17 who could go blind because of impatience, and an uncle who at 17 had committed suicide rather than put up with ordinary adolescent pressures. They had both too much resembled Mrs Hutton for their own good.

Mrs Hutton asked how Sean could be stopped.

TPA said 'How do *you* stop?', and added that if Sean saw a change in her he might follow suit. They would have to find out next time whom Mrs Hutton took after. Sean would be in a dangerous situation if he lost his eye.

Mrs Hutton said she was hurt because the specialist had told Sean he was doing well. Paradoxically, without that reassurance he might not have been so impatient.

TPA said people had told Geoffrey not to do things and he had done them. So, simply telling Sean something probably wouldn't have helped him either.

At the post-professionals' meeting they hoped that progress might have been made during the course of the meeting.

TPA thought that some change might become visible as a result of what was happening in the meetings now.

They pondered the contradiction in the fact that they saw Mrs Hutton's impatience as a fault and yet tended to criticise people who did nothing. It was remarked that Geoffrey had been stealing clothes from a convent school and his mother as a child had spent a great deal of time in a school run by nuns.

*

People were still fussing about the speed at which they were not going. Geoffrey had been a problem for fourteen years; they had had only seven meetings – that is seven hours. But that, says TPA, is the way people think. The subject of panic kept arising in this meeting and it looks to me as though Mrs Pannell and Mr King were in a bit of a panic themselves.

Mrs Hutton tried to imply that Louis's problems were all Geoffrey's fault, but if one troublesome child is removed from a family, often another child, still at home, promptly becomes a problem, taking upon himself the role of vehicle for the family's difficulties. This is one of the factors which can be used in an argument against the wisdom of removing a delinquent from his home. Even if he is considered to be 'doing well' in an institution, a sibling will almost certainly take up where he leaves off.

At the 6th meeting – the 'hedge' – the Huttons had made it clear that they wanted TPA to consider Geoffrey singly as an isolated aberration, even asking if their presence at the meetings was necessary. By the time this meeting came round they were beginning half-heartedly to acknowledge that further family problems were cropping up. They were reluctantly beginning to agree that just possibly it was the family which was the patient.

Despite all her experience, Mrs Pannell here seemed able only to pick up the points about panic on the overt level of the response created by Geoffrey's misdeeds, and was unable to see what TPA was talking about when he spoke of how Mrs Hutton in all innocence might have 'panicked' Geoffrey into speaking out of turn in the meeting. By the same token she might panic her family into doing the wrong thing, or things at the wrong time or in the wrong place.

TPA says that people squirm the most when the therapist is really on to something of significance, and that that is the moment when he has to hang on like grim death. I don't quite know why he said that then, but he did; so I have faithfully recorded it.

Towards the end of the meeting Mrs Hutton said that she had tried by words and exhortation to persuade Sean to wait and take things easy; but actions speak louder than words, if not so clearly, and she had betrayed her own impatient nature when she herself had encouraged Geoffrey to be impatient too and to speak out of turn in the meeting. The tendency to identify with one's mother's nature would far outweigh the good lady's hollow words. Geoffrey caricatured the hopelessness, the uselessness, of words. Example, not admonition, is likelier to achieve the desired result.

10. The short meeting

Venue: Clinic consulting-room   27th February 1978
Present: Dr Pitt-Aikens, Chairman
            Mr King, Local Authority Social Worker legally
               responsible for Geoffrey Hutton
            Mrs Pannell, link Social Worker at Orwell House
            Mr Quatermain, Houseparent and clerk to the meeting
            Mr & Mrs Hutton
            Geoffrey

At the preliminary professionals' meeting the minutes of the previous meeting were read as usual, and there were comments about allowing something to happen and doing nothing about it.

It was noted that Mr Hutton was aware that sometimes it was better to let Mrs Hutton see something through than interfere.

Mrs Pannell described Geoffrey's recent behaviour.

TPA couldn't see why he shouldn't leave Orwell House at 16.

At the joint meeting Mr Quatermain said he had mixed feelings about the case. Geoffrey was perhaps not old enough, or ready, to leave Orwell House and was trying to indicate this by his recent actions. He remembered the atmosphere at the first meetings as very different. They had been lighthearted, with Geoffrey's sisters laughing and smiling. Now things were much more tense. He wondered whether much was being gained at the moment.

Mr King too felt a significant change in the atmosphere. They had seen some of Mrs Hutton's impatience and the difficulties that unhappiness and uncertainty created. They had a duty to sort things out as best they could.

Mrs Pannell remarked that the word 'impatience' had been used a lot. She felt, however, that Orwell House had been too patient with Geoffrey's immaturity; that he should be made to face himself and build his own strength. They had cushioned him too much in the past, and Geoffrey needed to realise that. It would be painful for him, but it had to happen.

Mrs Hutton asked if Geoffrey was doing it on purpose 'to get others back', and the clerk had no idea what she meant by that.

Mr Hutton had 'nothing to say, really', and Geoffrey 'nothing'.

TPA said he was angry – in fact furious – that Sean hadn't been invited today, in view of what had been discussed at the last meeting. By not inviting Sean this time he had been abandoned, left alone with his eye problem and his impatience, while they all talked about, rather than to, him. While others had been speaking today, TPA had been thinking that they were acting out in the present something of the past. He had a horrible image of Mr Hutton's brother being cut off alone with, in all probability, problems similar to those they saw now in Sean. Kevin had needed some magical happening to let those around him know what was going on inside him, but it hadn't materialised. All the anxiety had been in him, and no doubt after his death everyone had wished that Kevin had only said something.

Mr Hutton said Kevin had attempted suicide several times, but it had all been covered up in an effort to spare feelings. He had himself had to do domestic chores about the house and hadn't been old enough to take his older brother in hand.

At the post-professionals' meeting TPA said that his feelings of history repeating itself were becoming more founded for this case.

Mrs Pannell observed that this certainly wasn't the first case in which they had seen that happen.

*

Mrs Pannell appears to have forgotten the point of the meetings and to be opting for the individualistic pull-yourself-together approach. I wonder why.

TPA seemed astounded that Sean hadn't been invited. He might be going blind, and yet everyone was more concerned than ever before with Geoffrey. Everyone was looking away from Sean, but if matters went ill with him they would probably, with apparent justification, cry that it was all Geoffrey's fault. It is common for families to blame upsets and illnesses on a delinquent child. 'Daddy would never have suffered cardiac arrest if you hadn't stolen that bus.'

This was an important meeting; so I don't know why it seems so short.

11. The gossips

Venue: Clinic consulting-room   25th May 1978
Present: Dr Pitt-Aikens, Chairman
           Mr King, Local Authority Social Worker legally
               responsible for Geoffrey Hutton and clerk to the
               meeting
           Mrs Pannell, link Social Worker at Orwell House
           Mr & Mrs Hutton

At the preliminary professionals' meeting it was emphasised that of course Geoffrey had now left Orwell House. TPA said that all the same he hoped that someone from the Orwell House Care Staff would be coming to today's meeting. They found it easy to slip into 'gossip' about what had been happening in the case and to the family in the absence of Mr and Mrs Hutton. He felt this was similar to what had gone on in Mr Hutton's own family thirty odd years before. Perhaps they had gossiped about Kevin without actually discussing his problems with him.

At the beginning of the joint meeting Mr and Mrs Hutton said that both Geoffrey and Sean had been invited but had declined to come. Mr Hutton said Geoffrey had refused because he had had two days off work already, and didn't want to anyway. Mrs Hutton said he *had* wanted to come. Sean was absent because he saw the meeting as a waste of time.

Orwell House staff had been invited but were unable to attend because of half-term holidays and staff shortages.

When the previous joint meeting's minutes were read Mrs Hutton said that the reference to Geoffrey trying to 'get others back' should have read 'get others' backs up'.

Mr Hutton wanted to clarify that a reference to 'first meetings' literally meant the first meetings.

Apart from that, the minutes were agreed to but were felt to be a foreshortened account.

Before beginning 'individual comments' those present decided the meeting's focus: 'anything felt to be relevant or important.'

Mrs Pannell said her main feeling was one of curiosity as to how Geoffrey and the family were getting on and whether he still had his difficulties. She had heard that he had a job – that was satisfactory. She wondered if things were going smoothly, what had changed from the time when he was at Orwell House causing problems and anxiety. If things had changed, was it because of living at home in a new situation, a sort of honeymoon period? She hadn't much to say but was curious and eager to hear.

Mrs Hutton said she was passing to her husband.

Mr Hutton said that when Geoffrey first came home he was extremely sensible. There were no serious problems, as there had been previously, but his immaturity was still evident. He had a group of friends who were still at school and tended to sponge off him. Geoffrey himself behaved rather like a 14-year-old when home from work in the evenings. Also, being sponged off may have led to a tendency to help himself to things – though that was only a suspicion. He had an unsettling influence on the rest of the family. For example, there had been an incident when Mr Hutton was watching one TV programme and Geoffrey had wanted another. When Mr Hutton put his foot down Geoffrey went into the next room and turned on his record player extremely loud, shouting the words over it deliberately to annoy. They had 'Top of the Pops' on weekly with some reluctance because it was something that Sean was allowed. Geoffrey insisted on watching what he wanted. He had to have his own way. He didn't wish to go on holiday with the family, but they were loth to leave him at home on his own and Mr Hutton couldn't think how to resolve this, though Geoffrey might have been able to stay with friends. It would have been impossible to leave him alone in the house since he was so destructive. Things just seemed to fall apart when he touched them. When they were out for the day they wondered what they would find when they returned. Geoffrey was perhaps best described as like an exuberant 14-year-old. His was not a well-paid job. Sean made more, though he wasn't well-paid either. Fares and smoking took a big chunk of Geoffrey's money. He didn't like the work, didn't understand it and wasn't working hard. He had applied for a job as an assistant sales rep for a double-glazing firm. Mr Hutton wasn't too happy about this, but felt they could do nothing about it. Geoffrey would have to find out for himself and learn a lesson.

Mr King remarked that there had obviously been many changes since the last meeting, which must have been quite dramatic for Geoffrey. Things had seemed to go wonderfully well at first – perhaps surprisingly. Now they all seemed to be waiting for the storm to break, wondering whether there would be a repetition of the previous problems. Geoffrey was making his presence well and truly felt in the household, and the family were beginning to worry about what he was getting up to. It was interesting that Mr Hutton had said that they hadn't yet had any repetition of the old problems. Did that mean the recent problems, which would have got him into trouble with the police, or did it refer to the old pattern of behaviour for which he had gone into care? It sounded as though the stealing, and the difficulty of controlling him within the home, was a replica in miniature of what had gone on before. If that was correct, nothing seemed to have changed since his return home.

TPA said he tended to study what happened at the meetings in the hope of understanding the background of a case. He had discovered that he and Mr King in the pre-professionals' meeting tended to 'gossip', talking of things they could well have discussed in company with Mr and Mrs Hutton but finding it easier to do so on their own. He alluded to the difference of opinion between Mr and Mrs Hutton on whether Geoffrey wanted to come to the meeting or not. That hadn't been sorted out. Things looked OK, but maybe they weren't. He had noticed words like 'old problems' and 'immature'. He felt they were still repeating Mr Hutton's problems relating to his older brother. People had looked for Kevin's problem but hadn't seen it. Mr Hutton had implied last time that he had been too immature to face his brother's problem, just as Mr and Mrs Hutton hadn't faced each other over Geoffrey's not coming to the present meeting. TPA guessed that Kevin had been talked about but not confronted before he died. What happened before Mr and Mrs Hutton took part in the meeting today might have happened with Kevin – people gossiped about him but didn't face him. This still went on. For example, when there was suspicion that Geoffrey had been stealing they perhaps talked about it but didn't face him. Regarding the holiday which would leave Geoffrey on his own, he had the impression that Sean wouldn't be going either and was rather frightened of what he might do in the Kevin sense while the family were away. People had a morbid tendency to discuss something awful. They almost enjoyed it, and only when it happened did they feel guilty or wicked. He felt there was a link between Kevin and Sean and added that he was interested in what was currently going on about Sean's eyes.

During the free discussion it was suggested that Mrs Pannell, TPA and Mr King had mistaken Mr and Mrs Hutton's agreement for disagreement. Geoffrey had wished to be at Orwell House again but not at the meeting. They heard an explanation of Sean's recent eye problems and also of his 'panic attacks'.

There was a discussion, headed by Mr and Mrs Hutton and TPA, regarding the family's talking in a 'friendly' fashion to Mrs Hutton in her kitchen, and this led on to a discussion about Kevin and how Mrs Hutton senior, who was a vicar's daughter, was very proud and disinclined to examine the possibility of things being 'wrong'. They also discussed the tendency shared by the local vicar and the GP make light of Kevin's past near-drownings and aspirin overdose. Mr and Mrs Hutton told the rather horrible story of how Kevin's family had avoided facing up to the fact that there was a spreading brown-red stain on the ceiling during the days before the discovery of his body in the loft. They talked about how devastated the grandmother must have been and yet she had refused to show it.

Mr Hutton disputed the Sean/Kevin correlation, thinking that Geoffrey/Kevin was more appropriate.

TPA said he would hate to be proved right in retrospect by seeing part of history repeating itself.

At the post-professionals' meeting Mrs Pannell said she wanted to introduce the subject of Geoffrey's not keeping the appointments with Dr Adams (Mr Butler, the Principal, had arranged for Geoffrey to have 'individual treatment', much to TPA's annoyance). This had almost been a condition of his return home. It was, in a sense, an example of letting things slide.

TPA made a comparison between Dr Adams and people who had offered to talk to Kevin. They had offered, but no one had actually confronted him.

It was also pointed out that Sean's panic attacks were apparently similar to something that happened to a relative of Mr Hutton. It seemed to be a family thing, a family problem.

*

The tendency to 'gossip' in the pre-professional part of this meeting is probably one of the clearest examples of the way in which the rigid structure can pick up unconscious family themes. Once upon a time there had perhaps been gossip about Kevin – people whispering in corners, reluctant to confront him for fear of what they might learn, afraid of hearing the unthinkable. Mr and Mrs Hutton had not spoken clearly to each other about the issue of Geoffrey's attendance at the meeting, and TPA thinks he didn't argue sufficiently strongly with Mr Butler about the idea – which he considered doomed to failure from the outset – that Geoffrey should have individual treatment. He had said it before and he said it again – delinquents by their very nature do not keep appointments. Certainly making this a condition of Geoffrey's returning home was a nonsense: doubly hypocritical because (a) it wouldn't work, and (b) the Orwell House staff were probably extremely keen to be rid of Geoffrey anyway. TPA says he voiced only slight annoyance when he should have been yelling his head off and, for a reason which I can only dimly discern, he blames this on the gossipy nature of the meeting he had had with Mr Butler. I think he is trying to tell me that gossip is always a bad thing, not merely because it is frequently unkind but because it is also almost invariably inaccurate, because it diverts attention from the main issue and because it is a shocking waste of time. It is, he says roundly, absolutely destructive. In this case it could also be seen as portraying projection, in that it could be described as immature – a soft option to a necessary confrontation projected on to Geoffrey, who then ended up labelled 'immature'. Furthermore, it is his 'old problems' which draw the flak, when the real 'old problem' is secretive gossiping. If by some fluke Geoffrey and his 'old problem' had gone along regularly to Dr Adams and had got 'better', then any chance of averting a family disaster, inevitable because of the secretive way they related to each other, would have been lost.

As a final illustration of this secrecy, TPA points out that Mrs Hutton keeps from herself the secret of whether her mother is alive or dead.

12. Double-glazed

Venue: Clinic consulting-room   17th July 1978
Present: Dr Pitt-Aikens, Chairman
            Mr King, Local Authority Social Worker legally
                responsible for Geoffrey Hutton
            Mrs Pannell, link Social Worker at Orwell House
            Mr Nuttall, Houseparent at Orwell House and clerk to the
                meeting
            Mr & Mrs Hutton

In the preliminary professionals' meeting TPA remarked that items in the last post-professionals' meeting were linked. The panic arising from fear of dying was evocative of Kevin not having 'achieved' a life-saving discussion.

It was stated that Orwell House staff would not be involved in future family meetings unless they wished to be – their professional obligation was now ended.

At the joint meeting 'anything relevant' was decided as the focus for discussion.

Only Mr and Mrs Hutton had been invited.

Mr Hutton said that at the start he had thought the meetings were to help Geoffrey. Now, after two years, he realised that they were to help them look at themselves. Geoffrey was far from settled and, though living in the house, seemed to be drifting away again. He was very intolerant of the other children. He was again in trouble with the police and Mr Hutton suspected that there were a number of incidents not known to them. He was particularly disappointed about one thing, the way Geoffrey had left Orwell House. It had been hurried, and Geoffrey had been unprepared. He failed the maths test for the navy and said he had never seen questions like them. They had also had great difficulty obtaining a National Health number for him and had been told it should have been organised by Orwell House.

Mrs Hutton said she would 'pass' and would have to leave to take her wandering children downstairs to the waiting-room since they could be heard outside the consulting-room in the corridor. She agreed with her husband that Geoffrey hadn't been prepared enough for the shock of leaving Orwell House and he certainly had been amazed at the questions in the navy exam. At this point, still talking she left the room.

Mrs Pannell said she wasn't surprised by the present outcome. She had failed to say last time that the arrangement between Geoffrey and Dr Adams seemed to have broken down. Geoffrey's departure from Orwell House had been accelerated by a feeling that they weren't really helping him. She had noticed that he had good marks for maths in his last report but could not believe that Orwell House's standards differed from the navy's. She felt they were understanding less rather than more.

Mrs Hutton returned to the meeting and sat down.

Mrs Pannell whispered something to the Chairman about needing to make up lost time because the meeting had started late.

The Chairman ignored her.

Mr King said he was finding it difficult to collect all the different strands of thought. Their anticipation that Geoffrey would again be in trouble with the police made it no less worrying. The departure from Orwell House had seemed to go smoothly at the time and it was only now that their feelings were becoming apparent. He was sorry he hadn't invited Geoffrey to this meeting.

Mrs Pannell kindly agreed to clerk while Mr Nuttall was making his 'individual comments'. He said he too felt sad about Geoffrey's problems, though not surprised. He also felt that the navy might well prove right for Geoffrey but thought Orwell House had found it difficult to decide how genuine Geoffrey's desire to join the navy really was. If he was really enthusiastic he should try to acquire the necessary knowledge and not just give up.

TPA thought that the theme of 'It's too late after the event' was extremely important. One ought to have some chance of being able to predict future events based on whatever clues one was given. How frustrating if the clues were useless or misleading. Mrs Hutton today, when it was her turn to speak, had told them she would 'pass' and then had proceeded to speak for three minutes – was that a lie? Was this the kind of thing that Geoffrey's lies reflected or caricatured? Certainly one would need to know what sort of maths test to expect if one was to have any hope of passing it. If you were born a boy it was a bit late to hope to be a girl, and even dressing up as one wouldn't do much good in that direction. Something connected with this had come up twice in the meeting. When Mrs Hutton was briefly out of the meeting Mrs Pannell had seemed to

want to take over and had pointed out that TPA, as Chairman, had
forgotten to mention the time they were short. She had been wrong
on two counts. It was one, not two, minutes; and he had already
done it. She also seemed to want to steal his job when Mr Nuttall
was speaking, saying 'Okay?' as though querying whether Mr
Nuttall had stopped talking. She might have just been doing her
temporary clerk's job, but TPA felt she was making a bid for power.
In the same way the social worker was actually the father figure at
the moment, and the parents the mother figure, in the sense that the
father's job is 'to see that children are looked after' and the mother's
'to look after them'. So in the past the mother figure had been Orwell
House. It was now mother and father, and the father figure, since
Geoffrey was still 'in care', was the social worker as before. Somehow
Mr King had forgotten that he was this important person and had
neglected to invite Geoffrey to this meeting, leaving it to the mother
figure (i.e. now mother and father). One of the important things a
father figure could do was to beat the tendency of always being wise
after the event: to be a 'good authority' – to be in charge of a
situation, anticipate difficulty and move before the disaster, not after
it. For instance, Mr Hutton had mentioned his reservations about
the double-glazing job, making it quite clear that he had forebodings
about it. He had shown he was apprehensive, and it might have been
a good idea if those 'future' thoughts had been acted upon. Geoffrey
wouldn't now be in a worse job – as he was – than previously. There
was something here again about the male, the father figure, not
coming forward and exercising his role as the person who speaks up
before something might happen. It was very difficult to say 'This will
happen; this *won't* happen' unless you had full authority, especially
when you had to make a decision about something that hadn't yet,
and might never, happen. One always chanced looking a fool. There
was probably something on those lines in the history of this case. Mr
Hutton senior had probably been a dominant kind of person and his
wife not the type to take a firm grip on things even after his death. In
the business of Kevin she must have said nothing where she could
have done; what came about was a tragic 'after the event' situation.
One of the main features would have been Mrs Hutton senior's
failure to take charge of what might or might not happen in the future
against a background of a rather more dominant Mr Hutton senior's
ghost. TPA believed they were still seeing this sort of thing depicted
in Geoffrey, but as usual he was more worried about Sean.

In the free discussion Mrs Hutton said she felt somewhat responsible
for the alienation between Mr King and Geoffrey, and cited a huge

angry row between herself and Geoffrey when he left the house.

The discussion then turned to the family 'atmosphere' in the five years between the death of Mr Hutton's father, aged 48, and his brother's death at 17, and it was discovered that Mr Hutton and his younger brother James had been evacuated during the war to the Lake District because their mother was afraid of bombs. Mr Hutton felt that his father, had he lived, might have made a different decision, but in any case the situation would have felt different. Certainly Mr Hutton and his younger brother had had a wonderful time there. His baby sister had been left with his mother and the 'more responsible' Kevin. Mr Hutton had often wondered since what it must have been like at home then.

It was suggested that there was a possible parallel between Mrs Hutton senior's 'dramatics' and the unreality evinced by Geoffrey, who didn't really believe that he was leaving Orwell House.

Towards the end of the meeting Mrs Hutton suddenly mentioned that Mr Hutton's relations never reached 50. Whether it was true or not, there were legends of a great-grandfather, two uncles and a grandfather dying before their 50th birthday.

Mr Hutton seemed to try to make a joke about all that, but everyone else was silent – for what seemed a long time.

There was no time for a post-professionals' meeting.

*

Timor mortis conturbat me. I think it conturbats most people, so I'm not too clear about the significance of the comments at the pre-professionals' meeting. Are panic attacks due to fear of dying? All I know is you're supposed to induce the sufferer to put his head in a brown paper bag.

Orwell House's obligation to Geoffrey was now at an end. Most institutions, I am told – certainly prisons – see their work as finished when the inmate leaves, assuming (not too surprisingly in my view) that he is happy to be out and away; but then, when you think about it, even a crowded prison cell is probably preferable to a damp cardboard box in a Soho street. This is beside the point. We are concerned with Geoffrey. Orwell House does recognise the short-sightedness of the above assumption and has various follow-up procedures, although the staff, being pressured by the influx of new inmates, still tend to forget the children when they leave and bow out relatively fast. Also, if the helpers have only scraped the surface of the problem and are colluding with the chimerical happy ending, they won't have earned much real gratitude from their clients.

For arcane reasons of his own TPA chose this moment to enlighten me as to the meaning of the term 'over-determination'. Throughout the case, he says, certain symptoms will have been interpreted in more than one way. If I had supposed that he was striking out in all directions trying to get it right I would have been wrong. All the interpretations could be right since a symptom may have multiples of meaning. This is what Freud called 'mental economy'.

When TPA describes the father figure as the one who 'sees that the children are looked after', as opposed to actually looking after them, he mentions the term 'good authority'. This is crucial to his way of thinking; it is something that the delinquent's parents never had, or lost in their own childhoods, and which they hope to redeem in the process of trying to cope with the embodiment of themselves in their own delinquent child: a belated but essential mourning.

It is worth noting that Mr Hutton is now 48 – the age his father was when he died. Apparently 50 is proverbially the maximum age for a male Hutton. The subject of wartime evacuation arose again, and TPA says that many parents in the war must have become strangers, occasional visitors, to their children, gradually losing the ability to pick up nuances which they wouldn't have missed if they had remained in close, day-by-day contact. It was now, he says, that he first began to think of loss of intuition as a major Hutton theme.

13. The Freudian slip

Venue: Clinic consulting-room   9th October 1978
Present: Dr Pitt-Aikens, Chairman
           Mr King, Local Authority Social Worker legally
               responsible for Geoffrey Hutton and clerk to the
               meeting
           Mrs Pannell, link Social Worker at Orwell House
           Mr & Mrs Hutton

At the preliminary professionals' meeting it was noted that they were
two minutes late in starting, and it was agreed to add this time on.

The minutes of the previous professionals' meeting were read and
approved, and it was noted how people who came to be involved in
this case found it fascinating. They wondered whether this was
because it was macabre, and referred to the 'stain appearing on the
ceiling'. They felt there might almost be an element of voyeurism in
the case.

Mr King said he was leaving the case, and this would therefore be
his last meeting.

They wondered whether Mr and Mrs Hutton would use the
change of social worker as an opportunity or excuse to drop out of the
meetings.

Mr and Mrs Hutton arrived for the joint meeting. Geoffrey had also
been invited but had declined, basically because he 'didn't want to
know about it'. Sean had again declined on the grounds that he
could see no point in it.

Anything relevant or 'important' was decided on as the focus for
discussion.

Mrs Pannell said she was conscious of feeling like an observer in
the case. Though she now had no direct role, she wanted to be
present because she was interested in what happened to Geoffrey. It
was a shame that Mr King was leaving but important that the
discussion about Geoffrey should go on.

Mr King agreed that it was regrettable that he was leaving at that stage. Quite a lot had happened in the family since the last meeting. Geoffrey had appeared in court and been fined £25 for the theft of a blouse. He was still working at a supermarket and that seemed to be going well. But it was getting more difficult for Mr and Mrs Hutton to cope with Geoffrey at home and they had made the difficult decision to request his removal. They had always treated him as their son and never rejected him, but the stress was now too much for the whole family. Mr King had contacted a hostel and they felt the move had been on the cards for a long time. It was better that it had happened now before there was a crisis and the police became involved. Geoffrey was denying the difficulties and avoiding speaking to him.

Mr Hutton made what he called a 'Freudian slip', saying that they were shocked to hear that *Geoffrey* was leaving, correcting it to being shocked that *Mr King* was leaving. He said Geoffrey refused to accept the problems and only saw Dr Adams when it was advantageous for him to do so, as when he had a court appearance hanging over him – having 'treatment' might impress the magistrate. Nor was he seeing Mr King, his social worker. He denied doing anything he wasn't actually caught doing. If not caught, he thought he couldn't be accused. Mr Hutton considered he honestly believed his own lies. The real concern now was for the rest of the family. Geoffrey still had his problem with clothing. He had damaged some of his sister's clothes and it was upsetting for them. Mr Hutton was also worried about the effect Geoffrey was having on Louis, who tended to mix with Geoffrey's rather unsavoury friends, and he didn't think that Geoffrey regarded himself as part of the family any more.

Mrs Hutton said she would pass, and agreed with her husband.

TPA said he thought that last time they had been on the right lines. Mr Hutton senior had been dominant in the family during his lifetime. He had then become the very opposite, since he wasn't there, because he was dead – very weak indeed. The saying 'when the cat's away the mice will play' came to mind. TPA wondered (in view of Mr Hutton's Freudian slip) about those who had left home between Mr Hutton senior's death and Kevin's. Hadn't it been he and his younger brother James? At the previous meeting Mr King at least had said that he 'regretted not inviting Geoffrey this time', almost anticipating his own 'professional death'. Inviting Geoffrey hadn't even been mentioned – he had allowed him to get away with saying 'no' to the parents, who couldn't legally make him come. TPA guessed that, in the original Hutton household, after the death of Mr Hutton senior there had been a theatrical atmosphere – an unreality reigning, as if they were all in a play. There may have been a belief that when Mr Hutton senior came back things would return to stark reality. Mrs Hutton, he observed, sometimes said in these meetings 'I pass or I go along with my husband'. She didn't seem to realise that she was alive and had something to say. On these occasions she looked more like a passive observer. If it carried on like that, time would pass; there would be no magic to bring everybody to life, only a wasting of time. As to the future of the meetings, although Mr King was leaving TPA felt they should continue. He speculated whether he should wait passively like Mrs Hutton until a new social worker was involved and could set up the meeting, or whether he should himself invite them and get a grip on it. It was easy to take the soft option. Mrs Hutton senior never really accepted her 'new male clothes' as the boss. She waited for her husband to return from the dead, and people were allowed to 'slip away'. TPA was tempted to do the same but wouldn't. He would arrange to see Mr and Mrs Hutton and ask Mr King to pass on the invitation to his successor. The trouble was of course that TPA had absolutely no say in the running of the family. He couldn't grab Sean by the hair and drag him into the front room for a long talk about his eyes, but if he were his father he certainly would.

In the free discussion Mr Hutton said there was no question of his mother having been the strong character and his father the weak one. His father had been an extremely strong character and his mother had very much needed the support of her husband. Then the meaning dawned very clearly that, since Mr Hutton senior had died five years before Kevin, this very strong man in fact became as weak as could be – in that he was totally absent. Mother had still been present but was unable to take on the responsibilities without her previous support. It was plain that Grandfather Hutton would never in a million years have done what Mr King did, viz. fail to invite Geoffrey, nor what Mr Hutton had done, viz. fail to act on his prediction that the double-glazing job would prove disastrous.

They went on to talk about the new job, which was proving successful and could lead to better things – management courses, etc. At that point they were interrupted by the children who had gathered outside, and Mrs Hutton went off to see what it was all about.

Mr Hutton seemed a little annoyed at being interrupted, because everyone had to sit in silence while the carry-on proceeded. (The Chairman stopped the meeting's progress while Mrs Hutton was out of the room.) When Mrs Hutton returned he spoke of Geoffrey's ambition to join the navy and how worried he had been about whether his 'record' would affect this. He likened Geoffrey's lack of urgency in doing things to a part of his own personality, though he alluded also to another part – his tendency to hang on to things, whereas Kevin had been somewhat butterfly-minded.

TPA, as Chairman, drew the discussion to a halt at this point, arranging the next meeting almost as an afterthought . He offered it to Mr and Mrs Hutton, Mrs Pannell and Mr King's successor – the invitees could in turn invite whoever else they wished.

*

This co-authorship is more complicated than I imagined it would be and is rather like playing tennis doubles. In my conscious mind I believe myself to be behaving in a beautiful, polite fashion: deferring to expert knowledge, not putting myself forward, and not treading on the toes of TPA (oops – sorry, partner).

'Rubbish,' says he.

'Do you mean I am not pulling my weight?' I enquire.

That isn't what he means at all. What he means is that I am contriving to make it appear that he is hogging the limelight, and that any readers who may pick up this book will remark that he is an awful nasty man who has pushed out that poor little woman, who used to be quite a good writer till he squashed her. I explain that I have a vulgar mind and that, unlike him, I find it immediately interesting that Geoffrey dresses up as a girl; my mind is also hopelessly given over to frivolity and I love the phrase 'Freudian slip' – I see it hanging on the washing line ready for Geoffrey to nick. I say humbly that I am intimidated by the stern masculine thought processes that he himself evinces and uncertain of my ability to interpret them correctly. I say, rather sneakily, that I have been infected by a 'Huttonism' and wish to be, like Anne in the meeting, merely a 'passive observer'. He refutes all this in his customary straightforward fashion and says that the truth is that I hate men, and have discovered a perfectly wonderful way in which to do one of them a bit of damage. I suppose he could be right, but it must be exhausting to think like that all the time. Back to the net.

TPA says that Mr King took the moral line of workers in the 'caring' professions (oh, bad luck, partner), considering that the client's 'motivation' was extremely important, even to the extent that the likelihood of a successful outcome to the case was dependent on it. I don't know why he said that, because it doesn't seem relevant to anything, but he concluded with the remark that underneath Mr King's proper professional concern there probably lay a Huttonian theme of 'things not being as you would have thought'. Although the suggestion arose that the meetings might be terminated, the Huttons carried on turning up for a further six years. The conventional way would have been to wait to see whether the new social worker wanted another meeting or not, but TPA says it was necessary to exorcise that conventional approach. He felt he had to get a grip on things and arrange future meetings despite the present non-existence of the new social worker. I wonder why? I bet it wasn't anything as simple as worry about what Geoffrey might do next. I sometimes get the feeling that TPA has left the court and gone off for a round of clock-golf all by himself.

Geoffrey was described by his father in the previous meeting as believing his own lies, and TPA observes that Mrs Hutton's behaviour is a kind of lie – she says she is going out of the room and then carries on talking – and it is very common for the dynamics of a meeting to precede and anticipate an actual happening. Speaking of Mr Hutton's widowed mother, TPA says that in his experience mothers who used to say to their disobedient children, 'Just wait till your father gets home' (two-person authority), often seem to feel too guilty when the husband dies to change the threat to 'I'll stop your pocket money' (one-person authority). What happens is that the child's naughtiness seems to become omnipotence and he rules the roost. Mrs Hutton senior did not take over her husband's role (change sex). It was as though she was waiting for him to return from the dead.

As an afterthought, TPA said that Geoffrey, as it were, lied by omission, denying the observer the luxury of facts and admission. He simply left people with their own intuitive convictions.

Looking back, it must have been shortly after this meeting that TPA and I first met.

14. The surprise

Venue: Clinic consulting-room   20th November 1978
Present: Dr Pitt-Aikens, Chairman and clerk to meeting
           Mrs Pannell, link Social Worker at Orwell House
           Mr & Mrs Hutton
           Margaret

At the preliminary professionals' meeting Mrs Pannell and TPA remembered with surprise that Mr King had left the case. They wondered whether his 'surprising' absence was reminiscent of Kevin's 'surprising' suicide, or of Grandfather's 'surprising' death. Were they experiencing a 'Huttonism'?

At the joint meeting it was learned that Sean and Geoffrey had been invited but had declined, both because of work and because they couldn't see any purpose in coming. The new social worker, Mr Tennant, would have liked to attend but had had to go to court.

Mrs Pannell said that it seemed strange without Mr King, and she was glad someone else had been appointed to the case. She was curious about what had been happening and wondered whether Geoffrey had left home yet. She was glad to see Margaret and wondered whether she was present at her own request or whether her parents had thought it a good idea.

Mr Hutton said that one thing had occurred to him about the meetings. He had the impression that TPA had either Sean or himself consigned as a possible suicide but wasn't quite sure which of them it was. If it was him they had no need to worry, as he just hadn't got the time for it. He had thought of it but had too many other things to do.

Here there was a roar of laughter from someone.

Mr Hutton explained that he had thought of it because an awful lot had happened at home since the last meeting. Geoffrey had gone to the hostel, come back at the weekend and announced that he was staying. This had been a complete surprise to everyone including the warden of the hostel since, when Geoffrey left for the weekend, he had said, I'll be seeing you.' Then they had Geoffrey hanging around the house, refusing to go back, and Mr Hutton had got his back up, refusing to allow him in. They had ended with Geoffrey wrapping himself in a blanket on the concrete floor of the garage on a bitterly cold night. Mr Hutton had previously discussed with the social worker what to do in such an eventuality and had been told that every time he gave in he made it more difficult. He had tried to harden his heart but at half past midnight could do so no longer and had gone out and dragged Geoffrey in. Geoffrey was nearly frozen stiff by then and Mr Hutton had a good talk with him. He hoped that that had had some effect because, to Mr Hutton's complete surprise, the next night Geoffrey went back to the hostel and had been there ever since, apart from his visits home. He had seen Mr Tennant, and at the moment everything was going marvellously. He thought that Geoffrey might have been testing them to see how far he could push things in the light of the move to the hostel and the change of social worker. But, whatever the reason, things were far better than they had been for a long time, and what he had said at the previous meeting about Geoffrey's not seeming part of the family was no longer true. He did seem part of the family again and was back in his old place.

Margaret said that in answer to Mrs Pannell's question she had come at her own request and really had nothing to say at the moment.

Mrs Hutton said that Margaret in fact had quite a lot to say but didn't know how to say it. She had said so before she came into the meeting. Geoffrey was quite good at the moment, but she was wondering how long it was going to last. As so often with Geoffrey, they would just settle down and cross their fingers hoping that everything was going all right. Then they would have a great upheaval again. So she wasn't putting too much store by him at the moment and she felt he was still a disturbance to the others. Here she asked Mr Hutton and Margaret whether they agreed with that and said she would leave it there.

TPA thought the word 'surprise' was important. It seemed to occur quite often on various occasions – past and present, professional and non-professional. For example, he and Mrs Pannell in the pre-professionals' meeting had been surprised not to see Mr King, although he had said a long time ago that he would be leaving. Then dying of a heart attack was a surprising business and not something that one could prepare for – like suicide. It was interesting that Mr Hutton thought that TPA had him in line for suicide. He hadn't, but he had been worried that something surprising – like dropping down dead – might happen to him. Mr Hutton had said he was too busy to contemplate suicide, and it was precisely people who were too busy to think about themselves to whom this surprising thing sometimes happened.

TPA had indeed been worried about suicide in respect of Sean, in so far as Sean was perhaps in danger of going through the sort of thing that Kevin had been through. He felt there was another theme which had come up that day. It was again to do with reality and unreality. He had noticed in the records of the previous meeting that he had, as Chairman, arranged the next Hutton meeting. Only subsequently had he realised that he should *invite* people. After all, they were quite at liberty to refuse. He had sounded very positive, almost pompous, and it was only moments later that he had used the term 'invite', which gave them the right to say, 'No, thank you.' He had also noticed that he had said that Mr and Mrs Hutton and the new social worker were allowed to invite whom they liked, and that again was only half the story. Mr Tennant could insist on Geoffrey coming. Mr and Mrs Hutton could insist on their children, over whom they had legal authority, coming – so there was some sort of muddle between making something happen and letting it drift. It could be that the two ideas – the 'surprising' and the 'letting things drift' – might have something in common. He was sorry Geoffrey had had to be put in the garage, but at least Mr Hutton hadn't let things drift. He had done it beautifully, leaving Geoffrey until he was stone-cold, or until at least he got the message. There had been no question of Geoffrey's twisting his father round his little finger. He was sure that Geoffrey had realised that the father talking was the one who was sorry for his son being cold, not the one who was saying 'OK, you can stay at home and mess us all around!'

TPA was reminded of something else on the 'surprising' list. The warden had been surprised at the turn around, having been convinced that Geoffrey would be coming back. How wrong could you be? He hoped Mr Hutton was looking after his health and not unrealisingly killing himself by not giving himself enough time for things. He hoped he didn't work at weekends, didn't drive when he was tired, ate the right things, went for long walks. He hoped they had a dog. Changing tack somewhat, he hoped the family didn't listen to Sean too much, overestimating his sense of responsibility, as perhaps Mr Hutton's family after Grandfather's death had overestimated Kevin's. Sean was probably not as responsible as he seemed and it might be a good idea if one of his parents asked him how he felt about suicide and wasn't palmed off by his saying something like 'You're talking stupid'. He was sure that that was what Sean would say but felt that Sean needed the same sort of persistence that Mr Hutton had shown towards Geoffrey.

Mrs Pannell started the free discussion recalling Mrs Hutton's anticipation of a 'nasty surprise' from Geoffrey.

TPA said that Geoffrey was perhaps a symbol of that theme.

They spoke of all the things that Mr Hutton got up to in his spare time – freelance writing, stamps, scouting, magazines, union work. It was remarked that Margaret had never known anybody to die suddenly, but there was talk of the family's various pets, who had indeed died in a surprising way.

They discussed the disappearance of Mr Hutton's job, and Mr Hutton said he liked something that was both exacting and interesting and he needed a challenge. He talked about the customs officers he dealt with, and Mrs Hutton and Margaret used words like 'strange' and 'peculiar' about the officers. There was apparently a danger of the group at Mr Hutton's work breaking up. Mr Hutton spoke of the necessity to be fast, friendly and therefore somewhat eccentric. A parallel was drawn between his outgoingness at work and his inwardness in a social situation, on the one hand, and Geoffrey's painful shyness together with his need almost to draw attention by dressing up in girl's clothing on the other. Mr Hutton said that perhaps he and Geoffrey found a way out of their shyness in their several ways of being extrovert: the clothes on the one hand and the job on the other. He underlined this by remarking that a colleague had been amazed that he managed to talk non-stop for three hours on a ship.

The meeting heard how Mr Hutton's job was potentially 'drying up' and involving more and more paperwork until there was a danger of the whole thing becoming paperwork. Mr Hutton used the word 'infuriating', and it was noted that the last time he had used it was in relation to the fantasy of his coronary. They noticed that time had gone very fast and were surprised at that. Mr Hutton concluded by reminding them that there was another aspect of 'surprise'. Not only had Geoffrey gone back to the hostel, but there had been no trouble.

At the post-professionals' meeting there was a discussion about Mrs Pannell's managing to come to the meetings. It was recognised that TPA was getting so used to her coming that he would be furious if she didn't (whereupon she too would be furious – after all she wasn't obliged to come). It was agreed that she would attend if possible.

There was another surprise when one of the clinic's staff rang the consulting-room to say that two other young members of the family were wandering round the building getting interested in it.

*

I sympathise with Mr Hutton's attitude to suicide. When I was an irreligious girl I used to think that if everything got too much, too crowded, too painful, it would be a simple matter to down a draught of some noxious herb or craftily save up a lethal amount of sleeping pills. I know better now. I have a conviction that you don't escape that easily, that the moment the light goes out you find yourself in another dimension, being informed that all the boiled cabbage and cod's head you have left on your plate will be served up at each meal until you have eaten every scrap. In the parlance of 'Snakes and Ladders', you would find yourself not up a ladder but down a snake; and I can see no circumstances, however dire, which would justify the bite on the cyanide capsule. It is hard, but it is one of the rules; and I hope that Kevin has by now, in eternity, worked his way through the left-overs.

Surprise kept bobbing up in this meeting. The professionals tossed around the idea that Mr King's surprising absence was reminiscent of Grandfather Hutton's surprising death and Kevin's surprising suicide. I know they have got to do that sort of thing, but I get a touch bored with it sometimes. I find Geoffrey's surprises more interesting. He is by now well established as a totally surprising boy, and he seldom lets one down. Once you are used to him being bad he does something good and people nearly fall over with astonishment. He went back to the hostel without a squeak and behaved for a while in a perfectly lamblike fashion. If I had been his parent I should have found this disconcerting, not to say alarming. Excellent behaviour in a child tends to make one nervous, since it can mean that he has just done, or is about to do, something dreadful. It is similar to the bunch of red roses which guilty husbands present to their wives – watertight grounds for divorce.

I find not surprising but bewildering the concern with the invitations, which will surface again in subsequent meetings and has caused me great confusion. It has all been explained to me many times but my brain can't get round it. Nor do I know how they remembered that Mr Hutton had used the word 'infuriating' in relation to the fantasy of his coronary, since it does not appear in any previous minutes, although I can well see why it would make him cross. It is a human characteristic to fly into a rage when some savant warns you that if you do not change your ways something nasty will leap out of the woodwork and get you.

15. The clerk's tale

Venue: Clinic consulting-room   22nd January 1979
Present: Dr Pitt-Aikens, Chairman
            Mr Tennant, Local Authority Social Worker legally
                responsible for Geoffrey Hutton
            Mr Hutton, clerk to the meeting
            Mrs Hutton

Mrs Pannell had been called away just before the meeting started.
Mr Hutton agreed to clerk.

At the joint meeting Mr Tennant – here for the first time – said that
he could see that the meetings were important to those present but
couldn't quite see the necessity for his own attendance.

TPA asked if anyone had been invited and not come. Both Sean
and Geoffrey had been invited and had both declined. Margaret was
walking the dog in the nearby park.

The topic was decided – 'anything relevant or important'.

Mrs Hutton said she thought Mr Tennant would like the family to
have Geoffrey home again, but that if they did it would undo all the
work that had been done, and as he was getting on well at the hostel
it would be a shame to take him away from there. Quite frankly, she
didn't think she would like him home again. His problems weren't as
bad as they had been and weren't showing at all at the hostel. She
explained that she was speaking of the dressing up. They had found
some clothes just before Christmas but didn't know how long they
had been there.

Mr Hutton said that the reason Margaret wasn't here today was
that the last time she had been present somebody had 'gone and
opened his mouth about dogs', and now they had a dog; and because
they had the dog with them Margaret wouldn't come to the meeting,
although she had meant to originally. It was a little puppy. He said
they didn't need that dog; he did quite enough walking in his job,
ambling up and down jetties and climbing goodness knew how many
gang-planks and companion ways in the course of his work. He got

more exercise than he could really cope with. He worked at weekends and in the last few weeks had thought about the business of heart attacks, and he hadn't got time for them either. He wasn't going to have one, and he wasn't going to worry about one. Getting to the main point – his wife had been talking about her view of having Geoffrey home, and he agreed that, at Christmas, by the time he had been home for a few days, their tempers were beginning to fray at the edges. Geoffrey had been getting worse-behaved than he had been to start with. He had been a nuisance with the other children and had thrown his weight around. The other problem they were concerned with – his dressing up in girls' clothes – was definitely true. They didn't have direct evidence of it, but there were enough clues around to suggest that it was still going on. He stuck to what he had said last time – that Geoffrey had found his place in the family again, but his place in the family, unfortunately, wasn't living permanently at home, and as he grew older he would have to make his own life for himself. As he and his wife saw it, what they had to provide was the family atmosphere for him to partake of, but they drew the line at having him there all the time, because that would destroy the whole works anyway – which wasn't a nice thing to have to say about your own son. When he came home for visits, for a while everything in the garden was rosy. Then it began to fall apart. Tempers were frayed and the good atmosphere disappeared.

Mr Tennant said the prime reason for his presence was connected with Geoffrey. It was nice to see things moving towards a workable balance between Geoffrey and his family. He was aware that Geoffrey still felt his roots were at home, and because of that he felt his body should be also. However, Geoffrey seemed to have accepted that that would not be feasible from the family's point of view and even admitted himself that there were dangers involved. Yet, said Mr Tennant, he was pleased to see that Geoffrey seemed able to stand a little more on his own feet outside the cosiness of home. He was coping with living in a hostel with older boys some of whom had more difficulties than himself. He was also dealing with a fairly demanding job. All in all, things didn't seem too bad all round.

TPA apologised for not being at his best. There had been an unrelated crisis in the clinic just before the family arrived and it seemed a shame that they had come all that way to get an analyst who wasn't firing on all cylinders. None the less he wanted to say something about Mrs Hutton, and about one of the ways in which, like Geoffrey, she didn't change either. She ought to know by this time how strange these meetings were. She knew that nobody was supposed to interrupt anybody else during 'individual comments', but twice while speaking she had turned to Mr Tennant for help with things she couldn't remember. He, of course, had obliged, since he had never been to a meeting before, and easily slipped into the trap. It seemed to be no good expecting Mrs Hutton to change. He had tried many times, and he had a suspicion that Mr Hutton's feelings about Geoffrey's not changing were connected. Maybe Geoffrey was still wearing girls' clothes. When he came home, the same old Geoffrey popped up again, and things began to fray at the edges. Mrs Hutton had been the same old Mrs Hutton interrupting on three or four occasions. Mr Tennant, new to the scene, might think that TPA was being petty, and in a way he was right, but it could be said that the rules in the 'meeting game' were petty. Mrs Hutton knew that and still broke them. Perhaps Geoffrey, a male wearing female clothing, was a living caricature of the breaking of petty rules, colourfully forcing on them a connection between petty rule-breaking and his mother's persisting in what she wished to do.

TPA wanted to know why Mrs Hutton had a plaster on her nose. He was worried too about the dog. It was almost as if he had said that they should get the blessed dog. He had hoped they had a dog to give Mr Hutton some exercise, and why the family had to give in to pressure to get the dog – which he felt they didn't want – God only knew. He could only suggest that they had given in to Margaret. If giving in to Geoffrey was a grave mistake the same must hold for Margaret. He added that the clinic staff had seemed to be concerned that the children were wandering round the clinic last time. He had been interested that those staff seemed so upset about it – upset and curious. His guess was that the children hadn't done any harm to anybody, but there had been something about their demeanour which had made the staff come up to him afterwards to ask about them. They had stuck in their memory for some reason or other. So there was something about the atmosphere emanating from the children that made people sit up and take notice while not knowing why. He hadn't really gone into it much with the staff, but he couldn't help noticing that it seemed to have made a tremendous impact on them. He wasn't sure in what way, but he felt it was important.

During the free discussion Mr Hutton explained his earlier reservation. At the last meeting TPA, worrying over the possibility of death by heart attack, had suggested that Mr Hutton get a dog and go for walks. The young children had promptly given him one for Christmas.

Mr Tennant asked why they went to the meetings, and there was some discussion between him and Mrs Hutton about Geoffrey's problems, with particular reference to a radio which had been given him for Christmas and had disappeared in somewhat inexplicable circumstances.

Mr Hutton spoke to TPA about Sean, giving details of the current state of his eyesight and saying that there was less worry about him than TPA seemed to think. They then talked about Mr Hutton's work, and Mr Hutton pointed out that he had to work at weekends. He had – not for the first time – just begun to question the purpose of the meetings when time ran out.

TPA asked if another meeting was wanted. Mr Hutton hesitated, and TPA pointed out that if another was agreed it could be cancelled easily, whereas if it wasn't it would be harder to arrange later.

There was no post-professional (or pre-professional) meeting since Mrs Pannell was not present and it was Mr Tennant's first meeting. They had been caught on the hop at the beginning of the hour, with everyone – family and new social worker – arriving in the consulting-room all at once. TPA didn't have the heart to turn the family away. Also, Mr Tennant would have been hard put to it to understand what was going on.

*

This meeting illustrates the charming artfulness of the little Huttons, who were clearly yearning for a dog and were swift to seize the opportunity – at the apparent behest of TPA – of buying one as a Christmas present for their father. The personalities of the family are apparent, and it is interesting that Mr Hutton clerked the meeting. His letter, which follows, also gives a good picture of him. (Having met Mrs Hutton, I can reveal that she is perhaps the only woman in the world who would still look appealing with a plaster on her nose.)

28th February 1979

Dear Dr Pitt-Aikens,

I enclose the minutes of the last meeting on 22nd January. I must apologise for the delay. As I have said at the meetings, there are never enough minutes to an hour for me, but nevertheless I really had meant to do it that evening. Unfortunately we got home very late and I put it away to do later. With me that is fatal, and of course it got forgotten. To make some excuse for myself, I have had a lot on my mind lately – more than usual, that is. Of course Geoffrey figures in this, but I will keep the details for the next meeting or we will have nothing to talk about. Also, you can set your mind at rest; it was not enforced walks with the dog that took up my time.

There are two main culprits. I had to attend a funeral a few weeks ago (not mine, unfortunately – sorry to disappoint you). My Group Scout Leader, who was also a great friend, had died and as a result I have had a lot of sorting out and administration to do. Secondly, I am currently involved in organising strikes, protests and so on in the course of my Union's pay claim.

Life does have its brighter side. The only reason you have belatedly got the minutes, and this epistle, is that Anne has badgered me into doing some redecorating. There is a great therapeutic value in this. Standing there wielding a paintbrush does not require a great degree of concentration and one can allow one's mind to wander. Having planned the future course of my stamp collection and worked out a couple of ideas on programmes for scout meetings, I progressed naturally to the sad loss of Sandy, my GSL and then on to my first conscious realisation of what my feelings on religion were. I was at complete peace with myself for a while. It was marvellous – I wonder if I can get my paint on the National Health next time. Anyway, the point is that somewhere in these mental perambulations you came up and I remembered the minutes. Please don't ask me the sequence of associations that brought you in – I can't even remember if you came before or after God. Anyway, I did and here they are, together with some ramblings that, I realise on reading them through, will either have you delirious with joy or jumping in the Thames.

Yours sincerely,
Ian Hutton.

16. Own sweet way

Venue: Clinic consulting-room   19th March 1979
Present: Dr Pitt-Aikens, Chairman and clerk to the meeting
            Mr & Mrs Hutton

Mr Tennant had been invited but saw no point in coming if Geoffrey
didn't. Nevertheless Mrs Hutton felt that Mr Tennant probably
would have come (considering a little bit of trouble that Geoffrey
had been in) if he hadn't been on holiday. Geoffrey couldn't take
time off work. Mrs Pannell had to go to the funeral of the mother of
an ex-Orwell House boy.

The minutes of the last meetings were read. Mrs Hutton's
explanation of the plaster on her nose (she had fallen over) had been
omitted – otherwise they were approved.

They agreed on 'anything relevant or important' as the topic.

Mr Hutton said that he first wanted to explain the new trouble
they had had with Geoffrey. He had appeared in court on a charge of
taking women's clothing. He was wearing it when arrested and the
court had bound him over! This had been reported in the local paper,
and as a result he had had to leave the hostel, mainly for his own
safety, since he had been threatened by the other boys. He was now
living in lodgings, which Mr Tennant had arranged for him.
Judgment in the case had been deferred for six months, during
which time he had to accept psychiatric help. That was the main
reason they hadn't wanted Margaret in the meeting, because they
would rather the children didn't know all the minute details of
Geoffrey's problems. Mr Hutton said that when he was taking the
minutes last time one thing that had struck him was – what were
they doing there? His concern was whether anything was being
achieved. He felt they were taking up valuable time with TPA which
might possibly be better given to other people. That, without
question, was all he had to say.

Mrs Hutton said she didn't know about anybody else, but she
thought it was doing her husband a world of good coming to the
meetings. She thought he got quite a lot from the meetings. She

didn't know if it was anything to do with the family, and wondered, in a round about way, if there was something not quite right in it. She asked if she could leave it at that, as she couldn't explain herself very well.

TPA remarked that Mrs Hutton was an amazing woman. She absolutely infuriated him at times and then came to the rescue at others. Mr Hutton had seemed to be saying he didn't understand the meetings but would patiently go along if they really wanted him to, without quite seeing the point. Then Mrs Hutton said that her husband seemed to be gaining something from them. It could be wishful thinking on her part, but his guess was that she was right. She, at least, went to the meetings, philosophically and guardedly. There was a tremendous difference between Mr Hutton, who also went, in spite of his reservations, and Mr Tennant who had only been to one and seemed to think they were nothing to do with him at all and couldn't possibly do him any good. He could be right, but there was no way of his finding out, if he didn't come. TPA was interested that the court had insisted that Geoffrey accept psychiatric help – whatever that meant. His guess was that when the six months 'binding over' were up no one would be able to put their hand on the Bible and say that Geoffrey had availed himself of such help. He might see someone during that time, but that would be about all. There did seem to be a theme of people going their own sweet way and perhaps landing in trouble. For instance, Geoffrey must have known what was likely to happen – the prejudice he would arouse by offending in the way he had done. Nothing seemed to be allowed to stand in his way. He had just pressed on and done it, and now the hostel didn't want him back. Mr Tennant had seen no point in attending the meetings if Geoffrey didn't, and TPA regarded that as going along with Geoffrey's omnipotence, at the very least. So, as it were, Mr Tennant was going along on Geoffrey's own sweet way. Mr Hutton, on the other hand, was somewhat different. He went to the meetings despite his reservations – was open to argument, discussion, reason, another point of view. Not so Sean, certainly not so Geoffrey. TPA wondered about Margaret, saying he had a funny idea she might be a little madam with a mind of her own. Perhaps she thought she knew best and then, wallop, she was in a mess, whereas she would be much better off if she could open up to, say, her mother. It would do her an awful lot more good to have open and free discussions with someone as life went by, than wait for a crisis, when she couldn't cope at all. He could almost hear Mrs Hutton saying to herself, 'That's all very fine, but you try and tell her that. She wouldn't listen.' He would be interested to know what the relationship had been between Mr Hutton and *his* sister when they were small and had gone through such a difficult time. He wondered how much real discussion there had been. Had people gone their own sweet way, or had they got together to make the most of each other in the difficult situation they were going through? He doubted the latter. He said, 'I bet they just pressed on.'

In the free discussion they spoke of the value of the meetings – for instance the 'keeping-in-touchness' which might not be appreciated.

Mr Hutton mentioned his opportunities to talk at work on the ships, and someone said 'minus Mum'.

Mrs Hutton said she was sometimes at screaming point over Geoffrey. She didn't see so much of her friend, who used to be a great help, since now they were both working. She did still have her intuitive feelings about Geoffrey, although she didn't get as agitated about them.

Talk proceeded to Mrs Hutton's loss of self-confidence. She said this had happened after some years of marriage. Geoffrey had knocked it out of her, and she mentioned a bill which someone said she had got wrong when in fact it was their own mistake.

There was then talk of Freda, the sister, who of course had been the only girl. She had been six months old when the father (who had always wanted this little girl) died. Mr Hutton had been 10½ with a 12-year-old and a 7-year-old brother. Freda had been the family pet. The mother had had to work and the older brothers did the organising. Mr Hutton said Freda had been 8 when he went into the navy and he enjoyed getting her all the things he had wanted when he was 8 during the war, particularly a special black paint-box. At some point during this story Mr Hutton used the expression 'had I been a girl'.

They wondered about the acquisition of the dog with its attendant moral blackmail, and went on to talk about the powerful unconscious forces which result in one's 'getting one's own sweet way'. They heard how both generations of children, especially if young and female, could be very self-centred, though all were seen to be selectively generous.

Mr Hutton used what TPA thought was a particularly Huttonian expression, viz. that Grandmother's devotion used to 'fray at the edges'. They then tried to make the Geoffrey/Freda connection and mentioned Kevin/Sean similarities. They heard that Kevin had been very popular and a leader. He had died at the age of 17 when Freda was 5. Mr Hutton said that Kevin had always 'done something' if a girl rejected him. He made the gesture on three occasions – 'drowning and aspirins'. At further mention of how a small child, especially a little girl, was able in an unconscious way to bring about what she wanted, Mr Hutton exclaimed, 'Oh yes.' They noted however that, unlike Freda, Geoffrey was both stubborn and untidy. Mr Hutton said that once he had been shocked to find himself trying to make his sister cry and had stopped. They heard that Margaret was indeed a little madam and Freda had been very strong-willed. Mr Hutton said Geoffrey didn't consider the consequences because he quickly denied the fact of his actions – reminiscent somehow of Margaret now and long ago – Freda perhaps denying their modus operandi – 'being young and female'.

TPA wondered whether Mr Hutton and his brothers and sister had tended to pay little heed to the difficulties of their widowed mother (Geoffrey's grandmother). It must have been especially hard for little Freda to resist exerting the power of 'Dead Daddy's little girl' when there was some advantage to be had.

Mr Hutton said he felt somewhat guilty at agreeing to another meeting, and TPA wondered if that word mightn't be significant. On that score he had a word with himself – the Chairman – the sense of which was that TPA would rather that his primary clients were Mr and Mrs Hutton from now on. Mr and Mrs Hutton were consistent attenders, Geoffrey's legal authority wasn't quite yet his own – he would be 'in care' for another nine months, and his social worker had approached another psychiatrist about him, and seemed to see his own attendance at the meetings as dependent on the decision of his client – a minor's decision.

The Chairman told Mr and Mrs Hutton that they could invite whoever they wished next time, e.g. Geoffrey as long as the acceptance was legally approved, i.e. by the local authority social worker.

*

TPA grows irritated with Mr Tennant who, he says, was kow-towing to Geoffrey. This, he avers, is fatal. One must stand up to the delinquent's sense of omnipotence as to the Devil, and deference is utterly counter-productive. Then why do people do it, I enquire? Well, obviously – I am told – a lot of professionals do it in order to get what they consider to be a 'good relationship' with their client. The delinquent then knows that the professional is not to be trusted because he won't stand up for what he believes in.

Poor Mr Hutton was again wondering what the meetings were achieving and whether they were wasting time which could be better expended on some other people. (This sounds to me like despair and reminds me of a man I knew who gave away all his dearest possessions before leaping under a train.) TPA says he can't have it both ways. Either the meetings are helpful and efficacious or they are not, and if they are not they wouldn't be helpful to other people either. One of their main purposes is simply 'keeping in touch' – a bland-sounding, but vitally important, aspect of human relationships which only a good authority can appreciate. Bad authority will realise too late that it has neglected to keep in touch when the negative aspects of this failure become apparent. (TPA didn't put it like that. *I* did, and it occurs to me that working in his mind is rather like working down a mine in cramped and dark surroundings.) Good authority however is not appreciated when things are going well; keeping in touch might even be seen as a blasted nuisance.

17. Locks, bolts and bars

Venue: Clinic consulting-room.   1st June 1979
Present: Dr Pitt-Aikens, Chairman and clerk to the meeting
           Mr & Mrs Hutton

Mr Tennant was not present, being on holiday, but hoped to attend next time. Mr Hutton didn't know whether Mr Tennant had invited Geoffrey or not. Mrs Pannell was also on holiday and sent her apologies.

The previous minutes were read and approved, except for Freda having been referred to as 'Margaret' and a few other details also to do with misnaming.

It was agreed that the topic for discussion today would be 'anything felt to be relevant or important'.

Mr Hutton said he had made a few notes while they were going through the previous minutes and would clear those up first. They had been to see Mr and Mrs Harris, Geoffrey's landlord and landlady. There had been a bit of trouble since the last meeting. Geoffrey had stormed out because, Mr Hutton thought, Mrs Harris had smacked his face. Geoffrey had been extremely awkward with her, as they knew he could be. The matter had been smoothed over, but he understood that (to use the Huttonian expression) she was getting a bit 'frayed at the edges' with him and they weren't sure what the position would be in the future. They had realised, as a result of a 'blow-up' a few weeks ago, that the children knew a lot more about Geoffrey's problems than they had imagined. Mr Tennant was quite willing to attend meetings now. Geoffrey was seeing a Dr Rogers, who was hoping this would continue – it would probably be a matter of years, since Dr Rogers considered that Geoffrey had a very deep-seated problem.

Mr Hutton went on to bring TPA up to date with their position. He said that things had been getting a little nasty lately and Geoffrey's self-willed atitude was wearing Mrs Harris down. Indeed, Geoffrey was wearing them all down. They had been away for a few days, camping with the small children, and Geoffrey had turned up at the house causing a lot of trouble one way and another. Sean, showing a bit of common sense, had called in the emergency social worker, and some of Geoffrey's friends eventually persuaded him to leave, but he had turned up again the next day. In other words, as soon as they were out of the way he was moving in and taking over the house. Well, said poor Mr Hutton, they particularly didn't like having Geoffrey by himself there (or rather *not* by himself, since he took all his friends in) because he was irresponsible. Once he was playing around with the gas stove, filling his mouth with gas, blowing it out and burning it. He did silly things like that, and they definitely didn't like the thought of his being in the house when they weren't there. He was beginning to be worried that Geoffrey would be 18 in December and would cease to be in the care of the local authority. They wondered what was going to happen to him then, because on his past record there was no way they could ask him back to live with them permanently. It would be far too upsetting for them and the other children. It was bad enough at the weekends. It was a terrible thing to have to say about one of your children but Geoffrey used them and used the house as a pied-à-terre. They were just a convenience to him. He seemed to have no feeling for family life, and of course once he was 18 he would be his own master. Already since the last short holiday Anne was beginning to talk about not going on the main holiday, unable to leave the house for fear that Geoffrey might get in again. He hoped to talk her out of that one, but it was going to mean an elaborate system of securing locks and windows and everything else to keep him out – and again that was a terrible thing to say about one of your own children. He thought he had rambled on enough and would let his wife add anything she could think of.

Mrs Hutton said she thought that Ian had said all there was to say about Geoffrey.

TPA said he was glad it had been arranged for Geoffrey to see Dr Rogers. It meant that at the very least he would be keeping within the bounds of the court's direction. He wondered, however, if he had been turning up to all his appointments. It was curious that at the end of the last meeting he as Chairman had told Mr and Mrs Hutton that *they* could invite Geoffrey if *they* wished, next time, provided Mr Tennant approved, and Mrs Hutton had just now said that she wasn't sure whether or not Mr Tennant had invited him. He had a funny feeling that this slip might be important. Inviting Geoffrey had been put in Mr and Mrs Hutton's control – it had been left up to them by the Chairman. He hadn't given licence to Mr Tennant to invite Geoffrey, so that if he had it would have been against a 'law of the meeting'. Geoffrey had been described as a bit out of control and, as it were, needing laws, regulations, secure locks and bolts; and it was clear that that particular metaphorical 'bolt' could become loosened – 'the bolt or the law of inviting'. He had a feeling in his bones that although it was only a small thing it could represent a subtly powerful small thing. It was very difficult to stop someone breaking into your house by means of bolts and bars or anything else. There was nothing you could do if they really set their minds to it, but when it came to inviting people to a meeting you had a tremendous amount of power in your hands. If you invited them they might come. If you didn't they certainly wouldn't. Certainly it could be said that the meeting, represented by the Chairman, would have been entitled to turn Geoffrey away, if he had been invited by Mr Tennant or anyone else – or if he had come of his own volition, but not if he had been asked by Mr and Mrs Hutton who were 'authorised to invite him', provided Geoffrey's acceptance was legally approved. That power to invite rested in Mr and Mrs Hutton and nobody else. That initial, rather ordinary authority had not only become shaky but somehow disappeared, as if only Mr Tennant, and not Mr and Mrs Hutton counted for anything. He added that he couldn't help, of course, but think about Geoffrey and the gas in connection with Kevin and his fulminate detonator. Someone blowing himself up with gas and then setting light to it did seem a bit reminiscent.

The free discussion was mainly on the subject of insistences and invitations, TPA saying that even if a person didn't comply that didn't mean that one's reason for insisting was wrong.

Mr Hutton, on the other hand, said that after a long time of insisting vis-à-vis Geoffrey he had come to the conclusion that his insistence must in some way have been wrong.

TPA suddenly realised that Mr Hutton's mother must have tortured herself over the years wondering what she had done wrong, or not done right, in respect of Kevin and that she might have found false consolation in the thought that her lack of insistence on the way she wanted things done, or not done, would have made no difference anyway – just as Mr Hutton seemed to be implying now about Geoffrey. They wondered whether she might be depressed.

TPA observed that, in spite of being deaf and living in Worcester, Grandmother could be invited to these meetings.

*

This misnaming which occurs frequently in the meetings is indicative of identity muddles. I don't know what the significance of this is, and if TPA has told me I have forgotten. I frequently muddle the names of my own children, though I don't think I have ever misaddressed the cat as Mrs Hutton once did the dog. I think myself that it is due to a sort of mild despair – 'Oh, sod it, let's just call everyone Fred': a sort of spiritual weariness when you are too tired to differentiate between personalities. I don't think saints ever do it.

Geoffrey had clearly been impossible and one must sympathise with Mrs Harris. What could have led her to smack his face? I don't think I have ever smacked the face of another person's child, though I have on occasion clouted my own.

TPA points out that with the realisation that the other children know more about Geoffrey's problems than had previously been supposed it becomes apparent that in this generation of Huttons the parents are at last prepared to acknowledge the possibility of this being so. Had the 'adult Mr Hutton' been pretending to himself that the 'child Mr Hutton' knew less than he actually did about Kevin's potential suicide – a guilt-laden secret portrayed only in the next generation? And had he been aware that even before Kevin's suicide his mother had been depressed, and that this was probably why she 'had left everything to the boys'? I used often to be told that maternal depression is never lost on the children and is deleterious to their little psyches. For this reason many miserable mothers go around with a grin plastered on their faces, which I am assured does not deceive the children in the slightest but only makes them worse, since they know the smiling lies and wonder what else is being concealed. It is really remarkably difficult being a mother, and it can't be all fun being a father. TPA reminds me that Mr Hutton had a lovely time in the Lake District when he was evacuated there during the war. Jolly good luck to him, say I. I feel extremely sorry for Mr Hutton, whose perfectly natural wish to evade too dreadful a sensation of guilt is constantly being leapt on as a prime cause of all the problems. 'Go out into the garden, Mr Hutton, and eat worms' is the feeling, although I am sure it is not intended.

The prospect of Geoffrey's 'moving in and taking over' reminds TPA of the way in which Kevin had taken over when Grandfather died, and he makes a correlation between Geoffrey's escapade with the gas and the gassing of Grandfather Hutton in the First World War. There was also, of course, Kevin's little effort when he filled a room with gas and sent in his brother to test the efficacy of a gas mask: three gas episodes in three generations, ending with Geoffrey literally playing with fire.

18. Two views through Maltese lace

Venue: Clinic consulting-room   10th August 1979
Present: Dr Pitt-Aikens, Chairman
           Mrs Pannell, link Social Worker at Orwell House and
             clerk to the meeting.
           Mr & Mrs Hutton

The meeting began two minutes late because of a misunderstanding between TPA and Mrs Pannell. Geoffrey had declined to come. Mr Tennant had been invited but wasn't very well and was taking the day off. He would however have made the effort to come, he said, if Geoffrey had been present.

Mrs Pannell said she was curious to know what was happening with Geoffrey and the family at the moment and had been quite surprised to be reminded that he was almost 18. She felt it was unusual, but good that Mr and Mrs Hutton were still interested enough to come to the meetings and she thought the reason must be that they felt they were of some value. She wondered whether this value, understanding, or whatever it was, would help indirectly when Geoffrey became his own master at 18.

Mr Hutton said that, first, Mr and Mrs Harris's frayed edges had become more like Maltese lace and Geoffrey had been 'slung out'. This had fortuitously coincided with the start of their holiday. Mr Hutton had taken the bull by the horns, not bothered about locks, bolts, screws or anything else, and told his wife she was coming anyway. Geoffrey had hung around at home for about a week but had then fixed himself up with new lodgings. He thought that Geoffrey was at last coming round to accept the fact that he hadn't got a permanent home with them. In fact he hadn't been too bad while they were away.

He then spoke of the matter of 'invitations', which had seemed to take up an awful lot of time at the last meeting. It was perfectly simple. He and his wife had somehow missed the little bit on the tail-end of the previous meeting about them inviting people. They had still been aware of something TPA had said at an earlier meeting

114

when he made it perfectly clear that it was the social worker who invited Geoffrey. Mr Hutton hadn't liked the way he put it – that Mr King was the father and he the mother. That had stuck in his mind and was the reason he hadn't invited Geoffrey. He assumed that the social worker would. Plus the fact that, as they knew anyway, 'you invite Geoffrey and he won't come'. His reason for not coming that time was that it was Friday and Friday was pay-day. In view of this he was going to ask whether, if they did have another meeting, it could be on another day. He and Mr Tennant had discussed it and both wanted Geoffrey to come. If he didn't he couldn't see much further point in their coming. They were going to try applying the strong arm to persuade him to come next time. He added that when the previous minutes were being read he had been struck by what he took to be a total misinterpretation of the incident with the gas. In his view there was no similarity between that and Kevin's business. Geoffrey was playing around doing something foolish, and that was the last thing you could say about Kevin. Whatever Kevin did, he knew what he was doing, and he certainly wouldn't do anything silly like that.

Mrs Hutton said that Mrs Pannell had observed that they were still coming. She didn't think there was any way they could help Geoffrey now if they tried. He was beyond help, but the meetings enabled them to see a little bit where they had gone wrong with Geoffrey and to take a different path with the others. As for Geoffrey doing no damage – she had spent the whole of the Saturday before she went away cleaning the house from top to bottom. Cigarette ends all over the carpet, her washing machine broken – she didn't consider that 'no damage'. Two different views there. Did they see her point?

TPA said he was positive that Mr Tennant didn't realise that Mr and Mrs Hutton were the people with the power to invite, or not to invite, him to come to the meetings. Otherwise he would have said: 'I'm awfully sorry, Mr and Mrs Hutton. Thank you very much for your invitation, but I really don't feel up to the meeting. I'm taking the day off.' What he said, in fact, was that if Geoffrey had come he would have come too. So he didn't believe that Mr Tennant had been properly invited, and he and the family were still giving Geoffrey the whip-hand. He certainly wasn't willing to make special arrangements to meet on any other day, unless it was a Thursday, at Orwell House. He wasn't prepared to be dictated to by somebody not quite 18. In fact the only people he would be inviting were Mr and Mrs Hutton and whoever *they* cared to invite – provided the acceptance was legally approved. He thought there might be something in the question of different views. Mr Hutton had said that there was surprisingly little damage at home – 'he hadn't been too bad' – and Mrs Hutton had said that there was. Perhaps Mr Hutton had meant that the place wasn't burnt down and therefore this was a tremendous achievement – the cigarettes safely stubbed out on the carpet – but there were certainly two views, and that was why an authority was needed. With similar views about the same thing people would probably go in the 'same direction'. However, if they chose to disagree about an item they might go off in different directions unless there was an overall authority. As to the 'invitations' – the direction that had been taken was that the Chairman invited Mr and Mrs Hutton – and they in turn had been empowered to invite whoever they cared to – certainly not that a meeting should happen at Geoffrey's pleasure, whether or not he had trouble with his pay-day.

TPA was also curious to know why nothing had happened about Grandmother. He still felt she might be depressed, and although she lived in Worcester he thought she ought to have been invited. He had a fantasy that she was a sad old lady who might have felt supported to have known she had been asked, even if she couldn't make it.

Lastly, he said, going on for another page, he wanted to say something about the start of the meeting. It was a hot day and both he and Mrs Pannell were feeling a bit frayed at the edges. When he had gone to the waiting-room, having heard from the switchboard that Mr and Mrs Hutton were there, he found they weren't. At that he had noticed in himself the beginnings of a feeling of bloody-mindedness and he had hung around (rather like Geoffrey) waiting for the family to appear, while a bit of him knew very well that they were probably upstairs in the consulting-room. He hadn't let himself think that perhaps Mrs Pannell had collected them, or that they had probably found their own way up. After all, the children, and probably even the dog, knew the clinic pretty well by now. So there was a feeling in him somewhere that they were 'up there', but he was aware also of a feeling of bloody-mindedness – very small but none the less there – and he hadn't wanted to go upstairs. It had reminded him of the dreadful business of Kevin's body in the loft. Perhaps because of their own frayed edges and bloody-mindedness, people hadn't really wanted to go and look, as perhaps later they felt they should have done. It would have been a bit like his sitting in the waiting-room for a whole hour – waiting for Mr and Mrs Hutton to appear, pretending to himself that they had gone for a walk in the park. If Kevin's mother felt she had behaved in some way like that she might still have it on her conscience. Certainly he would, even in the microcosm of the meeting. There was probably a slight element in Geoffrey of an avenging angel, as if he was somehow or other punishing the living for some unrecognised offence in the past. For instance, nobody need have known of TPA's bloody-mindedness downstairs in the waiting-room unless he had owned up to them, and if it had been a more serious matter he might never have mentioned it, being too ashamed or guilty to face up to it himself. He felt there was something like that going on, and it was possible that if he felt guilty in that kind of way he might find it more difficult to stand up to certain people. There was perhaps a fear of standing up to Geoffrey and, as Mrs Hutton had said, maybe to the other children too. This might be for fear they would accuse you, the proper authority, of having previously betrayed your trust. After all, he was supposed to be the authority at the meeting and it wasn't open to him to be foolish and pretend to himself that he didn't know that the Huttons were upstairs. An authority shouldn't behave like that. Children relied on authorities to forego the luxury of being bloody-minded. There could be a kind of reluctance to come into the open as an authority for fear you got it in the neck and were punished for previous sins of omission.

In the free discussion they talked about TPA's bloody-mindedness, and Mrs Pannell commented that perhaps it was *absent*-mindedness. This led on to a possible identification with Grandmother, who perhaps had been not so much absent-minded as 'frayed' because of having a large family and no husband.

Mrs Hutton then claimed to be the most absent-minded person on the face of the earth and said the children told her off about it.

Mr Hutton said that when he was a child and was sent to his room he would bloody-mindedly refuse to come down again (even if he wanted to) when he was told that his period of punishment was over. The family felt this single-minded or selfish Huttonian stance might land one in an impossible situation. TPA suggested that a boy dressing as a girl was like a pantomime of that.

There was a long discussion about invitations and the fact that even if Mr Tennant didn't accept an invitation or vetoed Mr and Mrs Hutton's invitation to Geoffrey because he was still 'in care', that didn't take away Mr and Mrs Hutton's power to invite. They realised there was a connection between that and the situation in Mr Hutton's own family when, on his father's death, Kevin, perhaps because of his physical size and strength, became titular head while his mother remained the actual authority. She might have become 'bloody-minded' and said, 'OK, if you think you're the boss, you get on with it, I won't interfere. I'll let it go on.'

Mr Hutton said that Mr Tennant was keen to take a strong line with Geoffrey, particularly as he was reaching 18, and admitted that he tended to compromise a little on this line.

They heard a bit about certain problems – Margaret's clothes had been strewn all over the house when the family returned.

They spoke more about the probable connection between what had happened to TPA at the start of the meeting and what had actually happened to Mr Hutton who, it transpired, had probably, in the back of his head, known that Kevin was upstairs in the loft all the time. They heard that the bloodstain had come through the ceiling on the Friday night and that Mr Hutton's mother had even pointed it out, but she was, as Mr Hutton remarked, the champion of all those who sweep things under the carpet. It was Mr Hutton, alone on the Monday, who found what he called an excuse – something about stamps – to go upstairs to the loft, where he saw his brother's body. Then he went to find his mother. It was mentioned that at one point, when Kevin was assuming the role of head of the family, he and his mother had a physical conflict. This was felt to underline the business of the power of invitation, the equivalent of poor Grandmother's legitimate authority, against the power of unwillingness to concur (Sean's illicit, physically superior power). It was also mentioned that Mr Hutton's mother had been so preoccupied with providing the essentials for her family that she hadn't been able to keep in contact with things as they happened. It was perhaps how Kevin had succeeded in assuming the role.

It was thought that bloody-mindedness might have a particularly taboo poignancy in a family who didn't want to know about a bloody stain creeping across their ceiling.

*

I am still very confused with the business of invitations, but am assured that it is all quite clear if I would only attend closely. I have to take this on trust.

Mrs Hutton brought up the subject of differing views, and several proceeded to emerge. Mr Hutton said it was quite wrong to compare Geoffrey and Kevin, since Geoffrey was silly and Kevin always knew what he was doing. One might think that Kevin was pretty damn silly with his gas-filled room. 'Two views there.' Then back to Geoffrey – his father was surprised and relieved that he hadn't burned the house down and considered that he had done no damage, whereas his mother had had to spend hours cleaning up after the very evident damage which he had done. Here TPA makes a noise like Sherlock Holmes and wonders aloud if it was at this point that Mr Hutton launched his attack on his wife's intuition; presumably not having noticed her (or having denied the evidence of his senses) on her hands and knees moiling and toiling. The significance of this observation will become clear later.

At some point everyone started wailing 'What are we doing here?' For reasons they didn't understand they kept on coming, and the chief reason was probably that the meetings kept people in contact. Grandmother Hutton, like the old woman who lived in a shoe, had lost contact with her children, enabling Kevin to make his take-over. I do sympathise with the poor woman. I have often felt that I would prefer not to know what the children were up to, but one has to grasp the nettle if chaos is not to follow. The meetings rub people's noses in it, provide a model of contact-keeping, are very salutary; yet everyone, including Mr Tennant, a professional, has been busy down-grading them.

What a thankless task is the therapist's.

19. Still bloody-minded

Venue: Orwell House   25th October 1979
Present: Dr Pitt-Aikens, Chairman
            Mr Tennant, Local Authority Social Worker legally
                responsible for Geoffrey Hutton
            Mrs Pannell, link Social Worker at Orwell House and
                clerk to meeting
            Mr & Mrs Hutton
            Geoffrey
            Margaret

Mr and Mrs Hutton were late, and Mrs Pannell suggested that they
might have lost their way. They didn't know which other invitations
might have been made indirectly. (The Chairman was two-thirds
through the reading of the previous 'free discussion' when Mr and
Mrs Hutton, Mr Tennant, Kevin and Margaret came through the
door [clerk's slip – not Kevin but Geoffrey]).

Mrs Pannell said she wouldn't say much because there were a lot
of them. She was pleased to see the family and to make the
acquaintance of Mr Tennant. She had felt sure they would turn up
but had been worried that they had got lost on the way. She was
really happy to see Geoffrey after all that time and interested to know
how things were going.

Geoffrey said he hadn't been to a meeting for a long time and
doubted if he would say anything now but was pleased to be at
Orwell House, in a way, rather than at the clinic.

Mr Tennant said he was pleased that Geoffrey was pleased to be at
the meeting and gave a summary of the confusion that the social
services had found while working with Geoffrey and his family. He
didn't know whether he should work to help Geoffrey rejoin his
family or not. That had been when he felt the family had rejected
Geoffrey. After a year he was still confused about whether to help or
not.

Margaret had nothing to say.

Mr Hutton said he didn't have a lot to say this time but thought
Mr Tennant hadn't quite got the problem pin-pointed. Geoffrey

hadn't been rejected by the family, but they weren't necessarily looking for ways of bringing him back in. Over the years he had pursued a certain course that had diverged from the course of the family, and what they were trying to do (he hoped his wife would agree with him) was to get those courses back more on a parallel so that Geoffrey remained in the family. But, having almost reached the age of 18 and having his own interests and a job, he had to live his own life. Mr Hutton said he found it a bit difficult to explain completely what he meant, but he hoped something would come of that. Sean was now presenting considerable problems, but perhaps his wife should talk about that.

Mrs Hutton said Sean had given up his job and gone back to college for a few years. She had advised him to think it out carefully first, especially how he would manage financially. She had wondered how long it would last – especially as he hadn't saved any money, in spite of her advice. He ignored whatever they said to him and thought they were old fuddy-duddies.

TPA said he was still intrigued by the business of bloody-mindedness and feared that he still had a dose of it himself, as evinced by his determination to start on time when the family were late. It was interesting that Mrs Hutton had emphasised the importance of Sean thinking things through. He himself in a way hadn't wanted to think things through. He didn't want to think that Mr and Mrs Hutton had been coming to the meetings for a long time, so were obviously keen to come. What, he asked himself, was he playing at, being so damn nasty as to start on time. They could have delayed for five minutes rather than just career on, but no one could accuse him of having done something shameful or wrong. After all, he was just sticking to the rules, but he thought he was, in part at any rate, being bloody-minded. That was enough evidence for him personally to feel that there was still bloody-mindedness going on in the Hutton household and that maybe it had moved on to Sean. Last time they had been wondering whether people who got themselves stuck in a bloody-minded situation were in an impossible situation. One of the many ideas about Geoffrey's cross-dressing was that he was demonstrating one of the most impossible situations that anyone could get stuck in. You might want to be a woman, but you were stuck with being a man and there was nothing you could do about it. You could cover yourself in a ton of women's underclothes and you would still end up a man. Geoffrey might be showing 'the absurdity of hanging on to some sort of bloody-mindedness' – 'I'm going to be a woman if it kills me. The fact that I'm a man isn't going to stop me.' He himself was a bit like that today. 'I'm the

Chairman. I'm going to start at 12 o'clock if it kills me.' He hadn't thought for a minute of the number of times he had lost his way to Orwell House. On one occasion he was four hours late. At least the family had arrived after four or five minutes. You could say that he had been a bit unkind, but he thought it was bloody-mindedness and somehow or other they had to get to the roots of the bloody-mindedness in the Hutton family. His guess was that it had been going on for a long time and needed to be driven out. Geoffrey seemed to be doing better than he had been, but perhaps only because Sean had taken over the bloody-mindedness.

In the free discussion Mr Hutton said it wasn't bloody-mindedness that had affected people in the case of Kevin. It was a matter of not facing facts.

A small argument ensued, with TPA claiming that the refusal to face facts was a good definition of bloody-mindedness. It was mentioned that Mr Hutton had a tendency not to open letters. This was compared to Sean's college plans and his failure to accept the facts of lack of money. TPA made it clear that he had only managed to stay bloody-minded by using the other Hutton-trait of absent-mindedness. He could only start at 12 o'clock with a free conscience if he was quite convinced that Mr and Mrs Hutton weren't at all the Mr and Mrs Hutton he knew well, the ones who always turned up. He preferred absent-mindedly to assume that Mr and Mrs Hutton were like many other families who didn't turn up when they said they would. Not true at all.

Mr Tennant spoke of his confusion and anger about the family's attitude towards Geoffrey. This led on to a discussion about whether there was a Hutton-family-fear of confusion. According to Mrs Hutton, Mr Hutton's father's mother was indeed extremely obsessional, with a need to line up jars, bottles and so on. Her children apparently presented a tremendous threat, almost personifying the danger of confusion for her.

Mr Tennant said the family experienced some of the difficult bits too. Mr Hutton said it was very important, with seven people living in a household, that relationships should be of a good sort.

TPA remarked that on the face of it Geoffrey didn't seem to be worried about what seemed his sexual confusion. It might well be that he 'was' partly the posing of a question – is it necessary or not to be upset about being confused?

*

TPA could seem annoyingly superior over the question of transvestism. He says he is bored by what he winsomely describes as 'the conscious parameters' of this phenomenon. To do him justice, he speaks no less than the truth and reminds me of a housemaid who is not at all interested in the fact that the painting on the landing is a Rubens, but only in the cobwebs and dead mice which have accumulated behind it and which it is her task to remove. He does not seem concerned with the excitement of the person busy dressing up as a person of the opposite sex, or in the vicarious frisson of the observer. He is thrilled to bits tracking down with mop and duster at least three unconscious meanings which have become apparent in the case. Geoffrey, it seems, has contrived in his cross-dressing to symbolise confusion, the attempt to achieve the impossible, the fact of unpredictability and the need for intuition. (I make that four, so don't know why my notes said three.) What is more, says TPA, warming to his theme, later on it could even be considered that Geoffrey is attempting to reverse his mother's dangerous tendency to lose her intuition – which, he says, looking sideways, is, as we all know, a female commodity.

I wonder what Mr Tennant meant by saying that the family experienced some of the difficult bits too. I would have thought that they experienced most of the difficult bits. I wish I knew apropos of what he said that.

20. The small suitcase

Venue: Orwell House   7th February 1980
Present: Dr Pitt-Aikens, Chairman and clerk to meeting
           Mr Tennant, Local Authority Social Worker legally
                responsible for Geoffrey Hutton
           Mrs Pannell, link Social worker at Orwell House
           Miss Tomlinson, postgraduate psychology student and
                participant observer
           Mr & Mrs Hutton
           Geoffrey

Mrs Pannell said she was surprised and happy to see so many of the Huttons at Orwell House again, and also Mr Tennant. She was particularly surprised because she thought Geoffrey mightn't have come again. The other children seemed a bit unhappy today, especially Margaret. She wasn't in the room with them and Mrs Pannell wondered what that meant.

Miss Tomlinson, a post-graduate student, said she had nothing to say except that she was delighted to see so many members of a family visiting Orwell House. She didn't think she had been to a meeting before where the whole family was present and she wondered what the other children were doing.

Mr Hutton said he had been to many meetings now and had the impression that dealing with his family was like trying to pack a suitcase that was too small for what was going into it. As fast as you shoved something in one side it came out the other. Geoffrey was back at home and everything was as near normal as possible. He was a bit of a nuisance, like any 18-year-old living at home, and that was about the sum of it with Geoffrey. Marvellous. A big change. Sean was definitely the problem now. He was getting impossible to live with, basically because he was so self-centred. There had been a bit of a bust-up a week or so back when they discovered that not only had he left work without making any reasonable provision for himself but he hadn't even been to college that year except once or twice. An argument arose and Mr Hutton was disgusted with him because, when Sean had to face any form of criticism, he immediately descended to obscene language, not just in front of, but directly at, his mother. Mr Hutton's reaction to that was to go violently off him, and at the moment he wasn't very happy at all. It would be interesting to hear what his wife had to say.

Mr Tennant said he was pleased to be there again and very pleased that Geoffrey was there. It seemed to have turned out a success story with Geoffrey, but he was unhappy to hear about Sean. It also seemed extraordinary that as soon as Geoffrey was out of their care his life should change and become far more normal and successful. He knew, however, that he should be more dubious, having congratulated himself and Mr Hutton on previous occasions that they were seeing a lasting and fundamental change.

Geoffrey had nothing to say.

Mrs Hutton said they were very pleased to have Geoffrey back. With Sean she thought that part of the problem was that it was usually she who found out what he was doing, and she didn't let him get away with it. She would come straight to the point and 'cop him' for what he'd done, so she got a lot of the backlash from Sean. He didn't like to think she knew what was going on. Margaret hadn't come in, because her leg was a bit stiff. She had hurt herself getting out of the car; the dog had jumped on her or something, and she was also going through a bit of a difficult time, as most girls do: up in the air one minute, and down the next.

TPA said he wished they had tape-recorded the family meetings, as he thought they would find that some things said about Sean had word-for-word been said about Geoffrey in the past, and that such recordings might be very useful for professionals who were trying to study the processes involved. He wasn't himself satisfied with an approach which directed itself to the so-called individual delinquent. He had a feeling that Geoffrey, at least currently, wasn't one of those. His eyes looked totally different. He looked much more like a real person than what TPA tended to call 'a bit of a thing', or an animal, as some people would say. He looked much more like real Geoffrey. There were whole systems set up to treat individuals, and what many people failed to appreciate was that even if you could do something about the individual, unbeknown to you there were other things going on: other members of the family whom you would completely ignore because you weren't paid to look in that direction. He thought that Mr Tennant had hinted at this with his ironic statement that it seemed that the best thing ever to happen to Geoffrey was his coming out of 'care'. He implied that the same phenomena which had featured noticeably around Geoffrey or which had happened to Geoffrey were now just as noticeably going on in

Sean. They were on quite new ground here. It might be seen as odd that they went on meeting in the way they did. The local authority care order had finished. Geoffrey was 18 – his own authority. Orwell House's obligation to care for him had ended, and yet they were still discovering things that not many of us knew about. Most attempts to understand delinquency didn't take into account the fact that 'the background' should be given priority. Because of these perhaps unusual meetings they really had a chance of learning something very interesting. It was sad that apart from Mrs Pannell there were no Orwell House staff present, since it would be professionally useful for them to understand the processes that went on. He was sure Mr Tennant wouldn't be there wasting his time if he didn't think there was something to be gained. He had found in the past that cousins sometimes shared a similar picture. Freda had been alive when her father and brother Kevin died and it was unlikely that her branch of the family would be unaffected by whatever was going on then. They didn't yet know enough about the way families could be affected by certain past events. TPA didn't think it need always show in delinquency; it might be shown by certain other out-of-control situations like illnesses. It was good that a doctor, social workers and a psychologist (Miss Tomlinson) should meet a family and see from their own professional angles the various ways that an old trauma could affect the family from one generation to the next. They were grateful to the Hutton family for giving them the chance to look into the unknown, because the sort of things they were learning weren't made available by the traditional ways of looking at delinquency.

In the 'free discussion' Mrs Hutton wondered whether transferring authority to the local authority had been a mistake in the first place. Nobody had really been in charge from then on. She pointed out her change of mind between then and now.

TPA mentioned Dr Rogers and his statement that Geoffrey would need therapy for a long time and wondered how one could know in advance. Both he and Geoffrey wondered whether Dr Rogers would think the same now.

They talked about the importance of seeing the family as a whole and how many professionals work as though the problem was centred in one individual. Mr Tennant pointed out the connection between his authority shielding the family from Geoffrey and the family shielding Sean from the reality that he needed to face.

They then spoke about the normal phasic behaviour of children, their ups and downs, and how unfortunate it was that one child could be caught in a bad phase and rubber-stamped from then on, fostering the delusion that he was bad and all the other children were good. Mr Hutton mentioned his childhood delusion – how on the face of it, he had seen himself as the most 'normal' among his siblings. As a child he had always felt that his younger brother had been extremely selfish and quite as nasty to their mother as Geoffrey and Sean had been to theirs.

Mr Tennant spoke of the confusion in the Hutton household and related it to the previous generation when Grandfather had died and a rather rigid family had become relaxed. They saw a parallel between that and Mr Tennant's view of the meetings – that he had at first seen them as rigid and sterile, whereas, paradoxically, what had resulted from the rigidity was a more productive relaxation. They saw that Mr Hutton's father hadn't been punitive but had had first-class organising ability and had supplied real relaxation, whereas when he died there had been a phoney relaxation, resulting in people doing what they liked and yelling at their mother. They realised that TPA might well wish to swear at Mrs Hutton and her traditional interruptings, but a part of him, akin to Grandfather, would have none of that. Mr Hutton spoke of his own hatred of chaos and his attempts to organise from behind, which didn't work.

Mr. Tennant ended by saying that the formality of the meetings might well 'flow into the various Huttonian creditors', and I haven't the faintest idea what he meant by that.

*

I am impressed here by TPA's percipience. He had been worrying about Sean for some time and been met with irritable dismissiveness: 'Sean gives no cause for concern at all. Geoffrey is the problem.' Now Geoffrey is much less of a problem, and Sean has behaved extremely badly, engaging in battle with his mother. Forty years before Kevin and his mother had had a bad argument, ending in physical conflict. The scenario is the same; only the cast is different. It is as though the meetings and the current family activity are capturing events of long ago. I find this faintly eerie. When I am in Wales I can only hear Irish radio with any degree of clarity and I have just heard about a man who has written a book putting forth the theory that all bad behaviour is due to ancestral control, that an old family spirit has entered the miscreant and that the only way to handle it is to hold a communion service and instruct the dead ancestor to depart. Once upon a time I would have been helpless with mirth at such a dotty conception, but now it sounds to me like a simplified tuppence-coloured version of TPA's own ideas, and I don't find it so funny. Whether genetically, spiritually or subliminally, our ancestors must affect us and, with the present fashion for seeing crime only in a sociological and environmental light, this has been forgotten. TPA has just said that I must constantly insist on the necessity for *mourning*; that denied or incomplete mourning gives rise to chaos; that we must admit and assimilate *all* our losses and griefs; and now I see the old, universal terror of ghosts as a perfectly sensible, albeit primitive, awareness of this. The unquiet spirit is rightly to be feared. He requires to be acknowledged and have his bones properly buried with all due ceremony, or he will not rest.

Mr Hutton went *violently* off Sean as, most probably, his mother had gone off Kevin. It is difficult to feel tenderly towards even your nearest and dearest if he has been swearing at you or beating you up. If Kevin's mother had indeed been hurt and outraged by his behaviour it would surely have increased her bloody-mindedness towards him. She would have stubbornly refused to notice, or care about, his unhappiness.

21. Dogs and sacred cows

Venue: Orwell House   30th April 1980
Present: Dr Pitt-Aikens, Chairman and clerk to the meeting
            Mrs Pannell, link Social Worker at Orwell House
            Miss Tomlinson, postgraduate psychology student and
                participant observer
            Mr & Mrs Hutton

Sean was invited but couldn't come. Geoffrey couldn't take time off work; nor could Mr Tennant.

Miss Tomlinson said she hadn't much to say, was delighted to see Mr and Mrs Hutton, was sorry not to see the rest of the family, and would be interested to hear what had been happening.

Mrs Pannell said much the same.

Mr Hutton began: 'Well, this will be our last meeting because we're on the move again.' He had thought of applying for a vacancy in Rhodesia, but he was too old for that now and they were going to Portsmouth instead. He had undertaken 'voluntary employment transfer'. There had been no problems with Geoffrey except for one which showed how things lingered on. One day, when Mr Hutton was on nights and therefore at home during the day, Geoffrey had returned saying he hadn't been to work because he wasn't feeling well. He had apparently started feeling unwell on the journey to work and had spent the intervening time on an underground train riding round the Circle Line hoping he might get better. Mr Hutton said it all sounded most peculiar to him and he had started worrying. No doubt he would continue to worry whenever anything unusual happened. Apart from that, Geoffrey had been behaving like any normal, noisy 18-year-old. Sean was a continuing problem. He was quite content to do the minimum amount of work to get a little bit of money to enjoy himself but wouldn't bother himself about anything. Mr Hutton had had to write off to the Ministry of Defence to claim money due to him because he hadn't bothered to do so. (Apparently Sean had been invalided out of some junior bit of the army.) He was still sure that Sean ought to have received more, but he was content to accept the opinions of his friends about this and not investigate

anything himself. Probably a factor in the family decision to move
was Sean's age. He was now 20 and, if they stayed where they were,
in ten years' time Mr Hutton thought he would still be living at
home. The move was going to involve a reduction in his take-home
pay and necessitate a smaller house, which wouldn't be big enough
for all of them. Sean was going to have to do something about his
own life.

Mr Hutton went on to clear up a point about Geoffrey's absence.
He could have come but would have lost a day's pay which he could
ill afford. And in view of the fact that this must of course be the final
meeting Mr Hutton hadn't insisted.

Mrs Hutton said she had nothing to say other than just to agree
with her husband.

TPA said he had at last realised the significance of the dog in the
Hutton household. The tail wagged the dog rather than the dog the
tail. (Mrs Hutton was interrupting here, muttering something
inaudible.) He had been cheered to hear Mr Hutton say something
like 'I realised there were going to be changes in my job situation
and I thought I would be the one to dictate the terms and decided to
move to Portsmouth.' He had thought, 'Heavens, that's not the tail
wagging the dog, that's the dog organising things for himself rather
than waiting to become a victim.' Then at the end Mr Hutton had
added a bit about Sean, who could be described as the tail, and TPA
had changed from being pleased to being pretty despondent. At the
same time he had realised why the children didn't come to the
meetings. He himself rather liked the formality, which gave the
freedom they had discussed last time, but he thought the children
were kept out for fear they would muck up the formality, which for
the family had perhaps become a sort of sacred cow. He would like to
test this theory to see whether the formality could cope with the
children. Would the children behave themselves in the formal
situation, or was the formality itself only preserved by their
exclusion? That sounded awfully like the idea of getting a smaller
house in order to exclude Sean and thereby keep the situation more
relaxed and controlled. He thought it was time the Huttons began
not to cheat, as he believed they had been doing in the meeting, and
that they should bring the children in to see if they could respond to
the formality. If they couldn't, there would be reason to worry. If
they could, maybe there was some chance of Mr and Mrs Hutton
being the dog wagging the tail rather than vice versa. There was
something of the tail in Mrs Hutton, who frequently mucked up the
proceedings. It was subtle, because she nearly always made them
laugh. For instance, when it was her 'individual comment' today she

had said she had nothing to say, and then when it was his turn to speak he heard her muttering away. He would speak to the Chairman – that is to say, his 'other self' – and the Chairman would ask the meeting if it agreed or not as to whether the children should join them. It then turned out that the children hadn't accompanied Mr and Mrs Hutton today and he regretted that they had missed the opportunity of testing the theory.

The free discussion was mainly taken up with the subject of structure and formality and how they help to enhance meaning. Mr Hutton spoke of Sean remembering something which had happened in a meeting a long time ago. Thanks to the formality and tradition of 'clerking' he had been able to correct Sean who had misunderstood a remark made by his father: something about Mr Hutton having said that if he did have a favourite it would have been Geoffrey.

They compared the ability to reveal meaning which a formal approach afforded with a mish-mash situation in which one might even feel like Sean the need to swear to get things across. TPA more or less accused Mrs Hutton of laying herself open to this. They had all heard how the children verbally abused her.

Mr Hutton related the background of his move and it was agreed that the necessity for Sean to live elsewhere could be regarded as a bonus, but in fact Mr Hutton had had to impose his own decision because of a worsening work situation. Mrs Hutton said the move might be a bonus in terms of Sean, but Margaret had to relinquish her place at a business school.

TPA went on at great length about what they were learning which might explain Geoffrey's behaviour – for instance, again, his cross-dressing. There was no doubt that in a tradition where males and females wore different clothing a man wearing women's clothes was startling. When formality was offended it made its presence felt.

Mrs Hutton said that Sean sometimes spoke to her about things which she would indeed not normally expect to hear from a son, and this seemed to illustrate the point that things might make more impact if they impinged on a traditional or formal structure. She talked about 'smoking LSD', and this was reckoned to be another example of a structure being broken – on at least two levels: LSD was illegal and one took it like tea with sugar.

They realised that arranging another meeting would present great difficulties. Nevertheless TPA insisted, against considerable opposition, that they should.

Indeed he went ahead and selected a date, agreeing reluctantly to the compromise that it should be six months away and saying that even if the family didn't attend he would.

*

In the 19th meeting TPA pinned down several meanings of tranvestism and has now discerned yet another. It is a personification of deviancy from the norm. People get carried away and blinded and bemused by its sexual aspect. Sex, like violence, is a very effective vehicle for a theme, but the vehicle itself resembles a double-decker bus bearing down on you unexpectedly as you cross the street. You are aware only of the bus and not of the passengers who give it its *raison d'être*. In the presence of threat and the unexpected, people feel fear or excitement, and the important, unconscious meaning tends to be lost.

TPA wasn't at all comforted to hear that the 'presenting delinquent' was behaving well, and was very anxious that the meetings shouldn't come to an end simply because this was so or because the family were moving. There were a great many relevant themes still crashing about – most notably and typically in another sibling. If there had been no siblings available for the themes to invade, no doubt one or other of the parents would have begun to portray them – probably in some medical condition. This is just the kind of time – says TPA darkly – when a professional, newly arriving on the scene and seeing that the presenting delinquent is as good as gold, would imagine that all was well and recommend closing the case. As though to bear out his implied forebodings, between this meeting – which Mr Hutton had suggested should be the last – and the next, Geoffrey pulled out all the stops, and all bureaucratic hell broke loose. The file contains two letters from Mr Hutton to TPA, two letters from TPA in answer, a reference to a telephone call from a probation officer, a written reply to him, a psychiatric report for the court from TPA, references to two telephone calls from yet another probation officer, a letter from Dr Rogers to TPA, a letter back, a letter from the second probation officer to TPA, two further reports, and one written for the court by the same probation officer.

Of all this we append part of Mr Hutton's letter and a request for a psychiatric report from yet another probation officer. Mr Hutton speaks for himself most clearly and eloquently, and his letter, contrasted with the distanced efficiency of the other, causes me to hear a horrid unnatural sizzle as the warmth of home meets the cold chill of the police cell. I would have been devastated if I had been in the Huttons' shoes. TPA is unsurprised and oddly unworried – almost, it seems, relieved – that the evil spirits are still where they can be recognised and observed.

Barking, Essex
Dear Dr Pitt-Aikens,   27th May 1980

I do hope you will forgive me for writing to you like this but quite frankly I do not know where to turn next and putting it down on paper will probably help. A few days after we saw you last Geoffrey was arrested on a charge of arson. He was remanded in custody for a week but is now home again on bail pending a hearing on the 13th June. I fear that that will not be the end of it and he will probably have to go to the County Court, or whatever it is.

The facts are these. He and a friend, who is jointly charged with him, broke into a building in the nearby cemetery on the May Day holiday. In the loft Geoffrey set fire to a towel in order to give some light. He subsequently stamped it out and left, but it must still have been smouldering for the building caught fire and was virtually destroyed, the damage amounting to some £42,000. That is the story as Geoffrey gives it but it goes beyond that. Two juveniles were involved and it was not the first time they had been in the building. We have heard bits from Louis, in whom Geoffrey confides, and it seems he wanted to 'blow up the immersion heater'. I do accept that it was not deliberate arson and this I gather is to be Geoffrey's defence, for what it is worth.

Coming, as it does, just when we are preparing to move, it has completely shattered both Anne and me. Indeed, I did at first wonder if it was a reaction by Geoffrey to our moving, etc.

Yours sincerely,
Ian Hutton

Dear Dr Pitt-Aikens,   12th June 1980

re: Geoffrey Hutton

Further to my telephone conversation with your secretary, I am writing to confirm that when the above-named appeared at the Magistrates' Court today the case was adjourned until the 10th July for the preparation of probation and psychiatric reports.

I understand that Geoffrey is known to you and in these circumstances I would be grateful if you could prepare the psychiatric report. He was charged on the 2nd June with indecent exposure and the theft of a lady's blouse from a washing line, and has been in police custody until today, when he was remanded on bail to live at the address of a family friend. I have no further details concerning the case but enclose a copy of his police antecedents.

Would you please send copies of your report direct to the Magistrates?

Yours sincerely,
Harold Nixon
Probation Officer

22. The world suddenly changed

Venue: Orwell House   19th November 1980
Present: Dr Pitt-Aikens, Chairman
           Mr Fuller, Probation Officer
           Mrs Jenkins, link Social Worker at Orwell House and
               clerk to the meeting
           Mr & Mrs Hutton (arrived late)

At the preliminary professionals' meeting Mr Fuller was welcomed and agreed to 'flounder'. it was noted that there had been no pre- or post-professionals' meetings for some time, as a tradition seemed to have become established that, since mostly only family members attended, the professionals' meetings had gone by default. They discussed the fact that they sometimes had had meetings back at Orwell House and took the view that these were a means of reminding the staff there that Geoffrey hadn't ceased to exist.

TPA's partial excuse for the abandonment of the professionals' meetings was that at one point Mr Tennant, the local authority social worker, had decided he didn't want to come to any more meetings whereas the Huttons always did. Nevertheless he remembered feeling a bit anxious about this fundamental change in their rather pernickety structure. They looked back to two years before – eight meetings ago – when the meetings 'just lost' their 'professionals only' quotient and found that Mr Tennant hadn't been very keen to be there, whereas the Huttons had arrived in the room, keen to be present. TPA could vaguely remember that, on one occasion, unusually for him, he had gone soft and as Chairman had decided not to hold the usual preliminary professionals' meeting – he hadn't had the heart temporarily to turn the family out of the room; also, he had thought Mr Tennant would 'wonder what was going on'. In other words he had 'castrated' himself as Chairman of this very structured procedure.

They pondered whether it was sensible to correlate the Chairman's self-emasculation in the meeting and Geoffrey's transvestism.

It was clarified that Geoffrey, being now 18, was no longer in care.

At the joint meeting, Mrs Jenkins asked the Chairman to explain Mr Fuller's presence and was told that he and TPA had come into contact over a court report regarding Geoffrey and that TPA had invited him to this meeting.

Mrs Jenkins said she wondered what had happened to Sean.

Mr Fuller said, 'I have little to say except that it seems that the Huttons' absence has some considerable relevance to their commitment to the future of these meetings, based on their comments at the last meeting.'

TPA said that by coincidence he worked at the same Borstal and in the same wing in which Geoffrey was a prisoner. Geoffrey hadn't approached him in spite of the fact that he had known him for so long. He referred back to the last meeting when, for Geoffrey, things had seemed on the face of it to be going better than they had for years and spoke of their realisation then that Mr Hutton had been fooling himself in imagining that the dog was actually wagging the tail. His despondency at that meeting seemed to have been justified by what had since happened to Geoffrey. On being approached by Mr Fuller to provide a psychiatric report for the court he had heard that Geoffrey had committed one not particularly serious sexual offence and also arson, which he thought had taken place in the loft of some building or other. In his report he had made the parallel between that and the fact that Geoffrey's uncle had blown himself up with a fulminate detonator in the loft of his family house. The family had always thought the connection between Geoffrey and his uncle was a big joke. He remembered talking about the similarities between Geoffrey and his uncle.

At this point Mr and Mrs Hutton came in, apologising for being late. TPA said he would prefer to stop because now the 'world had changed' quite suddenly. As Chairman he gave the latecomers a brief update on the meeting.

Mr Hutton said he hadn't anything to say because he presumed everyone was aware of the changed circumstances since the last meeting. What could he add?

Mrs Hutton said she was just going to sit back and listen to what was going on.

During the free discussion Mr Hutton said he was surprised and disappointed that the meeting was at such an advanced stage, since he had understood from Mr Fuller that it was due to start at 2.30. TPA expatiated on the tendency to want to cheat in this case: for instance the improper exclusion of the pre- and post-professionals' meetings and how they had now reverted to the usual format which would reduce even further the involvement of Mr and Mrs Hutton today since they would have to leave early because of the post-professionals' meeting. It was tempting to cheat again in order to allow more time for the latecomers. He pointed out, however, that at the last meeting Mr and Mrs Hutton had been present when today's meeting had been arranged for 2 p.m. Why had they listened to Mr Fuller's claim that it was 2.30? He hadn't even been there. Again, the tail wagging the dog.

Mrs Hutton said that they couldn't accept Geoffrey's latest crime although they had seen the warning signals – his burning the walls and burning a hole in the carpet.

They remembered that last time, when they were discussing the desirability of a further meeting, Mr Hutton's spontaneous reaction had been to consider the logistics of the event rather than the desirability of the event itself.

At the post-professionals' meeting TPA suggested that the family thought themselves only able to function in small units and that if everybody was present it would have to be chaos. Was that a legacy of 'evacuation thinking' from the war? He said that, tragically, imprisonments and deaths produced smaller units and people might unconsciously hope that as a consequence things would become more organised. The professionals guiltily agreed that the meeting – the 'microcosm' – had suddenly felt disordered when Mr and Mrs Hutton arrived. TPA in the middle of his individual comment had suddenly stopped on their arrival – like a small boy caught misbehaving. What had it been like when Father and younger brother James had returned from being evacuated? Had that been felt as disruptive?

*

TPA says dubiously that the attempt to correlate castration and cross-dressing could well have been a bit of the 'wild analysis' of which the responsible analyst is so wary. I am glad he said that, because I found it oddly irritating – glib and smart-alecky, like one of those maddening conversations with some chump who has been leafing through Freud and knowingly accuses you of penis envy if you borrow your husband's tie to keep your skirt around your waist. (When TPA first read through this bit he found I had said ' "up" around my waist'.)

He goes on to say that it is sad to hear Mrs Hutton talking about 'warning signals' when you think back to the 18th meeting and the topic of the 'two views'. Is she plaintively bemoaning the beginning of the killing of her intuition on that occasion? It had seemingly only been she who had noticed the burning on the walls and the holes in the carpet. Her husband, since the house was still standing, had seen no evidence of damage.

It was fortunate that by pure coincidence TPA was working at the Borstal where Geoffrey had been sent, because otherwise bureaucracy and ethical considerations might have made it difficult for him to follow the case. Establishments with their own professionals and psychiatrists could well take umbrage at an outsider muscling in. I am tempted to do my own bit of wild analysis and invoke the territorial instinct, but I won't. It is a boringly mundane political and bureaucratic matter.

23. Test scores

Venue: Borstal   13th March 1981
Present: Dr Pitt-Aikens, Chairman and clerk to the meeting
           Mrs Pannell, guest, retired link Social Worker at Orwell
               House, now a volunteer worker with the Probation
               Service
           Mrs Jenkins, link Social Worker at Orwell House
           Mr & Mrs Hutton
           Geoffrey

This meeting took place at the Borstal in which Geoffrey was incarcerated. Mr Fuller, the probation officer, had been invited but had telephoned at 4 p.m. the day before to say he was unable to attend owing to pressure of work.

Having made themselves reasonably comfortable, those present realised that they were in another 'Huttonian muddle' about the professional meetings. TPA as Chairman decided that rightly or wrongly, for better or for worse, they should carry on with the joint meeting and again not ask the Huttons temporarily to leave the room, as they would otherwise have to do. They then, however, found themselves in the invidious position of still having the previous pre- and post-professionals' minutes to read out. The Chairman decided to read them in the presence of the family but forbade the family to speak as he did so.

After the reading the family rejoined the meeting. It was agreed, as nearly always now, that the topic for discussion should be 'anything which those present felt was relevant and/or important'.

Mrs Jenkins said that today's meeting had come to her as something of a surprise since she hadn't noted it in her diary. She had noticed that when the topic for discussion was mentioned Mr Hutton had given a broad smile and she wondered why.

Mrs Pannell said that while she was pleased to see Mr and Mrs Hutton and Geoffrey again she was sorry that it was in these circumstances. She remembered that at the meeting before last Mr Hutton had said they wouldn't be able to attend any more meetings and TPA had been insistent that they should, and she wondered how it was that they were continuing – wasn't it because Geoffrey had got into further trouble that Mr and Mrs Hutton had changed their minds?

At this point Mrs Hutton interrupted, smiling, and remarked to TPA that she didn't know what was in her husband's mind.

Mrs Pannell went on to speculate that Geoffrey's parents kept coming hopefully along, thinking that one day somebody would find out what was in everybody's mind and they would become clearer about what was going on in their family. At the moment it seemed that even after all this time they weren't on the same wavelength. They would imagine they were; then something would happen and they would find they weren't. Having now worked for a time in the probation service she was saddened to see so many young men who had been to places like Orwell House. It seemed to be a continuous thing, as though the professionals weren't understanding them sufficiently or getting a message across.

Geoffrey said he hadn't got much to say really. The reason he had never spoken to TPA on his visits to the wing was that he hadn't anything to say. People said it was a bad place, but he saw it as a holiday camp. 'You know,' he remarked, 'you learn skills here.' He had taken English and maths O-levels and felt he had passed them both. He had learned a bit about carpentry and hoped to learn something about tailoring as well. Mrs Pannell had implied that the circumstances were bad, but they weren't that bad and there were many worse places than Borstal.

Mr Hutton first apologised for a rather crisp letter he had sent TPA and said he would have used milder terms if he had realised that TPA didn't have his new address. As to Mrs Jenkins's query about the smile at the words 'important or relevant', he had pondered about discussing the latest test scores. He just had that kind of mind. More seriously, over the last few months he had been making notes of things which he always meant to say at meetings and then forgot. When he and his wife had spoken to Geoffrey the night before his court appearance they had the impression that he sincerely regretted what he had done. At the last meeting but one, when Geoffrey had done something naughty but not been caught, there had been general agreement on his improvement. It had been one of the rare occasions when TPA gave a positive opinion: he seemed to think that Dr Rogers was wrong about the deep-seated problem, when obviously it was they who were wrong and Dr Rogers who was right.

Mr Hutton said he had previously expressed his own opinion that

Geoffrey had two personalities, and the danger was that anyone dealing with him almost always encountered the good side. The good Geoffrey knew that the bad Geoffrey existed but tried to play down the problem. His wife had once tried to link it to the moon's phases and was now attributing it to hyperactivity as a child, which someone had told her about. The Geoffrey they usually saw was a nice, friendly, helpful, likeable person – a bit self-willed and boisterous, but an attractive personality. Yet he had very few real interests and seemed unable to accomplish anything effectively. He was good at taking bicycles to pieces but not so good at putting them together again. The same went for washing machines. He thought this might have led to a frustration which manifested itself in various ways, resulting occasionally in violence. There had been a curious incident in 1973 at Summer Hill Grange when he was supposed to have smashed up a toilet, and there had been a time when his first social worker, Mr Dowe, had quite literally had to sit on him to calm him down. They had had to send for Mr Dowe, since Geoffrey had nearly killed Sean and the family had been helpless. Mr Dowe was the first, perhaps the only, social worker to have seen both sides of Geoffrey. Mr Hutton wondered whether it was frustration which led to the outbreaks of transvestism, since there certainly seemed to be a chronological link. He also remembered an occasion when he had remonstrated with Geoffrey over a minor disciplinary matter and Geoffrey had stormed out, stolen a bicycle and been arrested. That too was probably due to frustration, as were the many acts of vandalism which he had committed over the years.

There was also the problem that Geoffrey had difficulty in distinguishing between 'mine and thine'. These days it was easy to find reasons and explanations for this – social problems and deprivation and so on – and while he wasn't seeking to excuse Geoffrey's activities he did feel that there was an element of protest in the clumsy and pointless burglaries for which he was inevitably caught. The point of all that, he said, was that he and his wife had been aware for fourteen years of the problems in Geoffrey's character and all that time had been looking for help. He felt they had been banging their heads against a wall of sponge rubber. If a sea wall collapsed it was no good discussing the causes – you could talk about the wind and the tide at any time. Water was flooding in and had to be stopped and further collapse had to be prevented – it was no good just mopping up the water before dealing with the breach. He realised as he read through his notes that TPA would pick on this one, but there it was – he was extremely frustrated to see that something needed to be done and not get the help he needed. Perhaps he was getting help and not realising it, but it didn't feel like that. He and Anne felt they simply weren't getting the help they needed. The sessions they had been involved in for ages now were very interesting, and sometimes quite entertaining, but he sometimes got the feeling that he was no more than a guinea pig. No one seemed to be making any headway in settling the problems that bedevilled him and his wife.

Mrs Hutton said she was pleased that Geoffrey was doing something about his education while he was in Borstal but disappointed about his attitude. She wouldn't like to see him back there in a few months time because the place was a 'blooming holiday camp'. They had misunderstood Ian in the matter of money. Her husband's complaint hadn't been so much the fares as that he felt he was wasting time in coming here which he might have spent with his family. She knew he had mentioned that it was costing him a lot, but that wasn't exactly what he meant, and she had thought that after all this time they would have been able to understand him a little bit. Mind you, she added, she still found it hard to understand him after nearly twenty-five years.

TPA said that quite a few words had struck a cord with him. The first was the word 'castrate' from the minutes of the previous pre-professionals' meeting. The next were Mr Hutton's. He had used the words 'test scores' and TPA had thought for a second that he said 'testicles'. Then he had used the word 'protest'. There was a phenomenon known as the 'masculine protest'. Lastly, Mr Hutton talked about 'frustration': that had to do with feeling that his nose had been put out of joint partly through misunderstanding. He and Mr Hutton had now come the nearest yet to being on the same wavelength.

TPA then read out Mr Hutton's 'crisp' letter.

Dear Dr Pitt-Aikens

I received notification of the postponement of Friday's meeting less than an hour before we were due to set out. I am afraid that 30th March is not convenient for me. The only days I have free in March are Friday 18th or Monday 28th. Beyond that I have no idea at present of when I am likely to be free. Since I am apparently informed, not directly but via the probation officer, almost as an afterthought, let alone without prior consultation, it would appear that the presence of my wife and myself at these meetings is pretty low on the list of priorities. Maybe you could get along just as well without us. You managed pretty well last time. I have already used up two days of my annual leave on the aborted meetings and I am not prepared further to jeopardise time off which should be devoted to my family. Furthermore I am put to considerable expense – not only the travelling but meals out and so on – by attending these meetings and I am beginning to wonder if any further such drain on my resources is justified.

Yours sincerely
Ian Hutton

TPA continued with the observation that there could be two Mr Huttons – one 'good' one, who would realise that TPA wouldn't purposely inconvenience him, and one 'bad' one who could wilfully imagine that he would. How could Mr Hutton see himself as low on the list of priorities when they had been trying to help for so long? The only way he could have reached Mr Hutton's new address was via the probation officer, and he had sent the 'postponing letter' twenty-one days before the scheduled date – it simply hadn't been forwarded by the probation officer as requested, till virtually the last minute. Complications and misunderstandings could result in people feeling put down and 'low on the list of priorities'. He himself might feel put down by Dr Rogers, who had known Geoffrey for a very short while and was using terms like 'deep inner disturbances' and so on. What sort of idiot, he asked, did that make *him*? He still didn't believe that Geoffrey's personality was disturbed. It was rather that his whole personality got pushed to one side. From time to time he lost more or less of his personality, as though Geoffrey wasn't there any more but off waiting in the wings. There was nothing actually wrong with Geoffrey's self, but he was invaded from time to time by alien themes of frustration, helplessness – castration-like evil spirits. That made even the real Geoffrey angry – so angry that he did some pretty powerful things. There was a theory that an arsonist was always a bed-wetter, the idea being that there was some sort of connection between having a penis which was only worth peeing through, perhaps to dampen excitement, and the great power of setting fire to something and burning it down, the potency of blowing things to pieces. He also thought that for the first time they had seen a connection between Mr Hutton's rage and his confusion. Faced with a misunderstanding, he could have merely scratched his head, but he had chosen to be angry. It was strange that Mr Hutton should imagine that TPA wanted to put him down when, if you thought about it, surely the opposite should seem the case. He wondered how Mr Hutton would cope with retirement. Would he be happily confused, in the sense of 'Gosh what shall I do today? That's exciting' or would he feel that he had been castrated? Mr Hutton knew full well that TPA had always been a bit worried about what was going to happen to him, certainly till a year ago when he had passed 50.

In the free discussion Mr Hutton said he felt OK about retirement.

Mrs Pannell said that, when Geoffrey and she had spoken before the meeting, he had told her that he had been glad and sorry at the same time to leave 'his house': glad for his parents' sake, because he realised how much worry he had given them, but feeling also that sending him away was the worst thing they had ever done. Then it transpired that there was some misunderstanding between him and Mrs Pannell as to what he had actually meant by this 'glad and sorry' business. The powerfulness of their misunderstanding seemed to affect everyone in the room. Geoffrey tried to clarify by saying that his Mum and Dad had done a good thing, but he didn't feel ready to face the world by himself. He then started talking about his clothes and laundry, and somehow felt that he was wandering off the track.

TPA had an idea about tracks and parallel lines and said that maybe Geoffrey had a cross-over point. He asked Geoffrey whether he thought that if he were a woman he would be looked after.

Geoffrey shrugged. (The Clerk thought he had 'gone' in those few seconds.)

They then discussed Mr and Mrs Hutton and the fact that she had looked after him when they were first married. A little later in the marriage he had been away at sea and she had been very independent. Then, as the children arrived and Mr Hutton came home from the navy, she became more dependent on Mr Hutton and less capable of managing the responsibilities facing her. Mr Hutton seemed to assume these responsibilities; it was as if a cross-over point happened when Mr Hutton was away at sea. They wondered whether the two sides of Geoffrey portrayed this 'cross-over' and who would do the 'looking after' when Mr Hutton retired.

When the meeting was over, Mrs Pannell and Mrs Jenkins realised they had experienced a 'cross-over' of their own that afternoon. A few years before, Mrs Jenkins had been a social work student at Orwell House, supervised by Mrs Pannell; now Mrs Jenkins was the link worker, with Mrs Pannell alongside as Mrs Jenkins's guest.

*

Co-authorship is getting more difficult. TPA has been reading my notes on the earlier meetings and insists that I have still been leaving myself out of the narrative flow. I can't see this at all. I find myself intrusive and annoying, and I rather detest the woman who is writing this. As I have said before, I am like the Huttons in that I tend to get the giggles on serious occasions, such as chamber recitals and weddings, and I am wondering whether TPA might not be better off on his own. He repeats that I have been leaving myself out so that I can blame him. He, he says, and I quote, 'looks like a boring jerk', and I look excluded. What is all this self-doubt?

Now he wonders whether the Borstal might be offended by the word 'incarceration' and I feel giddy. I am changing my view of these institutions. Geoffrey, after all, sees the place as a 'holiday camp'. I can only assume it was a very unusual Borstal.

The Huttons had allowed themselves to be misled by Mr Fuller, who had given them the wrong time for the previous meeting, and might have been angry with the meeting itself had the misleading not become evident. Then the egregious Mr Fuller went along with the 'anti-meetingness' by referring to the family's lack of motivation. TPA, who had given them the right time, again found himself in the firing line in this meeting. The anger was directed at him (personifying the meeting) rather than at the Huttons' change of address and the failure of Mr Fuller to redirect the letter until the last minute. Moreover Mr Fuller, having played his part in the confusion, had sent his apologies less than twenty-four hours before the 23rd meeting and was therefore physically out of range. All the above, I am told, are common examples of misdirection of aggression and can only be seen properly by means of (a) a clear framework and (b) clear thinking. Does Geoffrey's imprisonment incorporate a similar phenomenon? When doubts and puzzles about the time of the meeting lead to chaos, the simplest thing is to blame the shrink, when in fact it is all much more complicated. The delinquent, like the shrink, is in the front line. Causing problems? Bang him in the slammer – end of problem.

TPA thought they had heard the real Geoffrey talking here and found him rather poignant, while at first I thought him cocky. Both Geoffreys were present: the bad one talking about holiday camps, and TPA's one talking about wandering off the track. TPA says that if anyone (not just the evicted delinquent) talks about 'my house' it indicates pride and affection more than the phrase 'my home'. I can see that. 'My home' has a rather genteel, self-righteous air.

When I eventually met Mrs Hutton she gave me a graphic description of the time Geoffrey nearly killed Sean. She was alone and was desperately trying to push one into the kitchen and one into the living room. She is brave and funny, but it must have been a dreadful situation until Mr Dowe came and sat on Geoffrey. I was lost in contemplation of this nightmare when TPA asked which was worse – Geoffrey actively *nearly* killing Sean, or Ian perhaps *really* killing Kevin by the sin of omission.

The subject of the cross-over of responsibilities arose again and obviously resonates with transvestism. I have lost count of the meanings of this determinedly over-determined syndrome. This must be the sixth or seventh to date. I have next noted: 'Even Geoffrey himself, or what remained of his true personality, might feel unjustly jailed.' And I don't know why I did so, unless it is connected with responsibility and where it truly lies.

Mr Hutton again attacks the family approach and I am enchanted to discover TPA carrying on like the proverbial analyst, hearing 'testicles' for 'test-scores' and warbling about the masculine protest, castration, etc. He redeems himself with a reminder that he had warned that Geoffrey was waiting in the wings, liable to revert to delinquency at any moment should the family approach be lost. The family had wanted to stop the meetings, and Geoffrey up in the proverbial loft had instantly tried to blow the top off a church, and that was why he was inside again.

24. Non-event

12th June 1981

This meeting was adjourned after two minutes since only TPA and Mrs Jenkins were present. The Huttons had 'mechanical trouble with their car'.

*

I wondered what could possibly be of any interest in this meeting which – to put it no higher – seemed to me a bit of a non-event. I grew seriously exasperated with TPA because he went on so about it. Two lines of adjournment. While he spoke he looked for an 'important piece of paper' on which the whole world seemed to depend. That *did* exist. That was important. I only realised the significance of the 24th meeting when I read the 'piece of paper' – Mr Hutton's letter – about it and felt the chill of the meaning of death, its proximity. This session was not only potentially the last of all the sessions but the end of Mr Hutton and, by extension, the family – and also the end of this book. That would perhaps not have been a tragedy but it brought home to me, in an oddly immediate way, the sheer surprise of sudden death.

We noticed that Geoffrey was released from Borstal on the day of the 'non-event'.

7th June 1981
Dear Dr Pitt-Aikens,

I regret to have to tell you that my wife and I will not be able to keep our appointment at the Clinic on Friday 12th June.

Unfortunately I have crashed my car and it is a complete write-off, so I am without transport. I am afraid that public transport is not a viable alternative, not only because of the cost but also because I have to be on duty at 15.30 that afternoon. Any future appointment will, I fear, be dependent on my being able to arrange a replacement for my car. I apologise for the shortness of notice I am giving but it did not

146

occur to me to have the crash earlier.

That's the trouble with the Huttons – everything is done at the last minute.

Yours somewhat bent but not broken,

Ian Hutton

25. Back to the holiday camp

Venue: Borstal   23rd September 1981
Present: Dr Pitt-Aikens, Chairman
            Mr Fuller, Probation Officer
            Mrs Jenkins, link Social Worker at Orwell House and
                clerk to the meeting
            Mr & Mrs Hutton

According to Mr Fuller, Geoffrey hadn't wanted to come.

Mrs Jenkins said she was puzzled about what Geoffrey was doing at the moment. She knew he had been released from Borstal, but Mr and Mrs Hutton seemed to have little idea where he was and she found that surprising. She was also surprised that they related Geoffrey's episodes in a humorous fashion and supposed that for reasons best known to themselves that was the way they felt able to cope with him. She had noticed that Mr Hutton had laughed when TPA read out the list of those present the last time they had met and thought it was because he and Mrs Hutton had seen themselves tagged on as 'also rans'. She wondered if he still had a 'low self-image of his attendance at the meetings'. Mrs Hutton had told her earlier that two or perhaps three of Geoffrey's friends had recently been killed and guessed that that would affect him quite a lot. She wondered whether Geoffrey had passed his exams and also what Mr and Mrs Hutton thought of her own attendance at the meetings: whether they saw her as a bit of the past, and whether that was a good thing, or whether they should actually be looking to the future.

Mr Fuller said he was going to be the bearer of bad news but could bring people up to date with what was happening to Geoffrey. He had been released from Borstal after doing an extra three weeks for getting into a fight. He had gone into bed-and-breakfast accommodation, but because of a misunderstanding over his social benefit payment had spent half the £100 giro cheque going to see his parents. This meant he had no rent money, and he had to go out and live with somebody else until he got back up to date with his rent.

Then, when he returned, the lady wouldn't let him in and he had to find yet another place. He had soon got into arrears there, had worked up considerable 'bar bills' and together with four others had been asked to leave because of having 'rowdy late-night parties with suspected cannabis smoking'. On the Monday he had gone to Mr Fuller to borrow money, and Mr Fuller had made it clear that he wasn't going to lend him any because he was such an appalling manager. He had appeared in court on August 20th charged with the theft of a ring valued at £170 and at the same time was charged with indecent assault – 'Sorry' said Mr Fuller – he had meant to say 'indecent exposure'. The burglary had occurred in broad daylight, and Geoffrey had been chased by several policemen and a number of police cars all round the middle of Ilford. Mr Fuller had been fortunate in finding him a bail hostel where he was able to go until the remand hearing. Geoffrey's general attitude was, at the moment, good; he was fitting in well at the hostel and co-operating with the regime there. Mr Fuller wanted to know what contact Geoffrey had had with TPA in Borstal and what plans TPA had for further contact. There had been contact with Dr Rogers and another psychotherapist, but Geoffrey hadn't actually seen them yet because he kept moving addresses and their letters never reached him. Mr Fuller said he wasn't sure where Geoffrey was going at the moment and wondered how valuable the sessions were, since Geoffrey's life was continuing without much relevance to them. He said he wanted to explain further that he had seen Geoffrey about two weeks before and Geoffrey had said that he didn't want to come today because he didn't want to be present when his parents heard about his latest offences.

Mrs Hutton said that, as to the drugs that had been mentioned, Sean had told them that Geoffrey and the other boys had been taking drugs of some description and also drinking quite heavily, and he was extremely worried about them. In between staying at the different hostels he had been to stay with someone the family knew and had also been kicked out of there. A valuable heavy gold bracelet had gone missing, but they couldn't be sure Geoffrey had taken it. They hadn't been informed officially, but Sean had told them that Geoffrey had taken money from the person he was staying with. It must have been a lot because £10 or £20 was nothing to his host. Geoffrey had then stayed with them for a day and completely wrecked Louis's bike, which had had to go back to the makers; and as for Geoffrey's dressing up, she had noticed that he tended to do it whenever anything happened that he didn't know how to deal with, and the same thing went for the indecent exposure. What, she asked, was likely to happen to Geoffrey?

Mr Hutton said that he had to confess he wasn't surprised that Geoffrey was in trouble again. He had felt it was only going to be a matter of time. He didn't know whether it had been precognition or what, but certainly during August and September, when Geoffrey was living with them, Mr Hutton had developed a 'twitch' when the phone rang. It was probably, he reflected, more a case of putting two and two together, having heard from Sean something of what was going on in Barking. There were some other things that he had been going to say today until he heard that news. Thinking about the meetings before coming here, he had tried to work out what they were attempting to do in order to find some point in them. He had noticed TPA dropping certain words to provoke, or gain, a reaction. One or two things which TPA appeared to attribute to him either consciously or subconsciously might be there, but how could he tell, if Mr Hutton didn't even subconsciously have a clue what TPA was talking about? Having never heard of the 'masculine protest', he couldn't see how it could have had any meaning for him.

TPA said he had had no individual dealings with Geoffrey while he was in Borstal. He would have seen him if he had felt he should, or if one of the officers, or Geoffrey himself, had wanted him to, because that was the way he worked. It had however been noticeable that Geoffrey hadn't made any moves towards him at all, which, on the face of it, was odd. He was trying to understand the situation in and around Geoffrey from another angle anyway, and still had no plans to see him individually, although in the unlikely event of Geoffrey making an approach he would be glad to see him. It was rare, he said, for him to make an offer to boys like Geoffrey, because in his experience was they didn't respond. He was sometimes surprised that professionals in this field didn't see the idea of a delinquent seeking therapy as almost a contradiction in terms. He would have considered it a waste of time chasing Geoffrey Hutton with lots of letters. In his way of working, in a case which by its very nature meant that the presenting person, or, as he would say, the 'personification', was difficult to relate to it would be a bit silly to pretend otherwise. His view was that one could maintain a solid connection with a case, primarily by means of existing professional relationships. Usually his offer would be to another professional, and even if that professional hated the idea of meeting him, if he had agreed to do so he jolly well had to, because he got paid for doing so and it would be unprofessional to renege on such an agreement. Non-professionals, even such as Mr and Mrs Hutton, weren't in that position. It was a real hardship for them to come whether they liked it or not. His way of working was to depend very much on the professional links, which should be a match for what could be called omnipotent and negative feelings that someone like Geoffrey had displayed – saying, 'No, I don't want to go to the meeting because I wouldn't like it.' He wondered, however, if in spite of having said all that he had made sense to Mr Fuller.

TPA continued that he was sorry Mr Hutton didn't understand what he was saying about the masculine protest business. Self-exposure was associated with masculine protest because on one level it was sexually showing-off. There were women who would screech and get very upset, and other women who would laugh and say, 'Who do you think you are, you little twit?' So you had both ends of the spectrum in this particular phenomenon. On the one hand you had masculinity symbolised in a powerful way with 'poor little women' rushing away, screaming, and at the other extreme you had 'poor little men' being put firmly in their place; so the masculine protest could go either way. He was curious about the boys who had got themselves killed and had forgotten who had told them about it. Were they the boys whom Sean was worried about, the ones he thought were taking drugs and drinking? He recollected that he had been going on for a long time about people in the family dying, and here was a situation where three of Geoffrey's friends were dead. There was absolutely no point in trying to help them now, not in this world anyway; but at least Geoffrey was still alive and kicking.

It felt peculiar that Mrs Pannell hadn't come today. She had been invited and wasn't there, and what did that mean? He knew she was still alive, but wondered if she would ever be back. She was gradually taking a back seat, while Mrs Jenkins came more and more into the foreground, and he wondered again how Mr Hutton was going to take retirement – he had looked pretty sad and almost despairing when he heard the news about Geoffrey. TPA hated to think of him being retired, if it meant being a shadow of his former self. He would like to think Mr Hutton wouldn't take his retirement lying down but would have some 'positive masculine protest' in him and make a good life.

He had had a fantasy about himself leaving and not attending any more meetings, whether or not they carried on. He thought of all the layers of professionals there must have been since the family first went to a child guidance clinic fifteen years before. It would seem sad if all the stories that he now knew, all the Huttonisms he was aware of, were lost: episodes such as, when he was comparing Geoffrey to Kevin in arsonist or blowing-up terms, Mr Hutton's saying that Geoffrey was nothing like his uncle: 'Good Lord, he had only exploded lighter-fuel cannisters stuck in a brick wall. My brother blew up an entire brickworks.' If he were to go, there would be new probation officers, new policemen, but all the things he knew would be forgotten, like an old book that had been burnt. There was something sad about losing all the stories, the family history, and it was tragic that sometimes all that was remembered about a person was how he had died. They all knew that Mr Hutton's brother had blown himself up, but not much about what he was actually like. It was depressing to hear that someone had been killed and all that people said was 'How did it happen?', as if that made any difference. The sad thing was that someone who had been known and loved – or hated – had just gone. It was perhaps relevant that people tended particularly to remember sex-offenders and also, as it were, 'to blow them up'. For instance, Mr Fuller had inadvertently said 'indecent assault' when he meant 'indecent exposure'. When very little was known about a person – for instance only what offence he had committed – people often made the most of that, even to the extent of telling lies, not perhaps knowingly, but almost as if they were compelled, since they knew so little about the real person.

Mr Hutton opened the free discussion by announcing that he had wrecked his car coming back from seeing his buddies. He had apparently gone to sleep while driving at 60 miles an hour and failed to take a bend. He regretted not confirming TPA's forebodings about him, but he had only been bruised; the car, however, was a write-off.

Mrs Hutton said she had somehow known there had been an accident. She had had the same sort of feeling when Geoffrey was a baby alone upstairs and had cut his head so badly he needed stitches.

On arranging the next meeting Mrs Hutton asked particularly that it shouldn't be held at the Borstal. The meeting was closed, whereupon Mrs Hutton asked what was likely to happen to Geoffrey.

*

Mrs Jenkins was 'puzzled as to what Geoffrey was doing at the moment'. I always wonder what Geoffrey is doing. He is so eclectic it could be anything.

Mr Fuller magnificently fulfils one of TPA's seeming predictions, saying 'indecent assault' for 'indecent exposure', and brings everyone up to date with what Geoffrey has been doing.

Mr Hutton talks about precognition, his 'twitch' – telling us in effect that he still has his intuition – which in theory he shouldn't have. TPA thinks he ought to have suppressed his intuition if that was the instrument which could have saved his brother. Geoffrey's telephone call demonstrates that he still has it, so where has his loss of intuition gone? It looks as though Mrs Hutton still has plenty of it too, since she was able to be intuitive about her husband's car crash.

TPA is still a little afraid that Mr Hutton is going to die, although on the face of it he is safe – having passed the traditional Hutton deadline of two score years and ten.

TPA sounds almost sentimental on the subject of the lost stories. He says lost stories relate to the lack of proper mourning. All those involved are buried, as it were, in unmarked graves. The longer he hangs on, the likelier it will be that the family history will become clear; and this, it must be remembered, is all thanks to Geoffrey, without whom the problems would never have become apparent. The family moves house, and this too contributes to the loss of continuity. The professionals leave unexpectedly and are not 'mourned', just as the victims of sudden death are seldom properly mourned. Sudden death is so shocking that people cannot cope. Illness and age are benevolent in so far as they give warning of death. Goodness, how depressing.

26. Wrong speed again

Venue: Clinic consulting-room   20th November 1981
Present: Dr Pitt-Aikens, Chairman
          Mr Fuller, Probation Officer
          Mrs Jenkins, link Social Worker at Orwell House and
              clerk to the meeting
          Mr & Mrs Hutton
          Geoffrey

> TPA and Mr & Mrs Hutton had spent the first three
> minutes of the meeting in 'preliminaries' when they
> were joined by everyone else – though not by Mrs
> Pannell.

Mr Fuller gave a quick up-date of the situation, saying that he
expected Geoffrey would fill in more: he was currently at a probation
hostel and due to go back to court shortly for sentencing. Mr Fuller
was still really trying to work out where the meetings were going. He
didn't know why, but it was almost as though he had picked up Mr
Hutton's confusion about what was happening, including the
problem of what all their roles were. He was thinking of the bits in
the last session about the professionals coming because they had to,
whether they wanted to or not, and wondering whether that was
valid. Geoffrey's experience in everyday life was different from the
sort of issues that were discussed in the meetings, and he had
originally intended to write to TPA saying that he wasn't coming
but had then phoned Geoffrey to see if he wanted to come. Hearing
that he did, he had decided that Geoffrey's commitment was
sufficient to induce him to come too. If Geoffrey didn't wish to come
in future, nor would he, because he didn't feel that a great deal was
being achieved.

Mrs Jenkins observed that Mr Fuller had just put a great onus on
Geoffrey Hutton. She had come late to the meeting and felt she
didn't know what was going on. Sitting there she felt she really did
admire Mr and Mrs Hutton for the way they came, for whatever
reason, to all the meetings and hoped they found them helpful,

adding that she recognised that Geoffrey had come but wondered what he was playing at. She was also mindful that they had purposely met at the clinic because they didn't want to go to the Borstal, and there were poor Geoffrey and Mrs Hutton having to stare at a photograph of the place. They were sitting bang in front of it. It was a pity, she remarked, that so many of Mr Hutton's comments at the last meeting hadn't been clerked. She hoped that wouldn't happen today, since his comments were very valuable.

Geoffrey said, Oh, um, he was glad he had got this probation hostel. He could now sort of sort himself out and he hoped he could just get on the right track of everything. He hadn't seen the minutes of the last meeting, but some of the things said were, he observed, untruthful. Of course he had had parties at the bed-and-breakfast place, but he had never touched drugs, and didn't want to, and he didn't know who had said he did. That was all he really wanted to say.

Mrs Hutton said she had noticed that Mr Fuller hadn't mentioned that since the last meeting Geoffrey had been up in court for taking and driving away a car. She had come to the conclusion that Geoffrey was the only one who could do anything about himself. None of them could develop him; it was up to him to grow up.

Mr Hutton said that perhaps he had been speaking too fast last time, playing himself at the wrong speed – and yes, he was still wondering why they went to the meetings: probably because Geoffrey had been a problem for so long and coming here was all they seemed able to do by way of sorting it out. What had always puzzled him, and what he still couldn't work out, was the aim of the meetings. What were they trying to achieve? Not knowing what you were trying to achieve was like his going to sleep in the car. If you didn't know what you were doing you couldn't point a car in the right direction. There seemed to be a repetitive pattern and, as Anne had said, just after the last meeting Geoffrey had been at it again. Like Anne, he was nearing the end of his tether. He didn't know what to do and was getting quite despairing about it.

TPA said he was quite clear why he felt it was worth his while going to the meetings. It was helpful for any group to have the chance to express, share and discuss feelings about important and relevant topics. He was part of this group, and he wanted to understand what it was that produced the kind of difficulties an intelligent boy like Geoffrey could get himself into. He was sure that the difficulties weren't caused by what could be thought of as logical. For instance, no one could say that Mr and Mrs Hutton were bad parents – a reason people often gave for delinquency. The evidence suggested that if Mr and Mrs Hutton could be faulted as parents it might be because they were too good. It certainly wasn't because they were irresponsible. So there had to be reasons which people on the whole didn't understand. On the other hand they were gradually nearing some understanding as to what it was all about. The kind of things they had been discussing might almost be called clairvoyance, as when Mrs Hutton had said she had a feeling about her husband at the time of his car crash. TPA said he had often felt he was battling against laughter when he voiced concern that Mr Hutton might die prematurely and then, sure enough, he escaped by the skin of his teeth. They had heard that Mr and Mrs Hutton had swapped over the dominant role in the family before, during and after Mr Hutton's time in the navy, illustrating that a man in a family can change from top-dog to bottom-dog according to what has been happening. That could relate to Geoffrey when he exposed himself to women who might either ridicule him or be frightened of him. It was important for Geoffrey to understand what this was all about, because otherwise, to use Mr Hutton's words, he might just despair and regard himself as a hopeless case, if he saw no reasons. Or he might even take false comfort by joining other people who had become invaded by similar sorts of themes, or 'aliens', and who also might have persuaded themselves that their behaviour was a normal response to a sick or repressive or uncaring society, or just a wish not to be bored. Either would be a shame. He confessed that he was back to gloom and doom – not about Geoffrey but about other family members. Mr Hutton himself didn't seem very well today and looked as though he could do with a good holiday. Did he look after himself well enough, or had it got to the state where the only way he could think of looking after himself was to forget about Geoffrey? It had to be a bit more positive than that. He agreed with Mrs Jenkins, that it wasn't a good idea for people to go to the meetings because Geoffrey wanted them to. That would support an idea that he was more powerful than he was. He himself would be quite happy if Mr Fuller and Mr and Mrs Hutton kept coming to the meetings without a clue as to why they were doing so, as long as they felt something inside them pushing them to come. There were a lot of secrets in the family which they hadn't yet uncovered and understood. What had happened to Geoffrey's uncle was a horribly important result of the loss of thought-communication, or whatever one might wish to call it. If he remembered rightly, Mr Hutton had known something was wrong with his brother all the time he wasn't there: it had been no surprise when he had been discovered dead. He was a bit disappointed that Geoffrey had had no chance to see all the minutes of the previous meetings and he should be given the opportunity to read them. He wondered what Geoffrey had thought about the amazing discussion TPA had had with his father, comparing Geoffrey with his uncle who had blown up the brickworks when Geoffrey had merely exploded lighter fuel in the wall. Mr Hutton, he believed, had been going for the difference of quantity rather than quality in order to destroy the connection.

Mr Hutton opened the free discussion by clarifying the difference between Kevin and Geoffrey. He considered that Kevin had been a leader, a person in control, whereas Geoffrey was not. Some of those present felt that the rejection and humiliation that Kevin had suffered as a boy of 17 might have been 'like death' to him.

Mrs Hutton said that people who took their own lives had to be very selfish. The subject of Mr Hutton's retirement came up again and she thought he would love it, as he had so many interests and hobbies. TPA had got it wrong and Mr Hutton needed more time for his interests, like stamps and moths and the articles he wrote. Sean, however, had a detached retina and had recently had a graft, which was knocked off when he was with some friends at a disco. He had panicked and his friends had put a paper bag over his head.

Geoffrey was asked how he would take it if Sean were to go blind and replied that he would be 'gutted'. Sean had a fear of hospitals but had necessitated his last operation by his own silly behaviour, and he still gave his need for a social life as an excuse for not spending the required amount of time in hospital. Mr Hutton then said that he didn't have favourites, but that if he had he supposed it would be Geoffrey. He had always thought that Kevin was the favourite in his family, and Kevin had thought it was him. Mr Hutton now thought it was probably his younger brother James.

*

I find it very peculiar that TPA should have a photograph of a Borstal on his consulting-room mantelpiece.

Mr Hutton 'playing himself at the wrong speed' reminds me of Geoffrey and the record-player, and of how very nasty and irritating the wrong speed is. TPA remembers in the 8th meeting wishing for a moment that they were going faster, and says that if Geoffrey is the personification of several decades of family history then trying to produce a symbolic precis within a short space of time might well cause him to experience confusion as to the pace of life. Geoffrey has also mentioned tracks several times. As well as being right or wrong, tracks can be slow or fast.

TPA talks about the fear of alien forces. He is always stressing that the delinquent is, to a lesser or greater degree, some or all of the time possessed by themes, spirits or what Winnicott called 'ego alien factors'. The individual's personality is squashed to one side, leaving the erstwhile occupant helplessly looking on. This is so alarming that even what remains of the squashed-aside personality will attempt to explain the phenomenon to himself using the most tenuous reasoning. Richard III, for example, excused his villainy by his deformity, and Sean explains his compulsion to risk blindness by his need of a 'social life'.

Perhaps anyone would rather think of himself as a monster of iniquity, or a feckless ass, than as a playground for extraneous forces. The sense of loss of autonomy must be as unnerving as finding oneself in a runaway train. TPA received a letter from an imprisoned patient which begins with a rather touching unconscious irony: 'My problem is I keep beating up the girl I want to marry.' It continues: 'I've also got two children now, one boy two months old and a girl 17 months old, and I'm scared I might hurt them as well. Please believe me, Doc, I don't mean it. I just can't help myself. It's almost as if I've got somebody behind me controlling my arms. I know I'm doing it, but I can't stop myself. I know it sounds like I'm exaggerating, but please help me. I can't stand it any more. I just want to live a happy life with my children or not live at all.'

This rather flies in the face of a popular belief that a violent criminal invariably pursues his activities for fun. TPA's remark that people might persuade themselves that their behaviour arises out of 'just a wish not to be bored' reminds me of a conversation I had recently with Someone who held that the Romantic movement with its regrettable results and adherents – Rousseau, Sade, Crowley ('Do what thou wilt shall be the whole of the law'), etc. etc., ending up in the 60s with such as Charles Manson – was initiated by people who had it in for their boring parents. After committing a few mass murders they feel they can claim that at least they've done something interesting.

Mr Fuller quite understandably still sees Geoffrey as the main problem, rather than as a mere personification, and doesn't see the point in coming to the meetings if he isn't there. He had written in January to say that he wouldn't be coming again but had reminded Geoffrey of the date of the next meeting, unable to grasp that the route to understanding Geoffrey lay through the professional links rather than through a boy who was not often himself.

27. Baby

Venue: Clinic consulting-room   29th January 1982
Present: Dr Pitt-Aikens, Chairman
            Mrs Jenkins, link Social Worker at Orwell House and
               clerk to the meeting
            Mr & Mrs Hutton

The Chairman read a letter from Mr Fuller which included the facts that his statutory obligation to Geoffrey had now been taken over by a colleague based at the probation hostel; the court had given Geoffrey two years' probation with six months' 'condition of residence' at that hostel. The letter continued that Mr Fuller was anxious about the value and infrequency of the meetings and the travelling difficulties they incurred for the family and Geoffrey.

Mr and Mrs Hutton had invited Geoffrey, who had agreed to come but had then telephoned to say (as was his wont) that he had pains in his stomach and was seeing a doctor. The new probation officer whose name was not known couldn't come. It was agreed that they would talk about anything which those present felt was important or relevant, whether they wanted to talk about it or not. Mrs Jenkins suggested they talk about something more specific, and Mrs Hutton proposed 'her feelings about Geoffrey not having had sufficient attention paid to him as a baby'. She described him as 'hectic'.

TPA asked if she was proposing that they should discuss Geoffrey as a baby, and she said she was. He found himself in a minority of one against the idea, so the topic for discussion was agreed to be 'Geoffrey as a baby'.

TPA had nothing to say, not knowing anything about Geoffrey as a baby.

Mrs Jenkins also said 'No comment' and then changed her mind, but the Chairman was reluctant to let her reclaim the floor.

Mr Hutton said he would rather come in after his wife, since she obviously had something to say and was already 'sort of hiding behind him'.

Mrs Hutton thought Geoffrey ought to have had help from the

time he was a baby, only she hadn't realised it. If she was to see such behaviour again – say, in one of her grandchildren – she would recognise that it was odd for a child of six months to go the whole length of the stairs to bed by himself. He could climb out of his cot before he was a year old, and it became too dangerous to let him sleep in it. When he was about 18 months old he had had to go to hospital with an infection, and when they visited him they found he had been tied to his cot because he had climbed on to a window sill two storeys up and nearly fallen out of the window. When she asked why he was tied down, the nurses said she should have warned them that he was a 'terrible climber'. She said, 'Well, all babies are like that', and the nurses said, 'Oh no, not like this one.' When they brought him home they had put an electric fire in his room, which they turned off at night, and one day discovered that he had taken it apart with a screwdriver and put it together again. At six months he had climbed over a fireguard to get at a lighter in the middle of the mantelpiece which he had also taken apart, and one day he put his little boots in the fire. Mrs Hutton had left him and Sean playing with Leggo in the middle of the floor, making various garages and things. She had gone upstairs to make the beds, thinking they were playing very nicely, and when she came down again he had taken off his boots and socks and burnt them. Another time she had decided they were again playing very nicely in the middle of the floor and had gone upstairs, and Ian had come in to find that Geoffrey had climbed the full length of the shelves right up to the top shelf, taken all the eggs and cornflakes and emptied them out of the window. 'Of course,' she said, in her Irish brogue, 'I didn't really take. I just thought he was quite all right. I thought Sean was the quiet one.' She had imagined there was something wrong with Sean, worrying that he should be doing this and that by his age. She had even let him start at school early, thinking he was well behind Geoffrey, and all the time it was Geoffrey she should have been worrying about.

In the free discussion TPA said he thought he had picked up a theme quite early on in the meeting, to do with 'knowing and not knowing'.

A parallel was attempted between TPA's omniscience – knowing, wrongly, that the meeting was going to be a failure because of the topic they had decided on; perhaps trying to prove it by starting off the 'individual comments', which was unusual, and having nothing to say; and then realising it wasn't going to be a disaster when it became clear that Mrs Hutton was speaking of things to which even TPA in his ignorance might be able to contribute later. They also noticed a tendency to 'cheat' exhibited both by Mrs Jenkins and Mr

Hutton who had had the notion that they might have a second 'individual comment' which, as they knew, was against the rules they imposed on themselves at these meetings.

Mrs Hutton said some more about her belief that Sean was slow, when the truth may have been that Geoffrey was quick. Since these were her first children, how could she have known which was relatively one or the other? But she now felt that she had made a mistake in not recognising this.

They again discussed Geoffrey's caricaturing someone who was expected to do the unexpected. He had painted his cars (and himself) with touch-up paint and at the age of five had startled the doctor (who had imagined it would be easy to look after him) by climbing up on the surgery roof.

Continuing the theme of the 'expected or not', TPA pointed out that Sean had gone to a disco, thereby risking blindness, and that Mr Hutton had cooked his own goose, as it were, by saying recently that it had to happen, when at an earlier meeting he had implied that such things weren't predictable.

They spoke again of Kevin's suicide, and TPA expressed some doubt that it had been intentional in the usual sense. Mr Hutton disputed that, and there ensued a long, complicated discussion which was too difficult to record clearly.

All the way through the meeting – especially during the 'free discussion' – the clerk complained about her difficulties in recording today's meeting. She was muddled about the order in which people had said things and knew she had left things out entirely. The corollary was drawn between the clerk's difficulties and someone trying to piece history and ideas together, having to leave things out and not being sure in which order they should go. Baby Geoffrey's mechanical efforts were of course mentioned in that context. More than usually, the meeting ended with a feeling that it was distinctly unfinished – again reminiscent of baby Geoffrey's uncompleted mechanical efforts.

*

Mr Fuller, never having quite understood the point of the meetings, has now left, though not without expressing a final doubt. I sympathise with him to some extent. I found the first one I went to confusing, and even the family took some time before beginning to understand their purpose.

I do not like babies in the usual sense. I do not seek them out, or lean over to look into their prams, but I find them touching. I wish that when I had my own I had realised fully just how important they were and had done more to ensure that their whole lives would be full and happy and straight. I know exactly what Mrs Hutton means when she regrets her lack of realisation of the implications of Geoffrey's demeanour in infancy. It seems absurd that we should be expected to know instinctively how to raise children when, if TPA is to be believed, intuition is contingent on close family bonds, and these some of us lack. Love is not enough.

Having said that, after reading through the meeting I look at my notes and see that I have written 'Geoffrey as intuition-carrier'. TPA had wondered how some very tiny children are capable of extraordinary feats – dismantling electric fires and lighters – when experience can certainly have taught them nothing, and now I am wondering whether Geoffrey had collared his mother's intuition, making her incapable of coping with him. What a strange idea.

There is an immediacy about the way in which Geoffrey's probation – following on his last court sentence – is spoken about. So much so that one has the feeling he is on probation for some new offence, but in fact it refers back to the mayhem in Ilford in August and he was only sentenced in December. Time plays tricks. What speed? What track? The image of the naughty lamb burning his little boots is most engaging, but there is nothing appealing about the boy's arson in his attempt at blowing up the loft.

28. What next?

Venue: Clinic consulting-room   19th March 1982
Present: Dr Pitt-Aikens, Chairman
            Mrs Jenkins, link Social Worker at Orwell House and
                clerk to the meeting
            Mr & Mrs Hutton

Geoffrey had been invited. Mr Hutton said he was pretty sure that he would have liked to come but didn't think he could make it.

The last minutes were read and corrected. Mrs Hutton interrupted to say that she sometimes worded things wrongly, but it was agreed that she had been clerked correctly. As the Chairman was asking what they were going to talk about she continued keenly to establish what she had worded wrongly in the previous meeting. TPA tried to coax those present back to deciding what they were going to talk about.

Mrs Hutton suggested they should carry on where they had left off.

Mrs Jenkins said it should be something specific.

Mr Hutton was happy as long as whatever it was gave him a chance to make comments on the minutes.

After some argy-bargy they agreed to continue the discussion where they had left it last time.

Mr Hutton said that, as often happened when he was driving down and wondering why he was coming here yet again, the business of the minutes had come into his head. He wondered why people seemed to get so hidebound with procedures. They had it in the stamp club, they had it in the union. Minutes were taken and read at the next meeting, and everyone agreed that they were correct; yet anyone coming in cold, and just picking up the minutes, wouldn't have a clue about what was going on, and any conclusion they drew would inevitably be wrong. He had been accused last time of trying to cheat by having a second bite at the cherry, and was still trying to work out how you could have a second bite when you hadn't had a first bite, since he had only asked if he could come in after Anne. (This Chairman allows people to make their 'individual comments' simply by going round the room in order of seating – nearly always clockwise – with himself last. Clerk.) The other thing was that he had been wondering what today's bombshell was going to be. The first suggestion as a subject for the last meeting was that it should be 'anything important or relevant'. Then they had decided that it should be something else, so presumably the something else wouldn't be important or relevant. He was, he explained, just pointing out the peculiarities that could arise from taking minutes. Anne had been making a few comments at home about the last meeting and its effects, and he had pointed out to her that it hadn't been the first time that the subject of Geoffrey as a baby had come up. The problems they had had with him and some of the anecdotes had been related several times. This showed that, in spite of all the set procedures, there was really no procedure at all, so he was still left worrying what on earth was going on.

Mrs Jenkins said, 'Poor Mr Hutton. It has been going on for so long and there must be something that has kept him coming to the meetings.' Perhaps it was hope. She didn't know. Perhaps Geoffrey's was one of the longest-running cases they had had family meetings around and therefore they must, unconsciously, get something from the meetings. Was Geoffrey aware of the areas they were exploring and why? It was strange that, with their belief that children mirrored their parents on and on for generations, they had heard so much about Mr Hutton's brother, whose life had ended so dramatically, and so little about both sets of grandparents. Might that be important?

Here Mrs Hutton interrupted to say she 'hadn't got any'.

The Chairman said he was tempted to slap her on the wrist and tell her that this interruption had been her 'individual comment'. This might be petty, but the episode was probably significant.

Mrs Jenkins supposed she might be thought to be getting off the subject of Geoffrey as a baby, but she didn't think she was, because the generational thing *was* so important. She would be curious to know about Mr and Mrs Hutton's parents.

Mrs Hutton said she had worried about Sean and his reading ability. They had had a terrible fight with the school, and it was only after a friend who taught backward children had tested Sean that they realised he wasn't hopeless and managed to get something done for him. Though she felt that Geoffrey was far ahead of Sean, in many ways he had never used the abilities he had but had thrown them away.

TPA said he thought he had made a discovery. At long last Mr Hutton's query 'What are we doing here?' had registered with him.

One of the reasons they kept on coming to the meetings might be that they were so keen to know what was going to happen. Some people – for instance previous professionals, like probation officers – had had an idea of what should or could happen, and when it didn't they were fed up. They had never discovered the excitement of not knowing what was going to happen, waiting to see, and then of its 'happening' – or, for that matter, 'not happening'. He couldn't help thinking that that was a 'primary Hutton theme'. The excitement of not knowing what was going to happen required a certain respect for one's own ignorance.

Mrs Hutton's interruptions were interesting, he thought: it was as though she wouldn't accept that interruptions shouldn't happen. One of the things you should be able to rely on in this life was that at these funny meetings interruptions during 'individual comments' didn't happen. But if it was a Hutton meeting, anyone making that assumption would be wrong. It was as though Mrs Hutton insisted that, whatever happened, you shouldn't be allowed to know what was going to happen even in something as strict as the meetings. He thought Geoffrey was the original what-will-he-do-next? boy. Good Lord, who would have thought that a male would put on girls' clothes! It just didn't happen. If it wasn't for the papers and television, most people would be immensely surprised to think of somebody of one sex dressing up as somebody of another sex. If artificial communications weren't so prevalent, it would be something so surprising that you would never believe it. The idea of the children was important here, in so far as most parents, rightly or wrongly, had a notion of milestones – what was liable to happen, at what time would they start to walk, talk, read, etc. For some reason Mrs Hutton hadn't had enough yardsticks in her head to give her an idea of the order and timing of events. It could, of course, have been due to her own upbringing, or she may have been so keen to find out 'what would happen' that the children obliged her. 'Never a dull moment' was the expression.

The free discussion was long and complicated. There was a lot of talk about Mr Hutton's family – his father who had been gassed in the First War, who had lost his own father at an inopportune time, who had used an insurance policy to cover the death expenses, and who didn't himself have a pension when he died. They spoke again of 17-year-old Kevin losing his prefectship at school and simultaneously losing his girlfriend, and as far as the clerk could gather they talked about authority figures.

Then they reverted to the topic of Mrs Hutton's interruptions. Mrs

Hutton agreed that she would probably continue to interrupt despite TPA's exhausted efforts to prevent her. The past repeated itself in the present and, sadly, might do so in the future.

Having spoken of Mr Hutton's forebears, they tried to balance this with some discussion of Mrs Hutton's parents and how she had lived with her grandmother until she was 5 when she found her dead. After that she had been brought up by nuns, who used to warn children abandoned by their parents to be wary if they made contact in the future since their motives would probably be entirely selfish. (The children would be old enough to earn money.)

TPA wondered whether what Mrs Hutton unconsciously believed was that her mother hadn't wished to interfere but had always wanted to know what was happening to her daughter, without affording herself the pleasure of actually finding out – unlike what they all did: look forward almost with pleasure to finding out what would happen at the next family meeting. It was sad to think that Mrs Hutton's mother might have been misunderstood all these years.

Had Mrs Hutton perhaps identified with that idea of her mother? At one point a comparison was made between the Chairman, who, for him, had become rather easygoing in the meetings, and Mr Hutton, who described himself similarly in relation to his family.

At the end of the meeting somebody asked about Geoffrey, and TPA predicted without explanation that, in theory at least, 'he should be all right for the moment'.

Mr Hutton confirmed that that was indeed the case and said he seemed much more of a person. He then spoiled the good news and mock-dismayed TPA by saying that Geoffrey was actually thinking of getting married.

*

Faced with a seemingly impossible problem I find I become childish and start wanting somebody to perform a miracle, or at least a spot of magic. It *cannot* be totally impossible, I argue. Not if God is good. There must be an answer, and I want it *now*. I don't think I am alone in this, but I am amazed at the patience of the Huttons, who suffered years of anxiety and retained their sanity and family unity. I have found it one of life's hardest lessons that there are few simple answers and one must endure confusion day after day. How wonderful it would be if one could seize hold of the wrong-headed and shake some sense into them. By now I should have got over this infantile yearning, since even in the god-like position of novelist it frequently happens that one's imaginary characters decline to conform to the plan one has made for them but develop in quite unexpected directions. This is, I suppose, because on some level one's imagination and desires are at odds with an acquired, if unrecognised, knowledge of human nature, and because what might be grandly termed one's artistic integrity refuses to allow one to 'lie'. I have intended heroines to represent womanhood at its finest and they have turned out the most frightful bitches. I have tried to pillory the type of person I do not care for and they have proved to have hearts of gold. This is irritating enough in fiction but not of any great importance. What is really annoying is the bewilderment engendered at the sight of somebody real who without apparent cause breaks all the rules – not only of society, but of natural expectation.

I think TPA still finds my attitude very stupid. I should know better by now. He is like an old gamekeeper, watchful and aware, cognisant of the wily ways of the game, while I, like most people, am an inexperienced, over-enthusiastic hunter charging and barging through the thickets and coverts without a hope in hell of bagging anything. The quiet patience of the professional is impressive. Perhaps a necessary quality in a novelist is a certain naiveté, and no one with a truly clear vision of the complexities of human nature would attempt to make sense of them – unless he were Dostoievsky.

TPA says that the Huttons come to the meetings apparently hoping for something magical to happen but really 'just to see what's *going* to happen'. This theme, he says puzzlingly, is epitomised merely by their coming, and Geoffrey (the what's-he-going-to-do-next? boy) is its personification. Bombshells are not surprising if you expect them. In fact they are not bombshells, and Geoffrey's surprises are not surprises. TPA predicts that he should be all right for the moment at least, since intuition is coming through as a primary theme and the family are beginning to get their teeth into it. When the family begin to grapple with the problem themselves there is less need for the personification to push itself forward. He concludes by wondering again whether being brought up in a rigid institution has lessened Mrs Hutton's need for intuition.

29. Somerset House

Venue: Clinic consulting-room   4th June 1982
Present: Dr Pitt-Aikens, Chairman
            Mrs Jenkins, link Social Worker at Orwell House and
               clerk to the meeting
            Mr & Mrs Hutton

Geoffrey and his new probation officer, Mr Fawley, were not present because they were in the Lake District. Both had been interested in coming, but the date of the meeting had been changed and now clashed with their trip.

The Chairman asked what they wanted to talk about and Mrs Hutton said she would leave it up to her husband, but he said he didn't know. TPA, against his present easygoing nature, became dictatorial and decreed that the topic for discussion should be 'anything that those present felt was relevant or important', though he supposed there was no actual ban on things felt to be irrelevant or unimportant.

Mr Hutton said that coming down the Kingston by-pass he had been thinking of the meetings, as he usually did, and had come to the conclusion that they were a habit now. It was as though you went to Weymouth on a fine weekend and down to the clinic on a Friday – as though it was a sort of outing. Listening to the last part of the minutes of the previous meeting, it had occurred to him that while he had liked his father very much, he had been rather strict, so that the father he liked wasn't always to the fore. As a result, he had gone completely the other way himself with his own family and in the Scout group had been criticised for being too easygoing. Geoffrey had left the hostel and moved into a flat. He had been to see them with his probation officer a couple of weeks ago and kept in touch by phone. All seemed to be going well.

Mrs Jenkins said she couldn't help feeling that Mr Hutton was absolutely right. She too thought the meetings had become a habit – a nice one, as it happened, but she wondered if there would be more effect now if they actually stopped the habit. She thought they all took it for granted that there would be another Hutton meeting, and all looked forward to it, but there should be more to it than that. She felt that they had gone back to the old regime and the usual topic, and she had found it a bit more hopeful when they had put their minds to it and decided on a specific focus for the meeting. She felt that, sadly perhaps, the meetings ought to stop, whether she actually wanted them to or not. Geoffrey hardly seemed to be part of the meetings any more. She remembered that Mr Hutton had said that Geoffrey had a girlfriend and was thinking of marriage, and she wondered whether Geoffrey still had her, bearing in mind the effect on his uncle when he lost his.

Would Geoffrey experience such a rejection in the same way? She also wondered whether he saw the minutes of the meetings and what he would think if he read his father's comment that they had become a habit. (A copy of the minutes was always sent to Mr and Mrs Hutton once typed.)

Mrs Hutton said she had nothing to say at this stage. She preferred to leave it to TPA.

TPA said he had got into the habit of expecting the unexpected from Mrs Hutton. When she had spoken just then, he had first thought 'Here we go again, Mrs Hutton interrupting', but she hadn't been interrupting – it was actually her turn to speak. She had fitted in with the format of the meeting. Mr Hutton had used the word habit which, of course, might mean clothes. One expected men to wear men's clothes and women to wear women's clothes, while one expected to find transvestites wearing unexpected clothes. To find a so-called transvestite wearing the clothes of his own sex was unexpected. In the same way he had come to expect Mrs Hutton to interrupt rather than speak within the format of the meetings. He didn't know whether they should stop the meetings or not, but if they did they should arrange a date a long time ahead, perhaps some time next year, so that it wouldn't be a shock – perhaps after the probation order had expired. Flicking through the minutes of the previous meeting, he had come across Mr Hutton's word 'bombshell', which meant something disastrous and unexpected. The whole theme of looking forward to what was going to happen was still very much alive, showing itself in mild ways, such as Mrs Hutton behaving usually instead of unusually. The family, of course, had experienced some very severe unexpected things, so there was still some work to be done on that. He was pleased to hear that Geoffrey was all right, and wanted to know about the other children. Were any of them behaving in unexpected ways? Had they been somehow or other caught up in this? He would have liked to hear something more about Mrs Hutton's mother. Had Mrs Hutton done any actual investigation? Had she been to Somerset House? Of course she hadn't. By that he meant he hadn't expected her to. He had expected her not to, and would like her to surprise them next time by announcing that she had, and that she had discovered whether her mother was alive or dead. The theme of 'I wonder what's happening to my daughter' was crucial and it was time the ghost was laid, or at least put back where it belonged, instead of dogging the rest of them. Mrs Jenkins, he thought, was taking a bit of a chance thinking about stopping the meetings. The time would come when they would have to take a chance on what might happen. That might be quite frightening. People might feel that they had to make something unexpected happen and, in some sort of artificial, almost contrived way, get rid of all the anxiety of not knowing. He would much rather make the themes go back where they belonged. He repeated that he thought the Huttons should at least find out whether Mrs Hutton's mother was alive or dead.

In the free discussion Mr Hutton said that three of his children were doing well but Sean was out of work and was 'sitting waiting for something to happen'.

They wondered if Sean had indeed taken on the 'Hutton curse', and whether Geoffrey was now free of it. Apparently he was still much more human. They felt that Sean should be invited to a meeting, or at least be given the opportunity of reading the minutes.

Mr Hutton had stopped worrying about Geoffrey, and Mrs Hutton reminded them what it had been like in the family, particularly regarding the children, when Geoffrey had been close to them during the summer.

TPA made a slip of the tongue, referring to Sean as 'Geoffrey', 'proving' to everyone's mocking satisfaction that perhaps Sean had unconsciously become the old Geoffrey.

Mr Hutton said that although it was difficult for him to feel affection for Geoffrey after all that had gone on, he still cared about him and his welfare. In the past Geoffrey 'provided a focal point for worry, particularly at times when there was very little to worry about in a real sense'.

Beginning a new sentence, he said 'Sean. Wrong – Geoffrey' and threw up his hands.

TPA asked him what he meant by that gesture, and he answered with the expression 'blow-up'.

They agreed that it had been perhaps in a time of relative calm, when things were just ticking along, that Kevin had literally blown himself up. They talked about the difficulty of deciding whether to end the meetings. The conventional thing would be to wait until everything was ticking along nicely and then stop them. That, of course, would be the very time when, Hutton-wise, things would be liable to blow up. No wonder they were frightened of stopping when things were OK. This implied that the Hutton meetings could continue for ever. They agreed to have another one, Mrs Hutton saying she wanted them, Mrs Jenkins that she did too but didn't think they should continue. Mr Hutton said he didn't mind, and TPA said he felt that for some reason they should have more – maybe until after the probation order expired, or all the children had safely reached their eighteenth birthday.

*

I am rather overwhelmed at the temerity of my position. TPA has been working in this field for years and years, whereas I am a recent convert to his way of thinking and unconfident of my ability to interpret it clearly and correctly. I must be careful. Sometimes I have grown seriously irritated with TPA, whose thought processes, when clothed in the inadequacy of language, can seem remote. Attempting to be accurate and not to miss anything, he knits himself, as it were, into a thicket where I cannot follow him. The danger is, to use another metaphor, that of throwing out Agamemnon with the bathwater. A nice clean bathroom is a delight to the eye but offers no evidence of crime to the upholders of the law, nor of passion to the artist. It is no good making the message simple if in the process the message is excluded.

It was round about the time of this meeting that I met several families with a delinquent member as we looked for a suitable subject for a book. I did not greatly care for most of them. Some of the parents had a long-suffering why-should-this-happen-to-me? air; some seemed simply utterly fed up with their child and clearly wished only to get shot of him; and some had so obviously provided fertile soil for delinquency to flourish that they were of no interest. I was briefly tempted by a family comprising an extraordinary mother with the build and immobility of a heathen idol, a girl of uncompromisingly half-witted appearance (she's 'glaikit', explained TPA, a Scotchman, kindly) and a tiny incoherent and disgruntled father. Mother and daughter sat side by side, staring straight ahead and conversing in asides through the corners of their mouths. The girl was manifestly a victim on her way to be murdered, and it was freely admitted by those responsible for her that they watched her like hawks because if harm came to her they, the social services, would get the blame. I have said that I would not be unkind about people, but these were not likable and I felt I could learn very little from them. I know God loves them, but I could not.

To return to meeting 29 and the Huttons, whom I am shortly to meet, I was struck by the coincidence of TPA's 'present easygoing nature' and Mr Hutton being criticised for 'being too easygoing'. It is not very interesting, but faintly odd. TPA says that now Sean, as Geoffrey had been, was 'possessed' by 'waiting for something to happen'.

30. Scaffolding poles

Venue: Clinic consulting-room   10th September 1982
Present: Dr Pitt-Aikens, Chairman
           Mrs Jenkins, link Social Worker at Orwell House and
               clerk to the meeting
           Mr & Mrs Hutton

The meeting started four minutes late because TPA had to go and
dig the notes out of the filing cabinet. When he came back, Mr and
Mrs Hutton and Mrs Jenkins were talking about police stations and
he was a bit cross that the meeting seemed to have started without
him. Mrs Jenkins was angry because she had 'nearly broken her
neck to get there on time'.

Geoffrey had been invited, and had meant to come, but was
extremely unlikely to be present, as he was in trouble with the police
again. The new female probation officer, whose name was not
known, had been invited by Mr and Mrs Hutton through Geoffrey
but had not replied. Mr Hutton said the other children had a
semi-open invitation. Mrs Hutton said they didn't want to come.

During the reading of the previous minutes quite a few corrections
and clarifications were made. They agreed, as usual, to discuss
anything relevant or important, although Mrs Jenkins would have
preferred to concentrate particularly on what was going to happen
once the meetings finished. She said (as she had said before) that as
she was driving along the Kingston by-pass in the pouring rain she
wondered yet again why Mr Hutton was driving along his Kingston
by-pass this morning, and she certainly wondered why she was. She
had forgotten that last time she had spoken about finishing the
meetings and the shock this would cause, but had felt exactly the
same as she drove, thinking that they had got into a habit and
perhaps needed a jolt, which stopping the meetings would provide. At
the moment things didn't seem to be too positive. She had
understood from Mr Hutton before the meeting started that
Geoffrey was again in trouble with the police, and she wondered
what he felt about continuing the meetings. She was also anxious to

know whether Mr and Mrs Hutton ever talked about the meetings, or whether, as Mr Hutton had seemed to imply, they were merely something that happened on occasional Fridays.

Mr Hutton said that, although he had tended to agree with Mrs Jenkins's proposal that they talk about the prospect of the meetings ending, he hadn't gone along with her because he had wanted further time to clear up some points arising from the last meeting. For example, on the question of invitations to the children, 'Well,' he said, 'We don't run our family as a departmental sub-committee or something like that,' so that, while the children knew they could come if they wanted to, they didn't go into the business of formally inviting them. It had also occurred to him while the last minutes were being read that you had to be very careful what you said and how you chose your words, because otherwise a word was liable to be picked up and turned into something it was never intended to be: for instance, the word 'habit'. He could, he observed, do a bit of that sort of thing himself, and he would like to point out that, if you expected the unexpected, it wasn't unexpected, and it was the expected which was unexpected. 'And you can sort that one out,' he added rather sadistically. Then, to bring the meeting up to date on Geoffrey, he said he believed the problem involved the theft of scaffolding poles, and he would be most intrigued to know what could be read into that one. All they knew was that Geoffrey had been released on bail. They had heard nothing from Geoffrey himself. A few days before they heard about the theft the phone rang one evening for Claire and Mr Hutton had 'twitched'. He thought, 'Oh, that's Geoffrey', and was soon proved only too right.

He went on to amplify what he had been saying about his feelings about Geoffrey now. In many senses he resented him, since Geoffrey had had a profound effect on his life, in as much as he had affected his career badly. In 1981 and 1980, when he was worried, he had become sloppy at work and made a serious error, which he was still paying for now. With this constantly to the fore, it was affecting his position in Portsmouth and made it difficult for him to think of Geoffrey in any kind of affectionate way. All the same, Geoffrey had been to stay with them for a few days since the last meeting. He did seem to have changed in many ways, but over the last ten years he had developed, as Mr Hutton had said before, a total lack of comprehension of the difference between mine and thine. Now that he was out of work they had expected that sooner or later he would be had up again for stealing.

Mrs Hutton said it was funny that Ian had 'twitched' when the phone rang. She had got back from work one day to find that somebody had got a letter which looked exactly like the letters you get from one of 'those places', and she had immediately twitched, hardly daring to open it in case it was from Geoffrey. 'Don't ask me why,' she said, 'and this was even before the phone call.' As for Mrs Jenkins asking what they got out of the meetings, she thought Ian got quite a lot out of them, because he might have had a nervous breakdown without an outlet. There had been a time when he was in a frightful state when Geoffrey was going through the worst and she had had a job trying to pull him and the rest of the family through. She didn't think they would have got through without the meetings. It may have seemed that it was quite a laugh to them when they came, but that was a way they had of not putting things over.

TPA sailed in saying he couldn't help feeling that there was something very important to do with intuition being discussed today, focusing particularly on the word 'twitch'. Then there was Mrs Hutton's feeling about the envelope. As she spoke of 'these places' she had pointed at the mantelpiece which held a photograph of the Borstal where Geoffrey had been for a while. He also thought that Mrs Jenkins's inclination to talk about ending the meetings also had to do with intuition, because if the topic for discussion was 'anything relevant or important' then of course that could include anything she wanted to talk about, but for some reason which she hadn't, perhaps couldn't, put into words, she had felt they should focus on that particular topic. He had been quite reluctant to overrule her because he had had an intuitive feeling, a twitch, that she was on to something. He had noticed that it wasn't just Mrs Hutton who interrupted. He himself, as Chairman, often interrupted, but he was, as it were, licensed to do so because he was Chairman. Quite often he did it just to make sure that everyone knew what they were talking about. Mr Hutton had said the family wasn't run like a sub-committee, but the meetings were.

They went cautiously through the minutes, correcting them meticulously. Obviously it was a mistake when Sean was referred to as 'she'; yet they faithfully spelled it out – not 'she' but 'he'. They could ask themselves, 'How daft can you get?' On the one hand they relied on intuition, twitching, and on the other were determined not to; not even trusting people to realise that the word 'she' in reference to Sean should read 'he'. They had to spell it out to all these terribly dumb people who might one day read the minutes. It could be connected with the transvestism. It was necessary to realise that a man dressed as a woman was a man none the less. A man 'in drag' didn't go round announcing 'I'm a man dressed as a woman'; it was just somehow understood that he was a man, and no one was fooled by the fact that he had women's clothes on.

TPA mused aloud in a convoluted fashion as to whether there were two strands here – one that Mrs Hutton's mother didn't know what was going on in her daughter's life and might even be dead, the other that there might be a strong unconscious feeling that by some kind of telepathy she did know. In fact it could apply to both of them. Then Mr Hutton couldn't have known that his brother was going to commit suicide, but on another level he might well have had a presentiment, a 'twitch', to which he paid no heed. In a way it would be comforting to imagine that the world ran only on common sense and the 'twitching' meant nothing, since Mr Hutton would then be blameless. If he had picked up something in the atmosphere, his brother's life might have been saved, and it was preferable after the event to believe that there had been no evidence at all. It was Geoffrey who kept ramming it down their throats that 'twitching' was a fact of life and very necessary. They all remembered how Geoffrey's life had been saved when his mother had a feeling that something was wrong and had gone upstairs and found her baby with his head bleeding profusely. TPA said he couldn't help feeling that this was connected with what had happened in Mr Hutton's job two years before. He had told them nothing about it at the time.

Mr Hutton here interrupted, annoying TPA, to say that he had known nothing about it at the time.

TPA replied that all he was getting at was that whatever had happened had somehow affected his career and he must, somehow or other, have had a suspicion at the back of his mind. Because nothing had been said straightforwardly he had gone blithely on as though nothing had happened. (I do not understand what I have written next. Clerk.)

In the free discussion Mr Hutton told them what had happened in his job. He had made an error in the record of the importation of somebody's car, and his behaviour had been investigated. This he heard about much later. The question was whether or not he had colluded with the owner of the car, who should have paid £200 duty. He quoted the case of a colleague who had been prosecuted for allowing two lighters through without duty. He himself would have been prosecuted if the woman, on being chased up, hadn't paid. Mr Hutton said that the job which he had once regarded as a vocation was now simply an occupation. It was more regimented and bureaucratic than in the days when one was allowed more discretion.

They then heard that Geoffrey's latest offence had been made known to the Huttons by his girlfriend, who had hoped he would contact them himself directly. According to Mr Hutton, that would have been out of character. The reason Geoffrey wasn't at the meeting was that he couldn't face them, not that he was in custody. Mr Hutton talked about how difficult it was to love Geoffrey, although he was still concerned and had been upset when Geoffrey was turned down for the merchant navy. When he had heard this he had thrown a glass, and then a jar of muddy water, which happened to be to hand, against his boss's office door. When he confessed this to his boss, his boss had promptly cried on his shoulder. Mr Hutton then told them a bit about his drinking, which, he claimed, made him maudlin – a condition which he cured by having a few more drinks.

Throughout all this Mrs Hutton seemed to be thinking and made the odd remark about breakdowns.

Mr Hutton said he might be becoming an alcoholic but wasn't going to break down.

Mrs Jenkins wondered whether the reason why the meeting had brought to light more information about feelings than was usual might be the shock element contained in the suggestion that the meetings should cease. She then asked if Geoffrey was still dressing up in women's clothes.

Mrs Hutton said she didn't know.

*

This begins ominously with talk of police stations. Yet another probation officer is on the scene. The turnover is great. It is as though a procession of people were to take up a book, read a passage where it falls open and then put it down again. They will, none of them, have a clear or accurate picture of the story line, especially if they don't meet and talk to the previous readers. Nor will they get to know the characters.

A point which arises again and again is the 'inhumanness' of delinquents: the emptiness, the quality, or lack of qualities, which causes them to be described as 'animals' or 'things'. TPA holds that this is because they *are* empty: merely living vessels, containers for old unacknowledged guilts and sorrows. Or, he says, they can be seen as flags, blowing in the wind – a sign that all is not well with those around them, a cry to 'watch this space'. They have been invaded by alien themes, are possessed and out of control. The police do not take this view.

Both the Huttons have been twitching again. Mrs Hutton had

been able to save baby Geoffrey's life because she had a 'feeling', and TPA again invites me to compare Great Uncle Michael Claud from Mr Hutton's family history who was wounded in the night in 1915 and crawled parallel to the lines until he died from lack of blood. Certainly his 'intuitive feelings' were not working for him; and certainly, as I have just discovered, because I had to think about it in order to write about it, if you really picture this scene it *is* almost unbearably sad.

At one point TPA entirely baffled both the clerk and me. When I first read the minutes of the meeting, I wrote: 'TPA then made an observation so abstruse that I am not even going to attempt to make sense of it.' He says I am mean to say 'abstruse', because I promised not to be unkind about people and he is people too. This is all very well, I mutter, but could he then please explain what he meant? What he meant was that Mr Hutton must have had a suspicion in the back of his mind about his employers having feelings about him, in the same way that it wasn't necessary pedantically to invite the children to the meeting or wait for a pedantic reply to be made. Parents and children just *knew* what the score was. I still find that fairly abstruse. He must have been annoyed with me, because he said I was as bad as Mrs Jenkins with her question about whether Geoffrey was still dressing up in women's clothes: the 1915 secret about Mr Hutton's poor great-uncle was far more poignant and interesting. This may be true, but I am reminded again of the difficulties of co-authorship. I again feel that it is rather like trying to drive a car from the passenger seat.

Mrs Hutton reveals that she is pleased with the meetings because they have helped her husband, which is both reassuring and gratifying. TPA wonders whether Mr Hutton's falling down on his job was connected with his losing his intuition.

31. Don't be rash

Venue: Clinic consulting-room   5th November 1982
Present: Dr Pitt-Aikens, Chairman
           Mrs Jenkins, link Social Worker at Orwell House and
              clerk to the meeting
           Mr & Mrs Hutton

Claire was invited to this meeting, and almost came; but then she decided that the proceedings there were 'too zany'. Mr Hutton said Geoffrey had said he would like to come but couldn't afford it – he didn't know whether or not that was the truth.

The beginning of the meeting was taken up with correcting the minutes of the last which contained numerous mistakes; for instance 'vocation' had been rendered '*vacation*', which caused considerable mirth, as did the remark about Mrs Hutton's 'thinking' which had occurred towards the end. They also left an equal number of mistakes uncorrected. There followed the usual discussion about what they should talk about.

Mr Hutton said they would be seeing Geoffrey after the meeting. The charges against him, to do with the scaffolding poles, had been dropped owing to lack of evidence. Sean had got a job and was also doing something about his eyes, and Louis was now at work in a training scheme in a shop. Still, everything wasn't rosy with the family. As soon as one thing got half-sorted something else popped up. At the moment the problem was poor old Margaret who had a skin complaint. 'Yes,' he continued, 'why do we come to these meetings?' They did discuss them in between times and Claire always read the minutes, finding them quite entertaining. He felt the reason the children didn't want to come was that they thought they ought to be able to say something, but couldn't, and would be embarrassed just sitting in their chairs kicking their heels. So they solved that problem by not coming at all.

Mrs Jenkins said she still wasn't clear in her mind who these meetings were for. She had thought they were for Geoffrey, and then that they could be for all the family. It was a pity that the children didn't come, because it might help Mr and Mrs Hutton if the children had some sort of insight into what was going on. She herself found these particular family meetings entertaining, probably because of the company of Mr and Mrs Hutton; but beneath that there was a deep, more serious element, and she thought it was a shame that the children wouldn't come because they felt they would have to speak, since it was possible to get a lot from a meeting just by being part of it. She was still anxious to know whether Geoffrey was dressing up in women's clothes and thought it was a pity he wasn't there. He was probably eligible for a travel warrant. Should the meetings continue minus Geoffrey?

Mrs Hutton said something which, as it was written, made no sense, but means, I think, that they were taking Geoffrey's girlfriend and a little baby back with them as well. The children kept telling her she was black. She felt there was something more to the scaffolding business with Geoffrey because it seemed so silly, and she wondered what exactly he was in trouble for. As for dressing up – she didn't know, because they hadn't had much contact with him at all. She said she reckoned Margaret's skin disease was due to some form of nerves; her skin was very bad, the rash all over her arms and legs. She had started to get it before the summer holidays; on holiday it had cleared up quite a bit, but it came back again worse than ever just afterwards. Margaret had had some pressure at work and also had a boyfriend who was pressing her 'to get married and engaged'. She wanted to be rid of him but found it difficult to tell him to clear off without hurting his feelings. She seemed to be very sensitive.

TPA observed that when they were reading the minutes of the last meeting they had corrected about ten mistakes and left about another ten uncorrected. All the mistakes in the early minutes had been corrected, either because they wanted to make things absolutely right, or because the corrections were necessary in order to avoid gross misunderstanding. As the minutes went on, their standards had declined, including his own, and they had corrected less, relying on people's good sense to understand what was meant. There was no reason to suppose, however, that people's sensitivity or intuition was any better at the end than at the beginning, but they had behaved as if it were so. In other words, it was as though, growing tired of making corrections, they had been hoping more and more that whoever read the minutes would be able to grow increasingly sensitive or intuitive, when actually they might be growing more and more exhausted and confused.

So there was something about intuition there, said TPA. Two examples had come up in this meeting. It was a pity that Margaret's boyfriend wasn't sufficiently intuitive to know that Margaret wanted nothing more to do with him, and didn't just take the hint and go. He wouldn't do that. He seemed, said TPA delicately, to have left it to Margaret to use an axe on him and tell him to go and get lost. It was as though he had ignored his own sensitivity and Margaret had had to become the one with the awkward sensitivity. Had he used his own sensitivity, even if it became awkward he would have concluded: 'This girl doesn't want me. Gosh, what a horrible thought, I'm quite intuitive; so I'm sure I'm correct', and gone away. Margaret somehow didn't let him do that. If she had said she didn't want him, the poor chap would at least have thought, 'Well, my sensitivity was all right', and gone. But somehow it was as though she had stolen, or damaged, his sensitivity.

In the second case there were times when he didn't think sensitivity was enough. For instance, Mrs Hutton had told them something which hadn't been said before – that Geoffrey's girlfriend would be visiting or going back with them with a little baby. 'Hang on,' implored TPA. (Mrs Hutton kept interrupting him here to try and put him right.) He said he really would prefer to rely on his sensitivity, or the lack of it, rather than be filled in – at least for the moment. Mrs Hutton hadn't made it clear whose baby this was. One could read into it that it was Geoffrey's baby, or that it was not Geoffrey's baby. Also, one could wonder whether it was the girlfriend or the baby who was black. If the baby was black, that might imply that the girlfriend was black as well, etc., etc. The story Mrs Hutton had told needed a few more explanatory notes, because intuition on its own wouldn't be sufficient to solve that puzzle, although in other situations intuition was sufficient. He had thought of Geoffrey the other day when he heard of a little boy aged two or three who had got out of the house at two in the morning and gone off and done the most amazing things. It sounded very like what they had heard of Geoffrey. How did young children manage to perform these feats? Could it be what was called intuition? Perhaps in these cases intuition was somehow being denied and split off by the parents and was 'poured' instead into the child, who then possessed all the intuition in the family and that was perhaps how these children managed to take clocks apart, and put them together again.

TPA went on to justify the meetings, saying that he couldn't think of any other situation sufficiently 'zany' to enable people to study these processes carefully. Where else would you have any chance of discussing the problem of when it was necessary to rely on intuition and when further objective clarification was needed? The police, he was sure, 'knew' that Geoffrey stole the poles – but they had no hard evidence. It was important that the Hutton family should have the chance of studying these kinds of issue. There were some difficulties about the past – for instance, as they had said last time, if you knew intuitively that your brother was going to kill himself you had a problem in owning that intuition because, if you failed to act on it, in a sense you had murdered your own brother, whereas if you had none you were blameless of murder. It was extremely important to know whether or not Mr Hutton was a murderer in his own unconscious mind, because that made the acceptability of intuition in the family very relevant. It would be difficult for the children to allow themselves to be effectively intuitive since that might imply that their father should have used his own intuition to save his brother. There was probably something similar in connection with Mrs Hutton and her mother. As to the decision about stopping the meetings – perhaps all they could do was toss a coin; or there might come a day when they would all know intuitively that they had come to the end of the line. If they proved to be correct and everything in the garden remained rosy, Mr Hutton might feel very bad, wondering why he hadn't used his intuition all those years before. If, on the other hand, they made a mess of it he could say: 'There you are, intuition is no good. I'm not to blame.'

In the free discussion Mrs Jenkins and Mr Hutton attempted to put the emphasis on the question of whether or not to continue the meetings and what was the value of them, but despite this they found themselves back concentrating on intuition.

For the first time Mr Hutton gave an account of how he had heard a bang when his brother had gone upstairs. It was the day after he had heard a garbled version of Kevin's difficulties at school. He had assumed that his brother had gone upstairs to get ready to MC the Youth Club Valentine Dance that evening and it was only the next day during an electricity strike that he thought perhaps he had gone off, not being able to face the music. It was on the Monday that he became possessed of the feeling that his brother was in the loft, though he thought he was alive. He could see nothing in the loft at first because of the power cut but went to get his cycle torch, still not wondering why his brother was saying nothing up in the loft in the dark. Then by the light of the torch he caught a glimpse of his coat and went for his mother, having now deduced quite clearly what had happened. There seemed at that time to be no intuitive deduction available to Mr Hutton. He told them that, by contrast, his grandmother had once appeared in a black dress instead of her usual one, not knowing why but feeling it appropriate for some reason or other. That day a telegram had arrived announcing that her husband , aged 48, had died. Mr Hutton seemed keen to stress that his twitches were always retrospective, not prospective.

They all agreed that on balance they wanted another meeting, though Mrs Jenkins was somewhat reticent.

*

My notes read: 'Me – her/black. Who?' I was inclined to change the line reading 'The children kept telling her she was black', which sounds as though Mrs Hutton had suddenly changed colour, so that it would make sense, but it is a neat example of the 'zaniness', the confusion, that is sometimes inherent in the meetings, echoing the family confusion.

This meeting underlined the fact that intuition, or the lack of it, is a number-one Huttonian theme. It dominates the whole meeting. Mr Hutton's grandmother had donned a black frock before hearing the news of her husband's death. Mr Hutton had not understood that his brother was bent on killing himself. The whole structure of the meetings, with the correction of some mistakes and the leaving of some for people to work out for themselves, relates to intuition.

The theme appears on multiple levels, even in the police who knew perfectly well that Geoffrey had made off with the scaffolding poles but had no hard evidence. Both intuition and suspicion are insufficient without hard evidence, and hard evidence on its own can be misleading. I cannot imagine how Geoffrey concealed his scaffolding poles, but a thought has just occurred to me apropos of evidence. Say Geoffrey was innocent of this crime and someone had planted the poles in his room in order to incriminate him. With his record, the police would have had no hesitation at all in arresting him, not being employed to realise intuitively that this was one misdemeanour of which he was not guilty.

Then there is Margaret and her skin condition coming between the unfortunate boyfriend and his own intuition. I find the whole thing confusing, and it is interesting that the family appear to be beginning to understand and accept the purpose and rationale of the meetings.

On yet another level Geoffrey himself prompts thought. Did he truly have no money to come to the meetings or, as his father intuitively suspected, was he telling lies?

Mr Hutton reveals for the first time that he had heard a bang when his brother went upstairs. I have not asked him about this because it is not my part to do so, nor did TPA follow it up specifically; but I wonder what Mr Hutton made of it at the time –

especially if we remember how he thought his father died? I have myself often ignored frightening signs because I didn't want to know. One stuffs the fingers in the ears, puts the head under the bedclothes, screws the eyes tight shut. If I were writing a novel how would I account for Mr Hutton's inaction? I think I would arrange to have a house nearby in the process of being demolished so that he could tell himself it was merely more falling bricks. I don't think I could convince the reader that he just went on sorting his stamps. I have often thought that novels are rather silly lying things, an attempt to make sense where sense is not. Perhaps this is why from time to time people essay 'experimental' novels. It is difficult to portray the illogical, incoherent ways of human kind without sounding half-witted yourself, so you impose an artificial order on the book and give it a beginning, a middle and an end, when really none of us knows where we began or where we are going. I joined the Hutton story like a child joining a skipping game in full swing and will leave before it is over.

32. The roar of Jenkins' ear

Venue: Clinic consulting-room   11th December 1982
Present: Dr Pitt-Aikens, Chairman and clerk to the meeting
           Mrs Jenkins (joined the meeting for 'individual comments'
               only via the loudspeaker telephone)
           Mr & Mrs Hutton
           Claire

Geoffrey was invited, but Mr Hutton didn't expect him to come. Mrs Jenkins was absent, but it was arranged that she would join part of the meeting on the loudspeaker telephone to make an 'individual comment'.

Mr Hutton said he had a feeling that one of the reasons they were having this meeting so soon after the last one was that the professionals in particular felt they were on the brink of understanding something about murky Huttonian secrets.

TPA thought he could be partly right, although it might also be that as Christmas was on the way they had felt that waiting until afterwards would have been to defer it too long.

This rather lax start to the meeting was cut across by the telephone ringing. It was Mrs Jenkins, who came roaring over the loudspeaker telephone saying, 'Hello, Mr and Mrs Hutton': she was terribly sorry not to be there with them but there were pressures at Orwell House which had to be given prior consideration. It was very difficult being on the phone, she said, because, while they could hear her, she couldn't hear them, and she was feeling very isolated. She hoped she would be at the next meeting. She had been giving it a lot of thought and wondered if they could perhaps set themselves some tasks in between meetings, thinking about what to discuss, what areas were giving particular concern and certainly about Geoffrey. She would really like to know more about what he was getting up to and wondered whether there was any way they could communicate between meetings – perhaps by telephone? – so that meetings weren't used only for information gathering. She almost felt that they should be setting themselves targets and aims because, while the meetings might he helpful, perhaps they could be made more worthwhile. She repeated that she hoped she could be there next time because she really didn't like missing them. She wondered again what Geoffrey was doing and what his, or perhaps Her Majesty's, plans were. She finished her 'individual comment' at this point and said goodbye.

Mr Hutton said he could give an answer to Mrs Jenkins's question, although it would be a long time before she heard it. Geoffrey was coming down on the following Friday to spend Christmas with them, by himself this time. He could also now answer a question of Anne's which had come up in the last minutes. When they last saw Geoffrey he had taken them up to his bed-sit, where they spent an hour or so with him. At one point Geoffrey had shown his father an aerial. 'Now,' said Mr Hutton, 'he is very keen on CB radio – this is one of the consolations he had in life, I believe. He was quite proud of this aerial, which is a very large, almost Alexandra-Palace-size thing, and he said to me, "You know what that's made from, don't you? Scaffolding poles." '

Mr Hutton added that Geoffrey seemed to be getting on well with his girl. 'A very nice girl and the little boy is a very nice little kiddy, about two and a half.' Geoffrey was sort of half-way between an uncle and a stepfather to him and got on very well with the boy although, added Mr Hutton, he had the distinct impression that Geoffrey hadn't yet really started to grow up. The business of the CB radio was an illustration of Geoffrey's basic loneliness, which Mr Hutton had always considered one of his problems. When he had been going through all the trouble in his teens he had never really had friends unless he bought them in one way or another. He hadn't made friends, he had got them in other ways, and in order to do that he had had to do certain things, many of which got him into trouble. As regards the rest of the family, said Mr Hutton cheerfully, there were no problems. Margaret was getting over her trouble; so, of course, she had an appointment with a specialist on Monday, which, he remarked, was just about par for the course: 'When it's almost cleared up she sees someone about it.' He himself was on one of the crests of the waves of his life at the moment although Portsmouth had virtually closed down. He was working in Dover at present and actually enjoying it. So he was going through a good patch.

Claire said she doubted if she had anything to say.

Mrs Hutton said she had been talking to Geoffrey's girlfriend, who said that sometimes he was absolutely lovely and the next moment right up in the air, and she didn't know how to cope with him: exactly the same problem as they had had. They would be going through a nice period and then he would be off the rails. She had found it quite interesting talking to the girl and finding out how

Geoffrey was and if he was changing at all. She concluded that although he had changed in many ways his behaviour was still a bit erratic.

TPA opened his mouth to speak – and Mrs Hutton said she wasn't sure whether she'd explained that all right or not.

TPA started again going on (and on and on) to say that he thought it worth returning to the subject of intuition versus factual evidence. Mrs Jenkins had been talking about collecting information. There were two sorts. One sort was gained by being told things and the other without being told. Whether or not it was to do with intuition, the scaffolding poles were very interesting. He was sure that Geoffrey hadn't said 'These, Dad – these scaffolding poles – are the scaffolding poles I stole. You may remember the case, I got off through "lack of evidence." I have made my aerial out of them.' In TPA's view Mr Hutton had used a bit of factual information (scaffolding poles had been mentioned at the last meeting) and also his intuition about his own son: a bit of information and a bit of feel.

(The clerk, TPA, cannot follow his own notes on what he himself said at this point. It looked like something that had been translated from Urdu into Ancient English.)

TPA wasn't at all surprised that Margaret's skin was better. The improvement, he was sure, related to what they had been talking about last time. She had caught an overdose of the intuition which her boyfriend had denied in himself, much as her father had denied his sensitivity when the fulminate detonator went off. Mr Hutton had used the expression 'murky secrets'. TPA supposed that murky secrets were secrets that you just felt. If it was a secret, by definition nobody was going to tell you about it, and if it was a murky secret it would have a layer of murk around it, so you wouldn't even know there was a secret. All was hidden. This thing called intuition, however, could let you know there was a secret, but there were those people who seemed to have no intuition some or all of the time. That appeared to be the case in and around the Hutton family. As to plain, clear information, he didn't know how many times he had asked Mrs Hutton to speak to the front plainly and clearly, and yet she still seemed to hope that the clerk would somehow pick up what she was saying even if she spoke quietly, sideways or into her lap. He hoped the clerk would always manage but thought she was relying on the clerk to be more able than he could be and was thereby taking a chance. The clerk wasn't a creature with perfect intuition; he wouldn't necessarily know what she was saying by her expression as her husband or daughter might. It was interesting that they might here have a combination of a fear of admitting to intuition because it hadn't been used to save Kevin and an overestimate of intuition – Mrs Hutton somehow having the idea that the clerk was bung full of it.

In the free discussion it was decided that TPA wanted another meeting but didn't know for sure whether they should have one. Mrs Hutton wanted one and thought they should. Claire felt the same, and Mr Hutton said he would go along with the others. Mrs Jenkins, of course, had already predicted that there would be further meetings and had spoken as though they were a *fait accompli*.

There was then a remark which the clerk's notes attribute to Mrs Hutton, but which doesn't sound at all like her. It went as follows: 'Certainly Mrs Jenkins had used her what we call intuition ... it certainly couldn't be deduction or what was termed "ordinary logical information" – to come up with a definite statement regarding future meetings.'

They talked some more about Kevin, and Mr Hutton reminded them that he had made several semi-attempts at suicide before the successful occasion (if it could be so called), when he had, as it were, got himself into a corner where he couldn't do anything else.

TPA expanded again on how guilty Mr Hutton might feel if intuition felt useful – for instance, in his job – and they spoke a bit more about Geoffrey and the scaffolding poles. He had described them as an aerial; yet father and son had each known what the other was referring to without a word about stealing or the provenance of the poles.

TPA then noticed that although they had agreed to have another meeting it hadn't yet been arranged. It would have been funny, would it not, if they had decided to have another meeting and then found themselves on the way home realising that there wasn't going to be one because of some administrative oversight.

Mrs Hutton said she thought TPA had said something about the room being hot. He hadn't, and she wondered if perhaps she was becoming deaf. TPA asked if anyone in her family was deaf. She said not as far as she knew, but Mr Hutton's grandmother had been deaf, his mother was very deaf and his sister wore a hearing-aid. There was little doubt in anybody's mind that people who were deaf had to rely on intuition and hunches more than people who could hear well. The family cryptically agreed that they thought the clinic was a little deaf.

*

Working with someone else continues to present problems. Chimpanzee TPA was today grooming what we already have of a MS for small errors while I – feeling peculiarly witless – was asking obvious questions and looking for reassurance that what I was doing was correct. It sometimes happens in mid-book that not only one's confidence, but all awareness of what one is supposed to be doing, abruptly disappears. It matters less if one is writing alone, since the sense of inadequacy need not extend into the guilt caused by the feeling that one has let another person down (oops – sorry again, partner). TPA grew irritated as I mourned that I had lost the drift of what I was saying. Writing is a solitary business. I think I am afraid of the secrets. I feel as though I am handling fragile porcelain and all my fingers have turned to thumbs. I think I should hate to be an analyst, as I should hate to be a surgeon. I don't want to look closely at anyone's psyche, any more than I want to peer at his insides. TPA has just told me of a particularly horrible incident among a group of delinquent girls and I don't think I want to know anything more about human beings at all. I have lost courage, and I wish I worked in a flower shop. I must think on those things that are lovely and of good report. The darker recesses of the human mind are full of rats and horrors. M.K. Bradley, a pleasantly lucid exponent of Freudian doctrine, writing in 1920, says: 'The worst calamities, the most appalling catastrophes, the most threatening dangers are faced with a calm and even mind by the man who has reckoned and come to terms with the enemies in his own unconscious.' She cites Joan of Arc and Thomas More as two ideal exemplars of the un-neurotic personality, and I am so delighted with this unfashionable appraisal that I feel cheered, although still uncomfortably aware that one needs to be extremely well in oneself to look closely at reality for any length of time.

Mrs Jenkins howling into the void with no immediate feedback reminds me of the lonely author, and I find it strangely coincidental to turn the page of the MS and discover that Mr Hutton is talking of Geoffrey's 'basic loneliness', to assuage which he had assembled his CB radio out of those scaffolding poles. Communication is remarkably difficult. I like listening to the wireless but hate talking on it. It is weirdly disconcerting to address a lot of people who are in no position to respond to you. When you have written a book you must wait for some time for reactions, and I remember uneasily those occasions when I have jumped up and down on some other person's book wishing only that it was his head. Perhaps all communication, apart from direct speech – person to person – is unnatural and frustrating. Now I am also cheered by the Huttons, their warmth and intelligence and humour, and I am glad that Margaret's skin – for whatever reason – is better. I find it odd yet again, having exercised myself about communication, to discover that the talk of deafness comes at the end of this meeting, and also that Mr Hutton had until now claimed to be deaf to the bang.

33. The meeting commits suicide

Venue: Clinic consulting-room   25th February 1983
Present: Dr Pitt-Aikens, Chairman and clerk to the meeting
         Mrs Jenkins, link Social Worker at Orwell House
         Mr & Mrs Hutton

Claire was invited, got as far as the clinic and then decided she
didn't want to go to the meeting on the grounds that the family and
TPA were mad. Mr Hutton said Geoffrey had been invited but they
hadn't been able to tell him of the changed date of the meeting since
they didn't know his new address.

At this point Mrs Jenkins and Mrs Hutton looked askance at each
other since they both knew full well that Geoffrey did know of the
changed time. Mrs Jenkins had telephoned Mr and Mrs Hutton and
got hold of Geoffrey, who had happened to be on the other end of the
phone, and had asked him to pass the message on.

Mr Hutton kindly agreed to read the account of the last meeting.

TPA then suggested that they talk about 'anything relevant or
important'.

Mr Hutton said, 'Why not, we always do', earning himself a
knowing look from Mrs Jenkins – presumably because what he had
said was totally untrue.

Mrs Jenkins said she had realised that, although one dreamed up
very good topics at times, they were usually squashed by the
Chairman, so now she was keeping quiet. She began 'individual
comments' by saying she thought they had had a unique experience
that morning. She hadn't been to a family meeting where a family
member had actually taken over the job of reading out the previous
minutes. It was almost as though they had put themselves in his
charge. She was now feeling a bit stupid sitting there, as though they
were three little kids in school and TPA was the schoolmaster, and
went on to explain why. The Huttons had come into the room and
she had thought they were all going to spread themselves around,
but they had all actually ended up sitting there in a tight row, and it
felt a bit crazy. She had also, knowing of the phone call, been
bewildered to hear Mr Hutton say that he couldn't invite Geoffrey to

the meeting. She added that this too was going to sound a bit crazy, but while the minutes were being read she had had a feeling that TPA had been thinking about other things. They had been discussing other Orwell House business before Mr and Mrs Hutton arrived and she wondered whether he was concentrating properly on the meeting. It had occurred to her that they had all perhaps arrived with preconceived ideas of what might happen today; people had come literally from different directions but also from different directions of thought. They all came in, and concentrated on one area for an hour; then they all went off home again. It seemed important to her because she felt they all had different viewpoints about what they thought was happening. She was disappointed not to see Geoffrey, who had told her in that brief phone call that he would be present today, and wondered if they should make greater efforts to get him there. True they often seemed to have got on to some general Huttonian themes, though they had apparently bypassed Geoffrey. Perhaps that was useful too. Perhaps Mr and Mrs Hutton would be able to tell them.

Mrs Hutton said that although she didn't discuss Geoffrey all that much the meetings had been extremely helpful in dealing with the other children. Geoffrey had been very good over Christmas and seemed to be on a very – she couldn't quite think of the word – a very good wave at the moment. He had joined the family and behaved himself.

The clerk noticed that Mrs Hutton was using a lot of hand gestures as she spoke.

Mr Hutton said that, regarding the invitation to Geoffrey, it was pure lapse of memory on his part. As soon as Mrs Jenkins had started explaining he had remembered. It was partly because he felt Geoffrey wouldn't be there anyway: he was very unlikely to go to the meetings unless he was dragged along. Mr Hutton thought he was probably 'sort of making excuses for him' without actually doing so. While going through the minutes he had been struck by the stressing of the word 'intuition'. He suspected that TPA and he probably interpreted the word differently. He took it as the subconscious gathering of facts, storing them and then presenting them to the conscious mind almost in the form of memory, but 'ahead'. He had to use intuition in his job quite a lot; his work would be impossible without it; he had to pick people to search who were likely to be smugglers. They didn't wear labels saying 'I am a smuggler', and you couldn't categorise them at all. You could only go on your feelings, and these feelings were quite obviously based on prior conversations which you didn't actively think about. They were just there in your mind, so that intuition was really the conscious mind being supplied with facts and provided by the subconscious and presented as a theory, an idea. This might explain two factors about Kevin. 'When it came to the actual evening,' said Mr Hutton, 'when I saw him that evening, I couldn't have had any intuition then because I'd got no facts to go on. At that time I didn't know about the previous attempts. That knowledge only came after the event and therefore there was nothing for me to be intuitive about, whereas on the following Monday when I got that feeling that he was up in the loft – that was a matter of my subconscious deducing the fact from all the various bits known to it which weren't present in my conscious mind, and they were presented to me then as a feeling that Kevin was up in the loft – and that's how I see intuition.'

TPA said he couldn't remember Claire being there last time. He couldn't even remember Mr Hutton reading out in the minutes what she had said last time, so his actual memory wasn't available to him in that respect. Luckily, as they had records of the meetings, he could now see plainly in typescript that Mr and Mrs Hutton and Claire were present on the 11th December 1982. There was, he said, certainly something about memory in this case that they needed to look at carefully. Claire for instance, according to the minutes, had said she thought they should have another meeting, had come all the way to the meeting today, and had then said or implied that all who were going were mad – presumably because they were going to it. He doubted whether Claire now remembered that she had been one of the people who wanted the meeting.

Still speaking of memory, TPA said that Mr Hutton had once said that they always talked about those things which were relevant and/or important; yet they had had great debates about that and on one occasion had talked specifically about Geoffrey's babyhood. As he remembered, it was Mrs Jenkins who had been particularly keen to make the focus something more central. Mr Hutton seemed to have forgotten that. TPA saw what Mr Hutton meant about requiring some basic information before you could make use of intuition, but wondered about all Mr Hutton's deaf relations. Did they have any bearing on this? Certainly deaf people had to rely on intuition more than the rest of us, since they couldn't expect the same amount of basic hard verbal information. Mrs Hutton had also exhibited something quite interesting when she was talking about Geoffrey being on a good plane or something. He thought she had used the word 'wave', but she had hesitated for a good minute as though she couldn't rely on their intuition to know exactly what she meant. She somehow *had* to find the right word, whereas if they had

194 _The Secrets of Strangers_

all been deaf she could have done what she was actually doing at the time – expressively moving her hands around – and that would have been quite sufficient. She hadn't really needed to use the word at all. They had all understood what she meant. He certainly had, but it seemed important for her to find that correct word; till then she couldn't 'let it go'.

He wondered also whether Mrs Jenkins understood how important she had been at the last meeting. She had been fairly negative about continuing the meetings at the meeting before last and yet, on the loudspeaker telephone, had talked about more, as though they were a foregone conclusion. Her intuition had gone against her previous feelings, showing just how powerful it was. Not only did you not need the information – you could have the opposite information – but your intuition would lead you to the right conclusion. It was all that mattered. So, in his view, poor Mr Hutton couldn't shift any rational or irrational guilt that he might feel. For the first time he thought that Mr Hutton was feeling upset about his brother. He himself had been wondering how he would feel if he had been in Mr Hutton's position – if something similar had happened to a brother of his own. It was almost light relief to think about Mrs Jenkins' question at other meetings about Geoffrey's cross-dressing. He imagined he wasn't doing it any more.

In the free discussion they first talked about the issue of another meeting. Mrs Jenkins said she thought they should. Mrs Hutton said she didn't mind, whereupon TPA observed that from where he was sitting he could see her face, and her expression was very different from a simple 'don't mind'. To him she looked 'ravenously keen' to have another meeting.

Mr Hutton said he would go along with the majority.

TPA indicated that he didn't know whether they should have another meeting or not. He emphasised that the majority, from what had been said, comprised Mrs Hutton and himself, who were half and half, but that Mrs Hutton's face had shown her to be even more positive than Mrs Jenkins. Mr Hutton had previously said something about not accepting things at face value, and TPA pointed out that, because of the seating arrangements, Mr Hutton couldn't see his wife's face as he himself could, and it was the look on her face combined with the hard fact that she had previously remarked that the meetings benefited her family that had convinced him that she clearly wanted another meeting. He asked Mr Hutton whether he had seen his brother's face just before the suicide.

Mr Hutton responded that he had, and it had been as normal.

that Mr Hutton's father had provided in the family, some sense of security about the future. Had Kevin taken on that mantle? Had she (clerk's or typist's slip of the pen – Clerk) symbolised certainty about the future so that even if her (clerk's or typist's slip of the pen – Clerk) face had looked different, exhibiting for instance, a streak of anxiety, it would have been impossible to foretell anything different from what one had grown to expect. If Kevin was going to be MC at a youth club function the next day then indeed he would be. Anything different would be 'unthinkable'. Neither intuition nor even hard facts would 'cut any ice against that sort of backcloth'.

Geoffrey now, he continued, had perhaps been giving them a crash course on intuition, or a crash course on '*not* counting your chickens'. They had heard nothing from him about how he was behaving. His absence and silence were saying in effect: 'You really cannot tell, can you, what has been going on since Mothers' Day, what is happening at this moment or what is going to happen tomorrow.' It could be very useful to be able to acknowledge that that was the true state of affairs.

Then, speaking of levity, if they were all dying they would probably still be laughing because, no matter what, levity was predictable in a Hutton meeting. The reading of the previous minutes was certainly a huge undertaking and sometimes took as long as a quarter of an hour. If in future they cut out the reading of the 'previous minutes', they might find to their surprise that the extra discussion time had become burdensome, rather than advantageous – who could know for sure? He didn't know why Mr Hutton felt that the reading of the previous minutes didn't give a true reflection of what had happened. He always found that they did, and wondered whether that was a kind of perversion on Mr Hutton's part in the following way. Was it really a distant past's future that he had been so sure about but wrong? This painful guilt-laden fact had perhaps been 'traded in' for a delusion that *today* was not as, in a more recent past, he had predicted it would be. Hence his frequent reflected experience of cynical disappointment in the minutes as well as in important real issues in his life. He wondered if Mrs Jenkins's ridiculous and inexplicable anxiety was guilt, due to the now near-conscious realisation that in her mind she had been tampering with the future – she had assumed the order of speaking. Not only that, but the 'tampering' (the tendency to ordain the future) would entail the extra 'sin' of violating the gift of intuition. Kevin had behaved in absolutely the opposite way to the way he had been scheduled in the minds of the family, who had grown used to having a predictable head.

In the free discussion the Chairman insisted that they should decide whether or not to have another meeting and should arrange one if so. He didn't want to fall into the same trap as last time when they had arranged the present meeting after the meeting had 'died'. .

Mrs Jenkins said she wanted another one but didn't think they should.

Mr Hutton said he didn't know whether they should have one or not, since he didn't know what they were trying to do; but, on balance, yes.

Mrs Hutton wanted another one.

ATE said that as it looked as though they all couldn't do without it she would say yes.

TPA didn't know whether he wanted one but certainly felt that they should.

Therefore, amidst much mirth, another meeting was arranged.

Mrs Hutton then said that the meetings certainly helped her with her relationship with her children. She was able to discuss things much more fully and deeply with them than she had with Geoffrey in the past.

TPA remarked that if they had waited until later to arrange another meeting, Mr Hutton, having heard his wife say that, wouldn't have been so equivocal.

Mr Hutton remarked with a grin that he certainly knew Mrs Hutton liked these meetings because they kept him sane. He spoke of Geoffrey as being unforecastable.

They went on chewing away at the topic of the blessed seating arrangements and the future and how Mr Hutton 'would have been second and not second and third respectively, to speak'. (And if I didn't scream about this earlier on I'm about to scream now – Clerk.)

The discussion went back (for a change) to Geoffrey and how he had left them with only the possibility of intuition to go on if they were to have any notion of what he might be up to. There was then a brief talk about the phone call which TPA had made to Mr Hutton the previous day to confirm that he would have ATE with him at the meeting. Mrs Hutton had said she had known for sure it would be TPA but had assumed he would be wanting to change the date of today's meeting. If he had, she said, she would have killed him. Mr Hutton said that at the first mention of ATE arriving as a 'colleague', he had assumed that TPA was planning to have him certified. Mirth. (Presumably an allusion to the necessity of having two psychiatrists to 'certify' a patient – Clerk.)

*

Well, here I am in a strange time warp. It feels as though I have known the Huttons for ages, and now I meet them for the first time. As Claire was not at this meeting she seemed infinitely remote to me in both time and distance. Since she was not there I somehow assumed that she had not been for years, and only now do I realise that all the time she was outside within throwing distance, staying in the fresh air because 'everyone was a bit mad up there'. I see quite well why Bishop Berkeley exercised himself about the tree in the quad. I find it difficult to remember that people continue to exist when I don't have my eyes on them. For some reason Geoffrey, whom I had never met either, seemed closer – perhaps only because he was the convenor of the meetings: crucial and concentrated.

I was astonished at the way TPA seemed able to stick to the point, to listen to everything that was said. After only a few minutes I was wool-gathering: thinking about something that had been said earlier, speculating on the decor of the room and the probable date of the building, wondering whether the butcher would still be open when I got home. But when it came to summing-up he seemed to have missed very little, remembering nuances of expression, complete phrases, fractured hints of meaning where people had been reluctant or incompetent to express themselves clearly. I told myself it was his training. He says he also relies on his free-floating attention, which analysts are always talking about. This obviously offers the greatest threat to the cringing analysand – a sudden unwary, unplanned movement in the undergrowth and the bird of prey is upon him. One old charge-nurse said that being in a meeting with TPA made the muscles of his brain grow tired. Quite so.

I stopped day-dreaming when the subject of Kevin arose again. He was not, from what we have heard, a shy or incapable boy, and I cannot understand why, as he was about to be MC at some youth club jollification, he should choose that moment to kill himself. I know people who would rather die than expose themselves to the limelight, but Kevin does not sound like one of them. If he had felt threatened by the prospect of a boring evening as a wallflower his decision would have been more comprehensible. Having lost his prefectship and his girl, was he saying, like an angry child, that the world wasn't going to get round him with any of its confidence tricks? If this was a novel, I should now be writing away about the thoughts which had passed through Kevin's mind as he ascended into the loft. I might even, perhaps, come close to the truth, but this is not my brief.

In this context TPA uses the word 'unthinkable' in its literal sense, wondering whether it was that everyone was so confident of Kevin's predictability that a change in his plans was as impossible to think about as climbing to the moon – that certainly a change of plan so drastic would have registered on no one, no matter what his demeanour.

Mrs Jenkins, I am told, here offers a good example of a professional being invaded by themes. She speaks of inexplicability, and it is precisely the inexplicable quality of delinquency that is significant.

Mr Hutton used the term 'some years ago' when talking of the 'test scores' meeting. In fact that meeting was two years and two months ago, or fourteen hours in meeting terms. TPA says this is a kind of transference in itself. Mr Hutton, he says, is imbued with feelings about what happened forty years ago and is transferring those self-same feelings on to what happened at the test-scores meeting. He even wondered after the meeting whether Mr Hutton's perversion of tenses might be personified by the good old cross-dressing. One looks into the future and hopes (and expects) that the child will be born a girl. One gets a boy. With a great deal of effort and make-up can the clock be turned back? No, it can't. It is as though Geoffrey keeps rubbing in this tiresome fact, indicating perhaps that his father had not been the little girl whom Grandfather had always wanted and who Aunt Freda turned out to be.

Having met the Huttons I realised fully for the first time that if I had set out to write a novel about a delinquent child I would not have given him this family background, and if I had chosen to write a novel about the Huttons I could not have given them a delinquent child.

35. Nautical

Venue: Clinic consulting-room   25th June 1983
Present: Dr Pitt-Aikens, Chairman and clerk to the meeting
           Mr & Mrs Hutton
           Alice Thomas Ellis, writer and participant observer

The family arrived a little late. Mrs Jenkins was off sick. Geoffrey had been 'mildly' invited by Mr and Mrs Hutton but had rumbled and muttered, which Mr Hutton had taken to be a negative response. Mrs Hutton thought she had invited the other children, saying that they knew they were welcome but they had made no overt response.

During the reading of the previous minutes they noted mistakes – Geoffrey being referred to as as 'she', and then muddles between 'he' and 'she' and 'his' and 'hers'. They went on to choose the usual topic: 'anything important or relevant.'

Mr Hutton said something like 'Well, first I'd like to clear up this point in the minutes of the last meeting … er … because if we go back to Mrs Jenkins individual comments she was quietly talking about … er … me being second and then transfers it to Anne being second. We can look at this either way: hm … if we take it from Dr Pitt-Aikens's point of view that actually I was second, Anne was third and not I was first and Anne was second, but from Mrs Jenkins's point of view that would be so anyway because I will be first after her and Anne will be second after me, the "after her" being assumed and not spoken. So I think that was a bit of a storm in a teacup, anyway.' (The clerk feels seasick here.)

Mr Hutton then, blessedly, resumed his customary lucidity and said that Geoffrey had been to see them not long after the last meeting and had brought the little boy but had left the mother behind. He thought she was having a break from Geoffrey. They had had a pleasant weekend with him and he seemed to be floating along with the tide all right, not actively doing anything (he was still unemployed) but not actively in any trouble at the moment. Nor from his manner, his general character, did he give them any impression he was likely to be. At the same time both he and Anne found that they were still uneasy in his presence. He was welcome to come home, they were glad to see him, but when he went they heaved a sigh of relief.

Mr Hutton went on to say that when reading through the last minutes he had been struck by one particular point – the levity. He had had some time to spare and had made some notes because it seemed to him a large factor in the meetings. He could remember saying at one of them many years ago that life itself was serious enough without spoiling it by taking it seriously. Humour was a great defence against the vicissitudes of life. If you were faced with a problem and could laugh at it, then straightaway you were on the way to solving it, or, if it was insoluble, at least to coping with it. It was a very defensive thing. There had been a time once in the navy when he had had a little too much rum and had made himself rather objectionable. He was sleeping it off, but wasn't asleep when he heard the fellows discussing him: one was saying rather plaintively, 'It's no good even thumping him, he would just come back and make a funny remark.' Humour could, of course, be offensive, but he was thinking of it in the opposite way. Life frequently showed that a complaint made with humour was more likely to be met and possibly satisfied than one just made baldly. He tended to use humour both as an offensive and as a defensive weapon to cope with problems.

He had noted down another point he said – about the minutes. What he had meant was that because they were a correct record they could be taken as meaning more than they should. He had been thinking of the time factor as well. Often TPA would make an incorrect statement, or draw a wrong conclusion, usually the latter, and because time was short they went down in the minutes and eventually became a record of what appeared to be fact. There was an example in the minutes they had been reading earlier to do with Kevin and his 'head of the family' attitude. Now the actual fact of the matter was that Kevin considered himself head of the family. His mother didn't, Mr Hutton didn't, his other brother didn't, and his sister had been too young at the time to have any opinions at all. Kevin had never even been in the position of acting temporary head of the family except in his own estimation.

Mrs Hutton wished to pass, and so did ATE.

TPA said that when he was speaking of Kevin he was concerned more with his quality of predictability, a quality which he suspected Mr Hutton's father had had as part of his 'weaponry', an aspect of his being head of the family. Even if Kevin had been the only one to see himself in this role, TPA was pretty sure that people had ascribed to him this very predictable quality: not necessarily in a good sense, maybe even in a bad sense, but it was part of the mantle which had previously gone with headship of the family. He was sure that Mr Hutton had taken it for granted that Kevin would be a certain sort of person in the near or even long-term future, whereas perhaps Geoffrey was the epitome of the opposite, giving everyone a feeling of unease, missing the security of apparent predictability. The his/her, he/she mistakes from last time, and today's business of Geoffrey 'bringing the little boy and leaving the mother', had reminded him of some history to do with Mr Hutton's time in the navy: something to do with the changeover of roles within the family when Mrs Hutton had first to assume more responsibility and then relinquish it. He thought that metaphorical change of sex was important and had recently been talking to ATE about it. It was probably significant that the two issues – of 'sex change' and predictability – were with them almost simultaneously.

TPA continued that he and ATE had experienced a Huttonian phenomenon, and ATE was now a fully-fledged 'honorary member of the Hutton family', as he had been for some time. ATE had asked him when he was going to let her have a spare copy of the Hutton minutes and he had said he'd already sent them. 'Fiddlesticks,' ATE had responded robustly, 'I always put important documents in a special safe place and if I had received them that was where they'd be and they were not.' He couldn't really remember having sent them; he just had a feeling that he had. But ATE was quite positive that she hadn't received them. She had efficiently and patronisingly suggested that he should approach the GPO and ask for a P58 form which might enable him to discover whether a package had got stuck somewhere, and he said disconsolately that he would do this, thereby half acknowledging that ATE was right, all logical and sensible, and he wrong with his 'silly hunch'. They had both agreed that while each would prefer to be right it would be most interesting in terms of understanding about intuition if his hunch should prove to be correct. Then, rooting about one day in the back of the drinks cupboard, ATE had discovered the very minutes. She couldn't imagine what they were doing in there, but in this case intuition had proved to be superior to logic, and TPA was pleased. He still thought it would be useful to understand where these themes of intuition and predictability were coming from, why they were such strong family themes and why they came over so powerfully. He had long had the idea that Mr Hutton might drop down dead before 50 – sooner than was necessary – and had been thrilled to bits when he had had his narrow escape in the car. 'Told you so' had been his feeling, although it would admittedly have been somewhat spoilt if Mr

Hutton had decided to go the whole hog.

The free discussion was difficult to record, as usual. It was noticed
that memories had proved unreliable in the meeting. Mrs Hutton
had asked what had happened to Mrs Pannell, had meant Mrs
Jenkins, and had already been told anyway; TPA had christened
ATE Mrs Hutton; ATE had intended to bring her most serious book
as a present for the Huttons and had brought her most frivolous one;
Mrs Hutton had called the dog Louis, etc., etc. Mr Hutton
wondered whether his extremely logical approach might have
interfered with his success at work and Mrs Hutton felt that,
certainly, he could have done much better than he had done. This
was partly blamed on Geoffrey who unarguably was the cause of
considerable worry. None the less TPA wondered whether he simply
personified what could happen to people's minds.

Then came the discussion about a further meeting. Mr Hutton
had no particular objection; Mrs Hutton felt the same, and so did
ATE; TPA said he didn't know but agreed.

Then it turned out, to everyone's astonishment, because there had
been a feeling of rush, that there was a whole three minutes of the
meeting left, and TPA wondered whether these meetings were a
reflection of the real situation within the family – that there was a
little more time than anticipated, not such a rush as had been
thought. Could it be that Mr Hutton needn't be depressed about his
future? After all he had lived over fifty years now – the maximum
time generally allowed to a male Hutton. Might he not have more
time left than he had imagined? Perhaps he could even change his
career and make a success there?

Mr Hutton shook his head negatively.

Mrs Hutton, 'after hours', said that there was no chance of
promotion within the department and he wasn't leaving it.

*

Mr Hutton again speaks of 'many years ago'. TPA and I reckon that
'many years' would mean a minimum of ten, and the meetings span
seven years. The choice of words seems to indicate yet again that the
actual time spanned by the thirty-five meetings represents a much
larger timespan in life. Mr Hutton goes on to talk about levity and I
find it very interesting since I have discovered that even in
unbearable grief some things have sometimes made me laugh and I
would never have believed it possible. When my son was dying I

spent a lot of time with a friend who was also dying – of catastrophic
cancer, and simultaneously suffering the miseries of chemotherapy –
and I don't think we laughed any less in the final weeks together
than we ever had. On one deplorable occasion we listened to a rather
high-flown wireless programme, presented in the poetic style, about a
child who had come to death's door, baffling the whole of medical
science with his symptons until they realised it was all because he'd
been eating dog shit. In the very shadow of the Grim Reaper we
laughed till we wept. It was almost as though he gave us licence since
no one could accuse us of being unaccustomed to his presence. It was
highly reprehensible, no doubt, but the mirth did not arise from any
sense of immunity, though perhaps at that time all our compassion
had been used up on ourselves. In between the spasms of gaiety there
were episodes of terrible sorrow, guilt, regret, apprehension – but the
laughter was there almost to the end. It might be easier to try and
see my dying friend as two people, but she seemed even more herself
when she laughed than when she suffered, even though the suffering
was rapidly taking her life away and might have been considered
overwhelmingly significant. I remember when I first observed a
group of delinquents and was surprised when one made a joke
because he suddenly became human. I think that laughter and grief
can coexist but laughter and evil cannot. Nor is madness funny.
Madness is a sort of slapstick and the people who laugh at slapstick
are probably those who would have taken the children to Bedlam for
a merry afternoon's treat watching the lunatics.

TPA notes that Mr Hutton wonders whether his 'extremely
logical approach might have interfered with his success at work' and
says this is the first time he has shown an overt thoughtfulness about
this aspect of himself.

When we started discussing this meeting I was tired and loath to
work, so TPA made us some tea laced with rum; whereupon, on
turning the page, we discovered Mr Hutton likewise drinking this
potable spirit. We found that – if you'll pardon the joke – faintly rum.

It was after this that I said I wanted to see the Huttons on their
home ground. I wanted to see their house and meet their children.
Although it was already established that it was my role to do
precisely this sort of thing, to see the family on ordinary human
terms, TPA was not enthusiastic. He couldn't see why it was
necessary – he learned all he needed in his rarefied clinical
atmosphere. What more did I want? Well, I wanted to walk through
their door and sit in their chairs and drink their tea and look out of
their windows and see what they saw daily. I wanted to talk to them
about their past, to gossip unreservedly in a way that was not easy for

me at family meetings. I simply wanted to know them better, not out of ghoulish literary curiosity but because I liked them. In the end he agreed rather grudgingly that I should go.

We drove to Portsmouth in a leisurely fashion. The friend, Janet, who was driving wasn't sure of the route, so we set off early and idled round the lanes of Hampshire. The pub we stopped at for lunch had run out of matches but the owner gave me a disposable lighter. I am superstitious about travelling but I thought it augured quite well. Portsmouth was a nasty disappointment. I had never been there before and was vaguely hoping that it might resemble Liverpool in the old days – be full of colourful foreign sailors, lascars holding hands, cheerful drunken Finns. I couldn't even see the sea anywhere, just the tops of some ships half concealed by the docks. We noticed one Victorian warehouse in a state of some disrepair but for the rest the developers had clearly been at work. We drove up to the Huttons' house to make sure that we would find it later in the evening and then wasted some time wondering where to stay. There were a number of small 'family' hotels along the roadside, one with a red light which I thought intriguing, but Janet said it was she who would be left alone there while I was talking to the Huttons and she preferred not to take any chances.

In the end we chose a hotel in the centre of town and then were told that dinner was between 7.30 and 9.30. As this was precisely the time I should be spending with the Huttons we asked if they could prepare some sandwiches for the late evening. They said 'no'. We are quite used to the extraordinary ways of English hoteliers, but this wasn't good for our tempers. We looked around for a restaurant which stayed open beyond ten and decided on a Chinese establishment, worrying a little about wandering around a seaport after dark; but the city has been rendered so characterless that we were unable to frighten ourselves properly – not in the midst of a pedestrian precinct surround by the depressingly familiar and ubiquitous chain-stores.

We found the Hutton house easily enough although it was dark now. I had to approach it through the back garden because the car couldn't be driven round to the front. I can't remember why. I remember the washing on the line because it reminded me of Geoffrey and I wondered whether if he had been there he would have removed the blouse.

Anne opened the door to me and I went into the kitchen and the familiar kitchen smell of tea and bleached sink. The rest of the family and the dog were in the sitting-room and we went through and sat down; a comfortable, orderly room, pleasantly furnished and warm. Anne brought in a plate of cakes, and Ian who has a rather formal, old-world manner, offered me whisky. I was pleased to accept because I was feeling faintly idiotic and intrusive in the house of these kind and pleasant people for the purpose of asking them questions, including queries about their troublesome son who had so recently seemed to have settled down. The children, Sean, Margaret and Louis, brought family photographs to show me and told me all they could remember about everything I asked. They were obliging and courteous and alert and attractive – as is Geoffrey. The photographs of him show a sensitive-looking handsome boy. They are all talented too. Sean, despite his eye problems, produces very well drawn, very rude comics, much in demand locally.

After a while I found that I was beginning to realise for the first time that I was in a seaport. Ian was telling me about his job as a Customs officer and I was enthralled. He gave me a 'special whisky' warning me that it was very potent. It was. I quite stopped worrying about the evening meal. He is witty and amusing and I think in some sense unfulfilled. His job gives him, for me, an air of peculiar glamour – tarry ropes and brandy and 'Watch the wall, my darlings, as the gentlemen go by!' I wouldn't find him so interesting if he were a smuggler, since now that they mostly traffick in drugs they have lost their romantic appeal. Rum and lace and tobacco and a run of tubs are one thing, heroin quite another. I think him fortunate to have spent so much time on ships, even stationary ones, where he goes to hunt out contraband and meets captains and seamen, and where the Chief Steward is always given the task of assisting and entertaining the excise man. I like the formality, the hint of ritual (something lacking in the lives of smugglers), the time-honoured courtesies. I like the framework and discipline and the exigencies of the law. Ian isn't merely law-abiding, he's a law-enforcer. He said that within that framework he has been known to commit peccadilloes – practical jokes, some fairly serious drinking – but he gives a great sense of overall decorum, of integrity. He spoke of some of the people he had met and I had an impression of nostalgia, of regret and loss. They have moved away from their old friends, having left Gravesend to live in Portsmouth because Ian had always planned to retire there. He said he feared it was lonely for Anne because the neighbours are so standoffish, but I sensed more loneliness in him despite his humour. Anne seemed content with her lot – her husband, her children and herself. She described a time when a neighbour fell and had to go to hospital and was subsequently amazed to find that Anne had not only looked after her child, but had given him breakfast. I said tentatively that I thought it rare to find a married couple who liked each other as much as Anne and Ian appeared to. He said, 'I don't know what I'd do without Anne.' Anne laughed and the children said 'Aahh!'

I thought of TPA while I was there: of how he might have disapproved of our cheerful gossip, would have wished us to keep to the point. I got quite annoyed with him in his absence since often I could imagine his comments, see his expression as Anne and the children and I giggled over some irrelevancy. Nevertheless it felt strange being with the Huttons without him since in my experience of them he had always been there. It seemed rather like bacon without the egg. Geoffrey's absence seemed less surprising because I was not accustomed to his presence.

I didn't want to leave when the time came.

36. Rather like the first

Venue: Clinic consulting-room   23rd September 1983
Present: Dr Pitt-Aikens, Chairman and clerk to the meeting
           Mrs Jenkins, link Social Worker at Orwell House
           Alice Thomas Ellis, writer and participant observer
           Mr & Mrs Hutton

Mrs Jenkins was late, so they waited five minutes for her. Mrs Hutton, who was in good time, apologised for being late. There was just time to hear that only Margaret had sent apologies when Mrs Jenkins arrived. The Chairman brought her up to date about the adjournment and Margaret's apology.

The professionals had forgotten to bring their copies of the minutes and had to rely on Mr Hutton who had remembered his. He pointed out that TPA had read aloud some of his marginal comments so, strictly speaking, the minutes weren't a correct record but included some of Mr Hutton's own pencilled additions as well as his 'ers' and 'hms'. There was a great deal of levity, led, in part, by the Chairman, who posed the possibility that they might talk about Mr Hutton's red-and-white harlequin socks and inadvertently said 'comic' when he meant 'comments'.

Mrs Jenkins said that when TPA had brought her up to date with the 'invitations' she hadn't heard that Geoffrey had been invited and had to keep reminding herself that she could only legitimise her presence at these meetings because they were instituted for him. She talked about role-changing and how if Mr Hutton hadn't brought his copy of the minutes they would have been at a loss. Then she observed that Mrs Hutton had referred to her as 'Mrs Pannell', and she remembered a previous meeting when they had noted that she and Mrs Pannell had swapped roles. Now, she said, she somehow felt that Mr Hutton was in charge of the meetings. In no other family meetings did TPA display levity as he sometimes did in these, and she felt that he had somehow handed over the serious part. The levity worried her a little because the situation they were in gave no cause for hilarity. Perhaps it was a defence mechanism, perhaps even a survival mechanism. She didn't know. She wondered what was happening to Geoffrey and how concerned people were about him. She was also worried, because she seemed to remember that the meetings were continuing for a specific reason and now she couldn't remember what it was. After, or maybe during, one meeting, she and TPA had got on to something which had seemed very alive and exciting at the time and she couldn't remember what that was either. She thought it was something to do with Mr Hutton and his intuition or his denial of it, but it had gone from her.

Mr Hutton said in answer that they had heard from Geoffrey a couple of times since the last meeting and had sent him some money for his holiday, for which he had thanked them by postcard. They heard from him again when he rang to tell them he had got some sort of employment, something on the lines of Manpower Training. They had also heard from Sean when he needed money. Mr Hutton then returned to the subject of the navy. On one ship the padre used to get people to talk over the internal broadcasting system about some event they had participated in and Mr Hutton had pointed out to one such person the number of times he had said 'er'. Then it had come to Mr Hutton's turn and as he gave his little talk he could hear himself going 'er' just when it was too late to stop it. He heard every 'er' that came out and there were an awful lot of them. It was then, he remarked, that he had had to accept that to 'er' was human. He still thought TPA hadn't got Kevin properly weighed up in his mind. Kevin was not predictable, certainly not after their father had died. He had always had a bit of a butterfly mind and would flit from one subject to another so that you could never be sure what his current interest was. 'After my father died,' said Mr Hutton, 'he sort of withdrew from the family predictability. You'd find out about it after it had happened and he was seldom there. He just went his own way and he wasn't a leading figure in the family. It was only when he was there that he imposed himself on one.'

Mrs Hutton said it was Claire she was a bit worried about at the moment. Claire kept talking about death and suicide, but not in a depressed way. She wasn't depressed. She was cheerful when she was talking about it and that was why Mrs Hutton felt a bit concerned. 'It's always at most peculiar times she keeps coming out with these things. It's almost like she belongs to another religion or something, but I know she doesn't and I'm not quite sure how to deal with it. At the moment I just tell her not to be a silly fool. Apart from that I've nothing to say.' Here she looked plaintively at TPA and said she thought that perhaps he would sort that one out.

ATE had nothing to say.

TPA took the floor, electing to talk about Mr Hutton's feeling that a false impression could be gained from the minutes simply because of their format: the fact that they had one hour and that was it. There was often no time to have long discussions to put matters right. They were landed with what they were landed with, and Mr Hutton felt that while things were 'technically' correct they weren't really so. It was interesting that he should have brought up the 'er' business, and he was delighted that the clerk had so faithfully recorded all the 'ers' in the last minutes. It had felt quite uncanny for some reason when Mr Hutton began to talk about how the 'ers' slip out and had then used the word 'er' in the sense of erring. 'Ers' were little errors which became prominent afterwards, not before. As to the vexed question of what they should discuss, he thought they all, including himself, felt that although it was fine to talk about anything relevant or important – levity could be included, babies, red-and-white-socks – nevertheless if the thing was broadened too much there was the danger that something specific might not be given sufficient attention. That seemed to be the worry, and that was perhaps why people grew almost angry at having to talk more generally. He thought the reason for those strong feelings which made no real logical sense was an unconscious realisation that there was *something* specific of great importance and unless they could pick on it it would somehow be lost. A grave error might be made. Mrs Hutton had been describing Claire talking about suicide and death at what she called 'peculiar times'. That made it very difficult to tune in on. How could you respond to somebody about serious topics if they chose peculiar times and kept the tone light? Then, when it came to suicide everyone said, when it was too late, what a pity it was. It was like saying 'er'. You knew afterwards that you had made a mistake, not before. There was something in the air about them all needing to know before, not afterwards. It could certainly have applied in Kevin's case. It was all very well for him, TPA, to say 'Ah, well, Mr Hutton, don't worry. We may have given the wrong impression by these minutes, but as you know we always have another meeting, don't we? We can always correct them later.' That was all very well as long as the topic was something which could wait, but there were some things which couldn't, and that was when you needed everything you'd got – all the logic and all the intuition. You had to spotlight whatever was going wrong before it went too far.

TPA wanted to know about Mrs Hutton's health, adding that she looked different. Had she put on or lost weight since they last saw her? (She, interrupting, indignantly denied this, but he insisted that what he said felt true.) He continued that he had always imagined

that if there was a danger of loss of intuition in this case it would
apply to Mr Hutton, but then he had realised that the phenomenon
called projection which he and Mrs Jenkins (and more and more
ATE) were always talking about was perhaps at work here.
Projection, he explained kindly, meant that one person's unconscious
business was pushed into another person, so he was wondering
whether we ought to be worrying more about Mrs Hutton. He
considered she would be a willing victim to the 'lack of intuition
stuff' because of the doubts and fantasies they had entertained about
her mother. Was this lady alive or dead? Did she wonder about her
daughter? Did Mrs Hutton wonder if she was wondering? All might
be questions to do with intuition. She might be in danger by not
making specific enquiries, and perhaps needed help in this, for
instance with regard to her health. It had been he, as we knew, who
had been worrying about death for ages, and in a funny sort of way
he was pleased that Claire had now taken it up as though supporting
him. She apparently laughed at herself, as Mr Hutton had used to
laugh at him. Mrs Jenkins was right. It was a serious business.

At the start of the free discussion the Chairman was keen to organise
another meeting (if people wanted one) in order to get the subject out
of the way.

Mr Hutton very positively said 'yes', which so surprised Mrs
Hutton and Mrs Jenkins that they commented on it. Mr Hutton
then began to talk about Claire and how introspective she could be.
She was reported as saying that she wanted to die now so that she
could remain the same age for ever and look down on herself as a
young girl for ever and a day.

This caused a faintly ecclesiastical discussion about the difference
between belief and faith, which ceased when TPA turned to Mrs
Hutton demanding to know intimate details about her health. Poor
Mrs Hutton was loath to say anything, and a parallel was drawn
between *this* awkward, peculiar situation – talking about medical,
indeed gynaecological, matters in a roomful of strangers – and
Claire talking about death at 'peculiar times'. Mrs Hutton
reluctantly admitted that, though her periods had stopped a long
time ago, recently they seemed to have come back again in an
irregular sort of way. She had also noticed a small lump in her groin.

TPA asked her what she was going to do about that.

Mrs Hutton said she supposed she had been waiting till the
children were off her hands.

TPA asked: 'So how old would they have to be and how old are
you?'

'Well', she replied, 'Claire's the youngest – she was 17 over a month ago – and I'll be 50 in three weeks'. She supposed she had been 'taking a chance'.

*

Any delicately-minded female would be loath to discuss these intimate matters in a room full of strangers, but delicacy is a form of secrecy, which in this case could result in death.

At the mention of 17 and 50 and the hint that Mrs Hutton might have cancer TPA grew wary, wondering whether here was the 'catastrophe on the time horizon' and whether at this point the task of writing the book might interfere with the therapy. I rang him from the country, to find he had been struck yet again, apparently this time with the force of revelation, by the idea that Mr Hutton might be 'murdering' his wife's intuition, undermining her ability to realise that there was something wrong with her health by invading her with his own loss of intuition. Intuition is commonly regarded as a feminine attribute, and the cervix is indisputably feminine. Was he launching an onslaught on the quality which had, unbeknown to his conscious mind, been oppressing him for so long? TPA's actual words were 'Is he a murderer?' and I was profoundly shocked. I gasped. Mr Hutton is gentle and brave and compassionate and he makes me laugh. Of course he isn't a murderer. What is more, TPA went on to speculate that Mr Hutton's rogue unconscious might be highly selective. It might permit his wife a remnant of intuition in regard to himself since she had 'twitched' when he had his car crash. I had to remind myself that all the horrors lurking in the unconscious are amoral – projections, aliens, evil spirits, or what you will – and have nothing to do with the real person.

Wondering about all this made TPA nervous. It was after all only a hypothesis, and yet there was a dreadful elegance about it. In terms of books, of plot, it would have fitted very neatly. Clinging to it could dangerously pervert it from what it really was – a hypothesis to be tested in a clinical setting. Listen to this: he even wondered out loud 'whether Geoffrey's attempts to portray himself as a female might have been his vulnerable unconscious internalised mother fighting off his destructively marauding unconscious father phallus, the cross-dressing producing a temporary sense of excitement, relief and safety.'

I was promptly banished from my privileged attendance at family meetings and turfed back out into the public realm. Anything that I heard from now on would be rather like overhearing secrets. I was no longer ranged alongside the analyst, seeing matters from that extraordinary perspective; my relationship with the Huttons had changed to something more remote, more usual. I went quietly, not only for the reasons set out above but for an added, slightly mad reason of my own, the possibility of which haunts many novelists. At its simplest we are frightened that what we write may come true, and I wanted no hand in any possible self-fulfilling prophecy which might distort the Huttons' destiny. I did not want to be tempted to forget that in this case I was only an observer with no brief to mould or to decorate.

When I telephoned them one day, a few weeks after my exclusion, just to see how they were, I heard that Mr Hutton's mother had died and was asked not to tell TPA, because they wanted to tell him themselves. I said nothing, but hoped for more news to emerge from the next and future family meetings. I learned from TPA that the family, on hearing that Grandmother wasn't well, had 'twitched', this time to excellent effect, and, instead of telling each other that she would probably be all right, had gone down to be with her. She had died at peace because Geoffrey and Gloria were happy and their own baby was on the way. At the funeral someone said to someone else that Grandmother had thought Geoffrey was her Kevin, and – this being the way talk goes at funerals – they remembered the time she had dreamed that she could see a gravestone inscribed with the name Hutton. Try as she might, she couldn't read the Christian name and feared that it might be her baby, Freda. Then two weeks later her husband had died. At her funeral, and in spite of the prevailing sadness, everyone had seemed to remark on Geoffrey's impeccable bearing.

Mrs Hutton's surgical treatment had proved successful. Mr Hutton, after some initial depression following his retirement, had become creative and was writing and drawing. Geoffrey was currently out of trouble and the other children healthy and cheerful. At one meeting, to TPA's amazement, after all the previous denial, Mrs Hutton suddenly announced that she had wanted to call Geoffrey 'Kevin'.

'Why didn't you?' asked TPA.

There was a long pause, and then Mr Hutton said he simply hadn't wanted it.

FOR THE BEST IN PAPERBACKS, LOOK FOR THE

In every corner of the world, on every subject under the sun, Penguin represents quality and variety – the very best in publishing today.

For complete information about books available from Penguin – including Pelicans, Puffins, Peregrines and Penguin Classics – and how to order them, write to us at the appropriate address below. Please note that for copyright reasons the selection of books varies from country to country.

In the United Kingdom: For a complete list of books available from Penguin in the U.K., please write to *Dept E.P., Penguin Books Ltd, Harmondsworth, Middlesex, UB7 0DA*

In the United States: For a complete list of books available from Penguin in the U.S., please write to *Dept BA, Penguin, 299 Murray Hill Parkway, East Rutherford, New Jersey 07073*

In Canada: For a complete list of books available from Penguin in Canada, please write to *Penguin Books Canada Ltd, 2801 John Street, Markham, Ontario L3R 1B4*

In Australia: For a complete list of books available from Penguin in Australia, please write to the *Marketing Department, Penguin Books Australia Ltd, P.O. Box 257, Ringwood, Victoria 3134*

In New Zealand: For a complete list of books available from Penguin in New Zealand, please write to the *Marketing Department, Penguin Books (NZ) Ltd, Private Bag, Takapuna, Auckland 9*

In India: For a complete list of books available from Penguin, please write to *Penguin Overseas Ltd, 706 Eros Apartments, 56 Nehru Place, New Delhi, 110019*

In Holland: For a complete list of books available from Penguin in Holland, please write to *Penguin Books Nederland B.V., Postbus 195, NL–1380AD Weesp, Netherlands*

In Germany: For a complete list of books available from Penguin, please write to *Penguin Books Ltd, Friedrichstrasse 10 – 12, D–6000 Frankfurt Main 1, Federal Republic of Germany*

In Spain: For a complete list of books available from Penguin in Spain, please write to *Longman Penguin España, Calle San Nicolas 15, E–28013 Madrid, Spain*